Jesus. Was it getting hot in here? Sudden, unwelcome warmth flooded his veins. He fumbled with the temperature controls, switching the air from warm to cool.

Dropping her hand from his arm, she sat back in her seat and laughed. "I can't believe I got you so mad you had to turn on the air-conditioning. We've only been together for five minutes. I think that might be a new record."

He could have told her that his reaction had absolutely nothing to do with anger and everything to do with the casual way she'd been touching him. But that definitely wasn't the best course of action. Not when he considered the fact at hand, which was that they were stuck planning this wedding together for the next couple of months. Not to mention that she was his best friend's baby sister. He had absolutely no business thinking about touching her right back.

So he let her think it was anger that was burning him up inside, and not that, somehow, a switch had been flipped, making him suddenly want her in the worst way. He was in a whole hell of a lot of trouble if he couldn't figure out how to flip that switch back.

A Wedding on
Sunshine Corner

A Wedding on Sunshine Corner

A Sunshine Corner Novel

Phoebe Mills

FOREVER
New York   Boston

Forever
Hachette Book Group
1290 Avenue of the Americas, New York, NY 10104
read-forever.com
twitter.com/readforeverpub

First Edition: March 2022

Forever is an imprint of Grand Central Publishing. The Forever name and logo are trademarks of Hachette Book Group, Inc.

The publisher is not responsible for websites (or their content) that are not owned by the publisher.

The Hachette Speakers Bureau provides a wide range of authors for speaking events. To find out more, go to www.hachettespeakersbureau.com or call (866) 376-6591.

ISBNs: 9781538753989 (mass market), 9781538753996 (ebook)

Printed in the United States of America

OPM

10 9 8 7 6 5 4 3 2 1

A Wedding on Sunshine Corner

Chapter One

If Savannah Lowe had known exactly how many butterflies would be occupying her stomach on the first day of her new job, she wasn't sure she ever would have agreed to accept it. Of course, that would mean letting down her best friend and boss, Abby Engel, which she wasn't inclined to do.

For years now, Savannah had been working with Abby at the Sunshine Corner, a day care center Abby owned and operated out of her and her grandmother's home. When Abby decided to remodel the second floor of the grand old historic building and turn it into a preschool, Savannah had been all for it. Right until Abby had tapped her to be lead teacher for the four-year-olds *and* to run the entire new addition. That included planning the curriculum, hiring new teachers, scheduling field trips and parent conferences. The works.

At first, Savannah had been proud to be entrusted with such a huge responsibility. But within minutes, an overwhelming feeling had sunk in her gut. She'd never been in charge of something like that—of anything, really. And yet, somehow, Abby had seen something in Savannah that made her think she was the woman for the job. But that was Abby... Not only was she the best friend a girl could ask for, but she was also the sole person in Savannah's life who believed in her, without question or hesitation.

Being the youngest child and only girl in a large family was... challenging, at times. Especially when they underestimated her at every turn. While she knew her brothers and parents didn't necessarily mean it as an insult, they hadn't exactly shown confidence in her decisions. And, okay, so maybe her decisions hadn't evoked much confidence, but was it her fault that she enjoyed trying new things but that nothing ever seemed to stick?

Savannah checked over the four-year-olds' classroom once more, making sure that the children's nameplates were still adhered to the backs of their chairs, that the alphabet signs still hung straight, and that the lists of colors on the wall were still in rainbow assortment. Yep, everything was in order, just as it'd been the past twenty times she'd looked.

"Savannah?" Abby called, poking her head into the room. She wore jeans and a bright green blouse, her light red hair swept away from her face in a side braid.

Her smile widened when she saw Savannah standing at the front of the classroom, and Savannah's nerves became turbocharged. That smile spoke of so much confidence. She just hoped she could deliver on the unspoken promise. "T-minus five minutes. Are you ready?"

Nope, but Savannah was willing to fake it till she made it.

"Yep!" she said as cheerily as possible. Her best friend had enough to worry about on this first day than to concern herself with Savannah's uncertainties too.

Abby cocked her head, her eyes intent on Savannah, and her smile softened the tiniest bit. "You're going to do great, you know."

"Of course I am." Except Savannah's voice wasn't firm enough to be believable, and their two decades of friendship meant that her best friend could see right through her facade.

Abby walked over to Savannah and wrapped an arm around her shoulders, squeezing slightly. "You *are*. I wouldn't have asked you to do this if I didn't think that you were one hundred and ten percent capable."

That much, at least, was true. Abby would never jeopardize her baby by putting its future into the hands of the incompetent. That was slightly reassuring, considering Abby had been there through all of Savannah's starts . . . as well as all her stops. Like when she'd dabbled in photography in high school, begging her parents to buy her a ridiculously expensive DSLR—one that she'd used for maybe a month before it died a lonely death in the bottom of her closet. Or when she'd gotten lost on Etsy one night in college and by morning had ordered all the supplies to make her own jewelry, intent on starting her own business. She wasn't sure she'd even opened the packages on those. Or when she'd bounced to three different majors before she'd finally been held over the fire and forced to choose.

Early childhood education hadn't seemed like a natural fit at first. She'd rarely spent much time around children who weren't her relatives or babysitting charges of Abby's. But with Abby opening up a day care and making big, hopeful doe eyes at her every time she mentioned needing a great staff, Savannah had figured why not give it a shot? She still wasn't convinced it was her calling in life, but she could do a lot worse. Working with kids was fun, and she got to spend her day surrounded by amazing, caring people.

"Speaking of," Savannah said, "I should check in with the other teachers and make sure they're all set for the day."

"See?" Abby said, smiling brilliantly. "Totally and completely capable." With one final squeeze, Abby swept out of the room, calling a quick hello to the other teachers milling about before she headed downstairs, no doubt to greet the incoming parents and children.

Savannah closed her eyes, inhaled a long, deep breath, and willed herself to exude a confidence she certainly did not feel today. After releasing her worries along with her exhale, she strode out of the classroom, nearly colliding with her brand-new teacher's assistant as she did so.

"Oh my gosh, I'm so sorry!" Tori said, her eyes wilder than Savannah had ever seen them. Tori was Korean American, petite in stature and young—definitely in her early twenties—with long, pin-straight black hair. Tori huffed out what might have passed as a laugh if it weren't for the tremble in her voice as she said, "I'm a mess."

"No worries." Savannah regarded the other woman and realized there was no hyperbole in her words. "Hey, are you okay?"

Tori laughed, a forced, high-pitched sound, and shook her head. "What gave me away?"

"Call it a hunch," Savannah said with a smile. "Anything I can do? What's going on?"

"Oh, you know..." Tori waved her hand through the air in a flourish. "Just the weight of fourteen four-year-olds' futures settling on my shoulders."

Ah...everything made sense now. Of course she'd be nervous on her first day—she'd never been in charge of something like this. Neither had Savannah, for that matter, but there certainly wasn't room in this scenario for two of them to be losing their minds with worry. That meant Savannah needed to swallow down every bit of apprehension and put on a brave face. If for nothing else than to make Tori's first day in childcare go off without a hitch.

"All you need to worry about is wrangling any wanderers, and I'll handle the rest today, okay? Plus, look on the bright side—we just have a couple of only children in the class."

Tori's brow furrowed, her dark brown eyes questioning as she regarded Savannah. "What does that have to do with anything?"

Savannah flashed her a smile. "It means if we screw the others up too badly, the parents will at least have other children to fall back on."

The joke did what Savannah had intended, and Tori laughed, her shoulders relaxing from where they'd been nearly pinned below her ears as relief appeared to wash over her.

"That's awful to say," Tori said on a giggle.

"And I will deny it with every breath in my body if you repeat it to anyone." Savannah leaned down closer and whispered, "But it worked, didn't it?"

Tori smiled and nodded, no longer wringing her hands. Once Savannah was confident that her teacher's assistant wasn't going to be the first one to vomit in their classroom, she set out to check in with Kiara and Jeremy, the teacher and assistant, respectively, who would be heading up the three-year-old room. Fortunately, they were faring much better than Savannah and Tori were, standing at the front of their room, ready to welcome in the new children. That gave Savannah more relief than it probably should have, but it was a tiny glimmer that maybe she'd done one thing right, at least.

Selecting the teaching staff for the Sunshine Corner's preschool had been one of the many responsibilities Abby had entrusted her with. But maybe she'd screwed up selecting Tori as her assistant instead of Jeremy— after all, it would have been nice to have one person who was confident in their abilities in the four-year-old room. But perhaps this was better. At least now Savannah didn't have a choice but to buck up.

Before she could dwell too much on her teacher-placement decisions, chaos in the form of excited three- and four-year-olds erupted in the preschool, the quick patter of feet on the curved stairs leading to their space on the second floor making her lips twitch.

"Miss Savannah! Miss Savannah!" Sofia was the first to reach her, her eyes bright in her excitement as she gripped Savannah's hand and jumped up and down. "It's the first day! What're we gonna do?"

It didn't surprise her in the least that Sofia was the first child to arrive. She'd been at the Sunshine Corner all of her four years, but besides that, she'd become a staple in Abby's life once Abby and Carter— Sofia's uncle—became a couple. She felt comfortable here and wasn't scared in the least for her new adventure.

Savannah squatted so she could meet Sofia at eye level and smiled at the little girl's excitement. "Well, we have a few activities planned, like getting to know your classmates. But we're also going to be drawing something special for the first day that will go in your portfolios to review at the end of the year. How does that sound?"

"So fun! Drawing's my favorite!"

Savannah smiled at Sofia's catchphrase and nodded. "I know it is. And I can't wait to see what you create."

Becca, Sofia's mom and Carter's sister, poked her head into the room and sighed. "You couldn't wait thirty seconds for me, bug?"

"You were going too slow, Mommy."

As Becca and Savannah shared a laugh, Savannah stood to her full height as Sofia ran to the landing area where the circle rug and activity stations sat, as well as the cubbies for each child to store their backpack and coat.

Becca shook her head. "I give her life...feed, clothe, bathe, and house her for four years, and this is how she repays me?" Becca heaved a dramatic sigh. "I suppose it's all downhill from here. Next thing you know, she'll want me to drop her off around the block so she's not seen with me anymore."

Savannah chuckled and shook her head. "I think you've still got a few years."

"I'm not so sure about that." She called over Savannah's shoulder toward her daughter, who was chatting with her best friend who'd just arrived, "Bye, bug! Love you."

Sofia's only response was a wave over her shoulder, and Becca snorted in response. "See?"

"She's four going on fourteen, huh?"

"You've got that right. I've gotta run, but I'll see you later." Becca jingled her keys in her hands and shot Savannah a smile. "And, hey—good luck today."

Savannah waved as Becca dodged the incoming children and their parents, and Savannah was immediately pulled in a dozen different directions by anxious kids and parents both. Katie's dad reminded her of Katie's strawberry allergy—something they, thankfully, had a chart to track. Phillip's mom let Savannah know he had a doctor's appointment so he would need to be picked up early today. After that, it was a whirlwind of excited squeals and a few tears—from both kids and parents alike.

Even though it had only been a weekend since she'd seen many of these children at the Sunshine Corner's day care on the main floor, it somehow felt like they were arriving at school after a long summer away. Because she'd worked with Abby since the Sunshine Corner's inception years ago, she'd had a hand in being part of many of these kids' lives that entire time. Of course, they hadn't had the dedicated day-care staff—or room—to accommodate all twenty-eight kids currently enrolled in the preschool, but Heart's Hope Bay was small enough that Savannah knew, or knew of, every single child who walked through their doors. Some more than others, and not necessarily for the best reasons.

"Stop! Stop it!" Austin, a rambunctious handful of a kid—if Savannah was being honest—shoved at his mom's face as she tried to kiss him goodbye. When she didn't let him go, he slapped her, then laughed before making his escape.

Yep, Savannah definitely knew some of these children better than others. She also knew it was going to be a very long year with that particular charmer in her class.

"Savannah." Megan, Austin's mom, acknowledged her stiffly, her assessing eyes scrutinizing the classroom as if looking for something to complain about.

Thankfully, Savannah, along with Abby, Jenn—a day-care worker who spent most of her days with the under-two crowd—and Hilde, Abby's grandma who owned the house the Sunshine Corner operated out of, had only been subjected to little Austin for a year thus far. But in that time, she and Abby both had had numerous discussions with Megan regarding her son's aggressive behavior. Predictably, his mom was quick to blame other children for her son's biting instances and rough-and-tumble tendencies—the whole *boys will be boys* adage that Savannah had little tolerance for.

She pasted on a smile that was little more than a baring of teeth. "How are you?"

Rather than answering the pleasantry or offering any of her own, Megan said, "I sent you an email last night and haven't heard back."

Savannah pressed her lips together and stared at the other woman for a beat. Yes, she definitely dropped everything and replied to emails after hours on the eve of a brand-new school year, especially from parents like this. "It must've come in after hours. I'll be sure to check it during lunch today. Unless you'd like to chat about it now?"

She sniffed and crossed her arms. "I'd like a copy of the proposed curriculum you intend to teach this year so I'm able to discuss any alterations I'll expect for Austin."

It was getting harder and harder to maintain this farce of a smile, but Savannah wasn't going to lose her cool before the first day had technically even started. "I'll be happy to set up an appointment for us to discuss any possible changes for Austin that will be necessary for his development."

"Great. I'll expect a copy via email by the end of the day."

What Savannah wouldn't give to be able to drop a house on this wicked witch. She held her fake smile in place as Megan left without another word and did a quick breathing exercise she'd learned during her brief stint as a yogi a few years ago. She may have collected hobbies like stamps and discarded them just as easily, but she'd been able to pick up a few things along the way that still came in handy.

Children and parents like that made this job hard and had her questioning her sanity on a daily basis. Of course, she liked what she did. You didn't consistently put yourself through daily multi-hour interactions with a dozen screaming-crying-laughing-jumping children and not enjoy it. That would just be masochistic.

Still, while she liked her job well enough, she wasn't sure she *loved* it. In all the time she'd spent exploring different majors in college, different jobs here and there, or different hobbies, she'd never found something she truly loved or that felt completely natural. That was probably why, despite being twenty-nine, she still didn't know what she wanted to truly do for the rest of her life.

Although, according to her brothers—and at least one of her brother's friends—that was something she was never going to figure out.

She straightened her shoulders, brushed back the blond flyaways from the ponytail she'd smoothed her hair into, and ran a hand down the front of her blouse. She'd show them. She may not know if this was her true vocation, but she knew one thing—she refused to let Abby down.

And if her succeeding just so happened to make her brothers eat crow, fine by her. All the better if her brother's obnoxious best friend, Noah, had some shoved down his throat too.

Savannah glanced down at her watch before darting her eyes around the space to take a mental roll call, noting how Tori's nerves had seemed to dissipate as she interacted with the children and showed them around. Thirteen of their fourteen kids had arrived, and it was already five after nine, so they should get started.

As she rounded the corner to make sure the missing child wasn't in the common space, she found who she was looking for. Rosie Adams hid behind her grandmother's legs, her wide, dark brown eyes shiny with tears. Savannah didn't have time to feel relief that Rosie's father—the aforementioned Noah—hadn't brought his daughter in. Instead, Savannah went straight into crisis mode and strode toward them with a smile.

She offered a silent wave to Cheryl, Rosie's grandmother, before turning her attention on the little girl, hoping that doing so would calm any anxieties she had. Making her voice as soothing as possible, Savannah said, "Hi, Rosie. I'm so excited you're in my class this year! We're going to have a lot of fun."

Rather than responding, Rosie burrowed farther behind Cheryl's legs, her backpack forgotten on the floor at her feet.

Savannah tried a different tactic. "Sofia is here already. Wanna go say hi?"

While Rosie hadn't attended the Sunshine Corner previously, the little girl had spent some time there in the weeks leading up to the start of the school year in an effort to make the transition easier. It was one of the many things Abby had thought of that went above and beyond and made the Sunshine Corner the best in Heart's Hope Bay.

Fortunately, Rosie and Sofia had hit it off, so the little girl would have at least one friend here today.

Unfortunately, the mention of her friend didn't

appear to hold much allure for her, as she didn't budge
an inch from the space behind her grandma.

Savannah glanced at Cheryl with a raised eyebrow,
her question clear.

"She's been this way since her mother moved away,"
Cheryl said in a quick, hushed tone. "It takes her a
while to warm up."

She'd only heard about Noah's divorce and his wife—
ex-wife—bailing to Houston through the grapevine,
but grapevines grew plentifully in a town the size of
Heart's Hope Bay. There'd been so many theories as to
why a woman would leave a man like Noah Adams,
each more outlandish and salacious than the last.
Savannah might not know much about Noah's life, but
she had a theory of her own. Their split was obviously
because he was an overbearing, judgmental jerk who
shoved his opinions where they didn't belong.

She had no idea what she'd done to attract his ire,
but one thing was for certain—he did not like her in
the least. That was fine. The feeling was mutual. True,
it'd been a little hard to get on that train initially—
after all, he was absolutely gorgeous, because of course
he was—and she'd met him when she was still a
naive preteen who'd blushed over every cute guy. But
even then, after a while, she'd been able to see him
for who he truly was. And of course, that particular
stance had been pushed even further along when he'd
started chasing off any boys who held even a modicum
of interest in her. He and Caleb—Savannah's second

oldest brother—had seemed to take great pleasure in denying her male attention.

Thankfully, she didn't see him as often now that Caleb had moved to San Francisco last year, but the little mood killer still hung out with her remaining three brothers who lived in town. And her opinion of him was always reconfirmed during every one of those inevitable run-ins, which was why it wasn't hard for her to presume why his ex-wife had left.

"Of course." She leaned in close and whispered low enough for only Cheryl to hear, "It might be best to leave without lingering. The prolonged goodbyes can sometimes make things worse."

Cheryl rested her hand on Rosie's dark brown locks and shot a worried look at her granddaughter. She looked back to Savannah, who gave her an encouraging nod. Cheryl leaned down to speak to Rosie.

Savannah gave them a bit of privacy, quickly checking in on the classroom and making sure that Tori was still rocking it, before circling back around.

"I'll see you tomorrow," Cheryl said. "Daddy's picking you up tonight, okay?"

"But I don't want—"

Without waiting for the little girl to finish, Savannah strode up and squatted to Rosie's height. "Oh, I'm so glad you're here, Rosie! I really need help with something. Do you think you can give me a hand?"

Rosie glanced from Savannah to her grandma and back again before giving a small nod.

Savannah exaggerated a relieved sigh. "Thank you. You're a lifesaver." She stood up and reached for Rosie's hand. "First, let's get your backpack hung up in your cubby. Do you think you can find your name?"

While Rosie was preoccupied looking for the name-plate that matched her name, Savannah lifted her chin toward Cheryl, who looked on with relief and gratitude before waving and silently slipping down the steps.

Even though Savannah wasn't sure this was what she'd spend the rest of her life doing, she couldn't deny the hint of pride that settled in her chest when she soothed a scared child, encouraged a friendship of a lonely one, or praised the activities of one with low self-esteem. That was enough to make her float through her morning, high on the idea that she was doing this. And not only that, but she was actually doing it well.

At least until she remembered what Cheryl had said earlier and that Noah would be picking up Rosie later. He was sure to be the rain on her parade.

Chapter Two

Most days in Heart's Hope Bay were downright boring for public safety officers. Other times—especially during full moons—Noah Adams could hardly find time to inhale something to eat between the calls. Today fell somewhere in the middle.

He and his partner, Cash, were on a run for a suspected broken hip of an elderly male. Since Cash was a paramedic, and thus higher ranking, he always called dibs on driving for the duration of the day. Although, that was probably best considering *Noah's* duration was half that of his partner's.

Noah and his ex-wife, Jess, had been slowly working their way through the process of separating for the better part of a year now. They'd fallen out of love even longer ago. When she'd announced that she wanted a divorce, his first thought had been for Rosie, which had told him everything he needed to know about his chances of salvaging their marriage. It had been tough, trying to figure out how they were going to co-parent their little girl as he started looking for apartments, but they'd made it work.

Until this summer, when Jess got a huge new job in Texas.

Since that moment, Noah's life had been turned upside down. They'd decided together that Rosie would stay here with him, where she was comfortable and where he had a support network—namely his mom. He wouldn't have it any other way, but he couldn't pretend it hadn't been a struggle. Out of nowhere, he had to figure out how to survive as a single father *and* as an EMT whose schedule didn't exactly lend itself to single parenthood.

Fortunately, his captain—a man he'd known his whole life…one of the benefits of living in a small town—had allowed for some temporary concessions to his typical schedule as he figured things out.

"I don't know why you don't just let me drive every day. You know I'm better at it." Noah glanced at Cash from the passenger's seat as they pulled up to 412 Maple Street.

Cash parked in front of their destination and snorted. "Only in your wildest fantasies, Adams."

"Hate to break it to you, but you're not even in the realm of my consciousness when I'm fantasizing."

"Your loss." Cash shrugged a single shoulder before

opening his door. "I'll grab the gear. You get the gurney."

"Sure, boss." The nickname Noah had given him years ago rolled right off the other man, who didn't even spare him a second glance.

They'd worked together for a few years now, and even though their routine had been disrupted by Noah's scheduling concessions, they still worked great together. It was like a dance most days, sometimes following and sometimes leading, always in sync and attuned to what the other one needed to get the job done.

By the time Noah made it to the front door, gurney in tow, Cash stood on the stoop, calling through the closed door. "Sir, we're with Heart's Hope Bay EMS. Can we come in?"

A muffled yes sounded from inside, so Cash tried the knob, and Noah exhaled a relieved breath when it turned with ease. Another plus to small-town living— no need to lock your doors in the middle of the day. Or ever. That made their entry into homes with single, elderly patients much easier.

Leaving the gurney out front for now, Noah followed Cash inside. The home was a small, cluttered ranch-style house, which allowed for minimal movable space. It was easy to see how someone could lose their footing and fall.

They found the older gentleman between the living room and the kitchen, prone on the ground, his face pinched with pain.

Noah and Cash made their way straight to the patient, their gear in tow. Cash squatted by the man's head, focusing on ABC first—airway, breathing, and circulation—while Noah went to the man's side in order to be in his line of sight.

"Hi there, I'm Noah. My partner Cash and I are going to get you all checked out. Can you tell me your name?"

"Bill Evers." The man's voice was tight with strain.

"Wish we were meeting under better circumstances, Mr. Evers, but we're going to get you squared away."

Cash took Mr. Evers's vitals as Noah asked for a detailed accounting of the fall so they could assess how best to treat him. It sounded fairly standard for what they usually saw—an elderly person, living alone, who overestimated their mobility and paid the price. Noah dreaded the possibility of ending up like that— alone and completely unable to take care of himself in an emergency. The thought was enough to give him hives.

Fortunately, Mr. Evers didn't have any complications. The drop-off at the hospital went quickly, and Noah was able to get the reports typed up on the laptop by the time they arrived at the firehouse. Raucous sounds came from inside even as they walked into the bay, and the noises only grew louder when Noah opened the door to the station. It was just before six, which meant dinnertime, and the dining area was filled with bodies of everyone currently on duty, the commotion resembling a large family meal—or what Noah assumed as such, anyway.

Things hadn't been like that for him growing up, as the only child of a single mom, but then again, he'd witnessed his fair share of family meals at his best friend's house. Since Caleb had moved to San Francisco, Noah hadn't spent as much time at the Lowe house as he had previously, but Caleb's parents still invited him and Rosie over once in a while. To say their house was loud would be like saying the roar of a jet engine was merely a whisper. Of course, that was bound to happen with five children consisting of four obnoxious boys and one opinionated, headstrong girl.

Before Noah could reminisce too much about his time at the Lowe household, Grant, a fellow EMT, shouted a greeting from the large dining table. "If you guys want to eat, you better hustle," he said, barely pausing long enough to get the words out between bites.

That was one thing Noah hadn't been prepared for when he'd become an EMT. He'd assumed there'd be plenty of food for all. Which, to be fair, there always was. But the rule at the firehouse was, if you didn't eat it fast, you didn't want it bad enough.

Cash clapped a hand on Noah's shoulder before striding straight to the stove to dish up a heaping bowl of chili. Instead of doing the same, Noah glanced down at his watch and cursed under his breath. He was already five minutes late to pick up Rosie at the Sunshine Corner. He hated this. Hated feeling like he was always dropping the ball, now that he was the one juggling all of them.

It was difficult enough making single fatherhood work for someone with a more traditional career, but Noah was working with unique scheduling confinements. Chuck, his captain, had agreed to give him some leeway while he and Rosie adjusted to being on their own. That meant instead of the typical twenty-four on, forty-eight off that his fellow public safety officers worked, Noah worked four twelve-hour shifts a week—and day shifts to boot. The fact that he'd had special allowances made for him had disrupted the camaraderie in the firehouse. While none of his coworkers would ever come right out and say it, he could tell it rankled by their "joking" remarks, hushed conversations, and derisive looks when they thought he wasn't paying attention.

The best course of action to defuse any animosity before it could even brew was generally making a joke, so Noah headed toward his locker, throwing over his shoulder, "I'll just eat at home and save this for you guys. You're looking a little ravenous, Grant."

The others' good-natured ribbing of Grant followed Noah back to his locker, where he quickly grabbed his things. As much as cutting out bothered him— and it did feel like cutting out, regardless of the fact that he was working just as much as the others—he couldn't hang around even if he wanted to. The Sunshine Corner technically closed at six, but Abby had been kind enough to agree to give him some latitude as he fumbled his way through this new normal. But that was sure to run out at some point, and Noah dreaded the day that he'd have to figure something else out.

God knew his mom would help him if only he asked, but she already did so much for them. She watched Rosie in the mornings from the time Noah had to be at the firehouse to when Rosie could be dropped off at school, as well as anytime a run kept him later than usual. Even though she insisted she wasn't put out by it and that she even *enjoyed* watching Rosie, he hated relying on his mom for help. He hated relying on *anyone* for help. In an ideal world, he'd be able to figure this out all on his own.

"I'll see you guys later," Noah said, striding through the dining area on his way out.

"Enjoy your beauty sleep, Adams," John, an older, seasoned firefighter, called, a slight edge to his tone—the only hint that the words weren't merely a joke.

Noah laughed it off, or put on a good show anyway, for those in the house. But the truth was, he was just as sick of his altered schedule as his coworkers seemed to be.

He just didn't see another way.

By the time he pulled up in front of the Sunshine Corner, he'd worked himself up into such a piss-poor mood, even the bright, sunshiny yellow door of the day care and preschool couldn't alleviate it. Some days skated by with little fanfare. Then there were others, like today, when he was reminded of every speed bump or pothole that had been thrown along his path since he and Jess split. One thing Noah didn't enjoy was having his failures tossed back in his face every time he took a step.

He rang the buzzer and hoped Rosie's first day of 4K went well. She hadn't attended preschool last year, though her former day care had offered a bit of schooling during her days there. She was so damn smart, though, he knew she'd excel, and he couldn't wait to hear about it.

"Hey, Noah," Abby said, opening the door with a kind smile.

While he and Abby didn't run in the same circles, they'd known each other for decades thanks to the Lowes. "Hey, Abby. Sorry I'm late. We had a—"

She held up a hand to stop him and shook her head. "Don't worry about it. I told you it was fine for her to stay a little after-hours."

A little after was one thing, but he knew from experience that consistently being thirty minutes late was quite another.

"Just make sure to bill me time and a half for it, all right?" He internally cringed as he said the words, mentally calculating his bank balance and how much these nights were going to cost him.

All those thoughts fell straight out of his head at the sound of Rosie crying. He rushed through the house to the great room at the back of the property, intent on finding out just what had his girl crying. When he got there, he froze in anger. It wasn't a *what* but a *who*. And that *who* was the bane of his existence.

Noah had been acquainted with Savannah for the better part of her life. Growing up, he'd been a surrogate member of the Lowe family, and he'd enjoyed every minute of it. The only sour note was how everyone in that household indulged the youngest Lowe. It annoyed him to no end that Savannah had always been treated like a princess who was in constant need of protection. First from school bullies, then later from guys with only one thing on their minds. And even, once in a while, from herself and her poor decisions.

Her family fawned over her so much that she'd never once had to stand on her own. That was one aspect of his life he was grateful for. He loved his mom with his whole heart, but it'd always been just the two of them. From a very young age, he'd had to take care of himself while his mom worked a couple jobs to support them. He'd gotten his work ethic from her, which was probably why the special circumstances he worked out with his captain rankled so badly.

Savannah, on the other hand, still lived with her folks at age twenty-nine. She'd had everything handed to her throughout her whole life. Which was probably why she stood there, in front of his daughter, completely unable to soothe her. She was clearly out of her depth here.

Yet, as he stood there, irritation seeping through his pores, there was no denying how utterly gorgeous she was, with her golden blond hair and legs that went on for miles. He glanced away, dousing that flare of interest that always sparked in her presence, despite how he felt about her. She was insufferably spoiled, and he had little time for that.

"Maybe instead of just standing there, you could actually try to soothe her," Noah snapped as he dodged Savannah and swept Rosie up in his arms.

"What? No, I—"

"Save it." His tone was cool and detached, but they'd known each other long enough that he had no doubt she'd be able to read the irritation in it. Good. Let her.

Rosie's face was buried in his neck, her arms wrapped tightly around him.

"Where's your backpack, squirt?"

When Rosie didn't so much as make a peep, he rubbed a soothing circle on her back and asked again. "Your backpack? We need to bring it home."

A throat cleared directly behind him, and he turned his head toward the sound. Savannah stood, arm outstretched and backpack dangling from two fingers.

He snatched the bag from her and strode to the front door without a backward glance.

"See you tomorrow, Rosie!" Savannah called, then mumbled something under her breath that he was probably better off not being able to decipher.

It was no secret that the two of them didn't get along. As a kid, he'd tolerated her always tagging along after him and her brothers, even when it ended in her tattling on them for inevitably getting into something they shouldn't. But as they'd gotten older, she'd continued to be an annoying thorn in his side. She was just always *there*, whether it was in the rec room at her house where he was trying to play foosball with his best friends or here at the Sunshine Corner where she was ineffectively trying to take care of his child. She aggravated him to no end, and she'd made it abundantly clear that he did the same. He didn't mind it. In fact, he reveled in it. It watered down the potency of his attraction to her, dousing the flame before it could get above a single spark.

Rosie quickly cheered up once they made it to the car and he drove home on autopilot, listening to her animatedly chat away about an episode of her favorite television show. No mention of her first day, her tears long forgotten. She'd always been quiet and a little clingy, but it'd gone to a whole new level after Jess had left. During the day, Rosie barely let him out of her sight to use the bathroom, and most mornings, he woke to find her curled up at his side, cocooned in her favorite blanket. He'd second-guessed everything he'd done since Jess had left, including switching Rosie's day care so she could attend preschool at the Sunshine Corner. He sure as hell hoped he hadn't made a mistake in doing so.

Since it was pretty close to seven by the time they arrived at home, he declared tonight's meal brinner—breakfast for dinner, Rosie's favorite—and poured them both bowls of cereal. He assuaged his guilt just barely by cutting up a banana and some strawberries to top hers and reminding himself that nights like these, when he was spread a little too thin to prepare a home-cooked meal, were why he didn't buy the sugary cereals, despite his mom trying to sneak them in every chance she got.

"How was your day?" he asked as they settled on the couch, their usual spot for brinner nights.

She only offered a shrug in response, and Noah glanced at her out of the corner of his eye. He figured she'd be tight-lipped—she usually was until after her bath when he was fixing her hair. Because of that, he didn't push for specifics until she was seated on the counter in the bathroom, facing the mirror as he brushed through her long, dark hair.

This hadn't come naturally to him, but he'd had to learn quickly after Jess left; fortunately, with his mom being a hairstylist, he'd had someone willing to teach him. Now he could braid her hair in five minutes flat.

He took his time tonight, knowing that she felt more comfortable talking when she wasn't facing him. Never mind that he could read every emotion that crossed her face thanks to the mirror. She was too preoccupied sorting through her different colored barrettes to pay him any attention.

"What did you do today?" he asked as he ran the brush gently through her hair.

She lifted a single shoulder and set out a purple and a lime-green barrette. "I can't tell you 'cause it's a surprise."

"Your whole first day is a surprise?"

"Uh-huh," she said seriously.

"Did someone tell you not to say anything?"

"Miss Savannah said our parents might like to be surprised. So don't tell Mommy I drew a special picture today, okay, Daddy?"

Noah smiled for half a second at her slip before the rest of her words sank in.

He didn't resent his ex-wife for leaving. They'd been well on their way to separating before she'd secretly interviewed for that out-of-state job. Jess had always been career-oriented, and the new position was a huge step for her. But he couldn't understand how she could so easily leave Rosie behind. How she could give up things like special pictures and time spent braiding their little girl's hair.

Worse, he hated that his daughter had to go through this. He knew what it was like growing up with only one parent present. And while Jess was still involved in Rosie's life—they still FaceTimed a few nights a week, and Rosie would see her for a little bit in the summer—Noah had sole custody, which meant it was just the two of them.

It was a big weight on his shoulders and something

he took seriously. He might've been trained in life-or-death situations, but he'd never felt pressure like he had when he'd realized Rosie's future sat on his shoulders and his alone.

Later, after Rosie was in bed and he'd collapsed into his own, his cell rang as he was watching a cooking video on it. Caleb's name flashed at the top of the screen, and he hesitated for a few seconds. He was exhausted and could barely cobble together a full sentence. He wanted nothing more than to mindlessly watch cooking videos to get ideas for meals he'd never have enough time to prepare, or maybe finally research ideas for how to redo the pantry shelves that were on the verge of falling down. But Caleb was his best friend, and that relationship was important to him. He'd been there for Noah when he and Jess had decided to file for divorce. He'd even come up the weekend Jess had left and stayed with him and Rosie, keeping both their minds off reality.

"Hey, man," he answered just before it could click over to voice mail.

"Screening my calls again?" A thread of humor wove through Caleb's voice, and Noah smiled, grateful he'd picked up.

"Nah, I'd have to care about you way more than I do to go to all that trouble."

Caleb snorted. "Glad to know where I stand."

"Were you unsure before?"

"With you? I don't think I could be."

There was so much truth to that statement, it was almost painful. Noah had never been able to keep his opinions to himself—for better or worse. For his friends, that meant they always knew where they stood with him. Everything was out in the open, and thus, they could get past it all the quicker. For those who weren't his friends, well… They didn't have to wonder, either.

"I know you're probably ready to crash for the night, but I wanted to catch you quick and see if you'd do me a favor."

"That depends on whether this one will end with me on my hands and knees, scrubbing your grandma's toilet like the last favor I did for you."

Caleb barked out a laugh. "Nothing quite as exciting, I'm afraid. I was hoping you'd head to my parents' place tomorrow after work for a group video chat."

Tomorrow night was Rosie's weekly ballet class, so his mom would be picking her up early and taking her to that before treating her to dinner out at a place of Rosie's choosing. He'd been looking forward to a couple hours of silence, but he knew that wasn't enough of an excuse to say no.

"A group video chat, huh? That's dramatic."

"Yeah, well, what I have to tell you is kind of a big deal."

Noah's eyebrows lifted, his curiosity piqued. "Yeah? Like what?"

"Nice try. You'll find out tomorrow, along with

everyone else," Caleb said. "And, hey, maybe you and Savannah can refrain from biting each other's heads off long enough to find out the news."

Considering Noah and Savannah's track record, that hope was utterly futile, and his best friend knew it.

Chapter Three

Savannah couldn't believe that today had only been the second day that she'd been running the Sunshine Corner's preschool. Even though she'd spent the past several years working with children, this was something else entirely. She didn't know if it was because she was solely in charge of this venture, because Abby was resting a great deal of responsibility on her shoulders, or if it had more to do with molding the minds of four-year-olds that made each day feel more momentous.

At least Noah's mom had been the one to pick up Rosie today. Savannah's temper still flared when she remembered how he'd glared at her at pickup the day before. If he'd been a jerk again, she wasn't sure she could have kept herself in check.

She pulled into her parents' driveway, looking forward to an evening of takeout and *Schitt's Creek* in her apartment above the garage. Most of the time, living this close to home wasn't a bad thing. She could sneak over for home-cooked meals whenever she wanted, borrow a cup of sugar—or an entire bag—and didn't have to worry about yard maintenance.

It also meant she lacked privacy and couldn't escape, even if she wanted to.

"Get in here, Savannah!" Jackson, her youngest brother—though still older than her—called out the back door before she was even fully out of her car. "Caleb's FaceTiming in fifteen, and he wants us all here."

Savannah blew out an exhausted breath, her shoulders slumping with disappointment and surrender as she trudged toward her parents' house.

"Did he get a promotion already?" Savannah asked, dropping her bag just inside the back door.

"Would one of you help your sister with her bag?" Savannah's mom snapped to the boys before turning a smile on Savannah. Pauline Lowe was gorgeous, a natural beauty who'd said goodbye to hair dye over the past two years and let her hair be its natural silver. "Are you hungry, sweetheart? I've got a plate of chicken pot pie in the oven for you, if you are. It'll probably be the only home-cooked meal you'll get, since I know you don't do much of that."

Savannah knew her mom never meant anything by what she said. None of her family ever meant anything by it. But the innocent comments still stung.

She sighed. "Sure, Mom. I was just going to order takeout tonight anyway."

"You can't have takeout all the time," her dad called over his shoulder from where he sat in the recliner facing the TV. Her brothers were scattered around him as they watched some sports highlights she couldn't care less about. "You know your mom always makes extra for you."

"Why doesn't she make extra for me?" Aaron, her second youngest brother, grumbled, crossing his arms.

"Or me," Spencer, firstborn and Mr. Perfect, chimed in.

Savannah rolled her eyes as her mom set a warm dish in front of her before patting her lightly on her shoulder. "What, no remarks out of you?" she asked Jackson, who sat at the table, shoveling in a piece of what appeared to be homemade cherry pie.

He gestured with his fork toward his almost clean plate. "I'm a little busy here," he said around a mouthful of food.

Savannah rolled her eyes. Her entire family acted as if she were the baby, when really Jackson was the one who acted like a child, if anyone were to ask her. He spent almost all of his free time surfing, and his table manners were *atrocious*. Sure, he also literally saved stray puppies as a volunteer at the local animal shelter, but that barely offset the rest.

Ignoring him, her mom pulled out a chair across from Savannah and folded her hands on the table, looking at Savannah expectantly. "Tell us about your first couple of days leading the preschool. Everything go okay?"

The apprehensive note in her mom's voice was probably something no one else would pick up on. Certainly, if they did, they'd tell Savannah she was overreacting or reading too much into it. But it was comments like that that made her self-conscious in her endeavors. It was why she rarely told her family when she was excited to try something new. That was 100 percent saved for Abby. This, though, wasn't something she had the luxury of hiding. Whether she succeeded at this or failed, it'd be fodder for the entire town before she could so much as blink.

"Pretty good, I think." Savannah shrugged and blew on a bite of chicken pot pie before bringing it to her lips.

Jackson snorted and leaned back in his chair, regarding her with a bemused expression. "You can't seriously think you're going to get off that easy."

Apparently, even eating did not excuse her from regaling her family with all the hairy details.

"I think it's going pretty well. Or at least Abby hasn't received any angry phone calls yet."

No angry calls, true, but there was the incident of Noah walking in on her when she'd been trying to distract Rosie from the fact that her dad was late picking her up. Of course, Noah being Noah, the jerk didn't think twice before blaming *her* and cutting off all attempts to correct him. She hadn't even bothered to restrain herself from giving his back a one-finger salute. After all, Rosie had been the last child at the Sunshine Corner for at least thirty minutes, so she didn't need to worry about impressionable eyes witnessing her impulsive reaction.

"No angry parents is most definitely a good thing." Her mom reached out and tapped Savannah's hand gently. "I think you're doing *great*."

Savannah fought not to roll her eyes.

Which was worse? Her mom subtly commenting on her lack of enthusiasm for cooking, or her subtly condescending encouragement? It made her feel like one of her students. When you were four, it was cool to be told you were doing a great job for cutting along a straight line. When you were almost thirty? Not so much.

She was an adult for heaven's sake, and she didn't need her parents fluffing up her ego.

Then again, she also didn't need her every action questioned.

"What's Savannah doing 'great' at?" a deep voice rumbled from behind her, the back door closing punctuating the question.

Savannah concentrated very hard on restraining her physical reaction to Noah's voice, or his question, or his smug, perfect face. As if it wasn't enough that she had to interact with him daily at the Sunshine Corner, now he was infiltrating her family time too?

"What are *you* doing here?" She couldn't keep the hostile edge out of her voice, and apparently she wasn't the only one who noticed.

"Damn, Noah, what'd you do to piss off Savannah?" Jackson asked, laughing.

Noah slid into the chair directly across from her, his deep, brown eyes piercing hers. "I assume it's because I woke up alive today."

Savannah narrowed her gaze at Noah, her hand tightening around her fork. Did he have any idea how much willpower it was taking her not to stab him with this? Growing up with four older brothers, she was no stranger to the incessant irritation of men, especially those related to her. But Noah was on a whole different level, even if he wasn't related. Or maybe *because* he wasn't related to her.

Beneath the table, his foot nudged hers. It had to be an accident, but the casual touch made her shiver all the same.

Jerking her leg back, she pasted on a saccharine smile. "Am I that transparent?"

Noah's nostrils flared—the only sign of his frustration—as he stared her down, and a dormant butterfly fluttered to life in her stomach. "Pretty sure I've always seen through you."

The butterfly was suddenly crushed under the avalanche of his words, and she exhaled a relieved breath. Noah was drop-dead gorgeous, in that brooding, arrogant, know-it-all kind of way. And his good looks sometimes made her lose her head a bit around him. Fortunately, he couldn't help but shine his true colors around her, and they always served to extinguish any fire sparked by pure attraction.

Before she could retort, her mom's phone rang, indicating an incoming FaceTime call.

"Alan! Boys! Get in here," her mom said, grabbing her laptop to answer from there. "Caleb's calling."

Savannah scooted her chair closer to her mom's and leaned in.

"Hi, honey!" Her mom leaned too close to the screen, grinning at Caleb and Issa.

"Hey, Mom." Caleb's deep voice boomed from the laptop, his dark blond hair a rumpled mess. He shifted his laptop so they could all see his girlfriend, Issa, seated next to him. Her deep brown complexion glowed as she grinned widely, her crown of ebony, corkscrew curls framing her face.

Savannah smiled at the sight of them. While her brothers irritated her beyond compare most days, she still missed having them all here. "What about me?" she asked, poking her head into the screen.

"Hi to you, too, Savannah. Where's everyone else?"

A chorus of greetings went up around her as her dad and brothers crowded around Savannah and her mom. Savannah knew immediately that it wasn't one of her brothers standing directly behind her because her hair stood on end, goose bumps rippling across her skin. Only one person evoked that reaction in her—no doubt underlying rage bubbling to the surface—and he most certainly wasn't related to her.

Noah rested his hands on the back of her chair, his fingers just barely grazing her skin through the thin fabric of her shirt. His scent engulfed her, like pine trees and fresh ocean air, and she couldn't help but to inhale as covertly as possible.

Why had she never realized before just how good he smelled?

She shifted forward to get away from him before she lost all her sense, but with them all crowded in together, there wasn't far to go.

"What's this all about, son?" Savannah's dad asked as he braced himself on the back of his wife's chair. "You moving back home?"

Caleb huffed out a laugh and shook his head, glancing toward Issa. A smile overtook his face, mirroring hers, and Savannah felt an answering one sweep over her mouth. Caleb and Issa had met not long after he moved to San Francisco. They'd only been dating for a year, but Savannah had gotten to know Issa well in that time, and now counted her among her closest friends. Seeing her happy—seeing *them* happy—lit her up inside.

"No," Caleb said, finally turning his attention back to the screen. "But I do have news. Well, *we* have news, actually."

Savannah's eyes went wide as she held her breath, pretty sure her brother was about to tell them—

"We're engaged!"

Issa smiled widely and swept her hand toward the camera, holding it out so the new solitaire diamond sparkled on the screen.

Grumbles of "Oh great, now Mom will never get off my back" and "I'm never going to hear the end of this" came from her brothers, but they were instantly drowned out by her and her mom's squeals of excitement.

"Oh my God!" Savannah said, leaning closer to the screen, as if it'd be possible to get a better look at the ring that way. "Tell me everything! When did he do it? *How*? And when is the wedding?"

Issa laughed. "He asked me Saturday night."

"*Saturday*," Savannah and her mom said in unison, betrayal evident in both their voices.

"I wanted to make sure you could all be there before we told you." Caleb wrapped an arm around Issa and tugged her into his side, kissing his fiancée's temple. "Plus, it was kind of nice having this secret to ourselves for a while."

"Well, there'll be no more of that." Savannah's mom narrowed her eyes at the screen and pointed a finger toward Caleb and Issa. "Now, answer the rest of your sister's questions before I get in my car and drive down there to get a response in person."

"Better listen to her, son," her dad piped in. "I don't want your mother driving in the middle of the night just to wring your neck."

"Well," Issa said, glancing at Caleb with a bright smile. "He filled the day with all my favorite things—"

"So basically you toured all the libraries in the area?" Savannah asked dryly.

Issa giggled. "Basically. He chartered a boat for a private wine tasting, and I started to wonder if he was going to propose."

"You proposed to her on a private boat? What a douch—" Jackson cut off on an *oof* when their mom reached back and smacked him.

"No, he didn't." Issa glanced at Caleb, a small smile playing on her lips. "He totally threw me off. When we docked and got off the boat without him asking, I wrote it off. But then he took me to the Garden of Shakespeare's Flowers, and...honestly, I don't remember much about it. One second, we're walking through and I'm pointing out some of the flowers and what books they were in, and the next, he's down on one knee, holding a ring out in front of him."

Savannah and her mom sighed in unison.

"Oh, Issa, that sounds so special and just perfect for you!" her mom gushed. "Nicely done, sweetheart."

"I'm just glad she said yes."

"More like shocked. Us too," Aaron cut in, never one to let an opportunity to insult his siblings pass by.

"When's the big day?" Noah asked, his breath fanning over Savannah's skin in a way that had her responding in wholly inappropriate ways. Wholly inappropriate because for one thing, she was literally surrounded by her family, and for another because this was *Noah*, and she absolutely wasn't going there with him.

"Better question," Jackson said, "is which of your brothers are you going to ask to be your best man? It's me, isn't it?"

"Actually," Caleb said, his eyes now trained above Savannah's head. "I was hoping Noah would be my best man. I figured that'd be the only way to avoid bloodshed among you three idiots. So, what do you say, man? Want to help me out and make sure they don't kill each other?"

"Well, when you put it like that," Noah said, a wry tinge to his voice. "Of course I will."

"And, Savannah," Issa said, "I'd love if you'd be one of my bridesmaids. Will you?"

"Um, *obviously*." Savannah shifted, accidentally bringing her back into contact with Noah's fingers for a brief second before he seemed to realize how close they were and pulled away. "So, what date are you guys thinking about?"

"It depends on everyone's schedule," Caleb said, glancing over at Issa. "But we were hoping for some time around Christmas."

"Of this year?" Savannah nearly shrieked.

Issa laughed and nodded. "Yeah. We want to make it official as soon as possible."

"Oh, my." Savannah's mom pressed a hand to her chest. "That's so soon. But I suppose I can make a few trips down there to help out, if you think it would be useful?"

"Actually, Mom, we'd like to have the wedding in Heart's Hope Bay. But we're both so busy with work, and with the cost of a wedding, we're going to be a little strapped for cash and won't be able to make any trips home to plan." He glanced to Savannah and then above her to where Noah stood. "That's where you guys come in."

"How so?" The tinge of apprehension in Noah's voice mirrored her feelings.

"Well, we were hoping you two would help us with planning the details up there. You know, check out reception sites, taste-test cakes, find a ceremony location, that kind of thing."

"We know it's a lot to ask," Issa interjected, sitting up straighter. "We'll take care of as much as possible from here, of course. Send you lists of places to check out. But we really need eyes on the ground for some of these things, you know?"

Was that a hint of wistfulness Savannah caught in Issa's tone? "You sure you wouldn't be missing out? A girl only gets to plan her wedding once."

"Hopefully," Aaron muttered behind her. He grunted at a not-so-subtle jab of their mother's elbow into his side.

"I'm sure," Issa said, all sign of hesitation gone. She smiled and leaned into Caleb again. "All I care about is the groom."

Said groom flushed, even as he curled his arm back around her. Addressing the screen, he asked, "So, what do you guys say? Noah? Savannah? Can we count on you?"

An immediate yes leaped to her tongue, but she paused. She had so much on her plate already. The responsibility of running the new preschool program was the biggest commitment she'd ever taken on. And now she was going to pile this on top of it?

For Caleb and Issa, she'd make it work.

But the utterance of Noah's name reminded her that she was signing on for more than just cakes and flowers and venues. Biting the inside of her cheek, she snuck a glance over her shoulder at him.

Months of even more interaction with the one man who seemed to drive her out of her ever-loving mind, all while being entrenched in the most romantic ventures possible? What could go wrong?

Chapter Four

What was Noah supposed to say? Although that didn't matter much, because he found he couldn't say much of anything. He just stared slack-jawed at the computer screen where Caleb and Issa stared back at him expectantly.

Noah could barely string together enough blocks of time to get a passable amount of sleep each night. He was burning the candle at both ends—had been for months—and he wasn't sure he'd ever catch up. But, yeah, sure, he had plenty of time to plan a wedding that wasn't even his own.

That said, of course he was going to do it. This was Caleb he was talking about. The same guy who drove ten hours home the day Jess moved out. The same guy who opened his childhood home to Noah when they were younger, while his mom had been working hard to support them. The same guy who would give anything to Noah, *do* anything for Noah.

"Sure," he said, gripping the back of Savannah's chair. "We'll take care of everything on this end."

Chatter erupted around him, but he couldn't focus on any of it. Not with the way Savannah slowly turned around to face him, her blue eyes narrowed on him and her lips pursed. His gaze darted down to those full beauties, only briefly entertaining ill-advised thoughts before snapping his attention back up to her eyes. He didn't know if Savannah was so pissed because they were about to be stuck together for the next several months outside of preschool interactions, or if it was because he answered for her.

Growing up, she'd always been a little bit prickly about that. Protesting when he or her brothers would challenge something she wanted to do. She firmly re-iterated that she was perfectly capable of taking care of herself, but in the twenty-odd years he'd known her, he failed to see how that could possibly be true.

Take tonight, for instance. She was almost thirty, but her mom still prepared her dinner and served it to her on a—okay, not silver, but still—platter. And could it even really count as moving out if your parents were thirty feet away?

Noah tuned back in in time to catch the round of goodbyes from everyone.

"Seriously, thank you guys so much for doing this." Caleb stared back at him, gratitude shining in his eyes.

"Yeah, I don't know what we'd do without you two," Issa said, her genuine smile showcasing her relief.

"Maybe don't thank us until after the wedding," Savannah said. "What if we book your reception at the bowling alley?"

"Don't joke about that, Savannah Rose." Pauline lightly slapped Savannah's arm and shot her a scathing look.

"Relax, Mom. I'm not *actually* going to book the bowling alley. I'm not an idiot."

"You two understand us so well." Issa bit her lip. "I know you don't always get along with each other, but there's no one either of us trusts more."

Aaron and Jackson immediately erupted into protests, only for Spencer to mime cuffing them both on the head. "Case in point," Spencer muttered.

"We know you'll make good decisions," Issa said, ignoring them all.

Caleb nodded. "Noah can be practical and keep us on budget."

Well, he wasn't wrong there.

"And Savannah will make sure it's dreamy and swoony and *not* in a bowling alley," Issa added.

"And of course we'll help as much as we can from here," Caleb said.

That was the issue, though, wasn't it? Caleb and Issa would be there for *discussing* these items, but not putting in the legwork. That would fall on his and Savannah's shoulders. Actually, if he knew Savannah—

and he did know Savannah—this was going to fall solely on *his* shoulders. Savannah rarely stayed focused on anything for long. She might share Issa's love of all things "dreamy and swoony," and she was the only local bridesmaid, but he didn't know how the happy couple expected her to see this commitment through.

Caleb and Issa set up a time to talk to Savannah and Noah about budget and finances and all that stuff the following day. The call ended with good cheer and best wishes from everyone in the room.

When they finally logged off, Savannah abruptly stood from her chair and turned to face Noah. "Can I talk to you for a second?"

It was less question and more demand, and Noah barely refrained from giving an eye roll. It wouldn't have mattered anyway, because she didn't wait for any kind of response from him before she headed off in the direction of the den.

"Good luck with that," Spencer said, clapping a hand on Noah's shoulder. "I'm just glad she's not pissed off at me for once."

With a sigh, Noah strode toward where Savannah had disappeared to, wishing he could sit in front of the game and watch for a while with all the guys. But nope, thanks to his big mouth and unwavering loyalty to his best friend, every spare minute would now be filled with all things wedding. And at every turn throughout, he'd face a reminder that his own marriage had failed and that he wasn't faring much better on his own.

"'Sure,'" Savannah mocked as soon as Noah rounded the corner into the den. "'We'll take care of it'? *Seriously*? You might not have a lot on your plate, but I do."

Noah barked out an incredulous laugh. "Pretty sure I've got more than you, princess. But what, exactly, would you have liked me to say to your brother when he asked for our help? 'Sucks to be you, figure it out on your own'?"

Savannah blew out a heavy breath, her shoulders sagging as she ran a hand through her long, blond hair. He fought not to get distracted by the way the golden strands fanned across her shoulders.

"No, of course not. But the whole, 'We'll take care of everything on our end' thing?"

Noah sighed. "Look, I get it. You're probably busier than usual with your preschool class—"

"You realize I'm *running* that preschool, right? I don't just have my curriculum to worry about but the whole program."

Actually, no, he hadn't realized that. He knew she and Abby were tight, but wow. Abby had really taken a chance on that one.

As if she could hear his thoughts, she narrowed her eyes. "Your faith in me is astounding."

He shook his head and ran a hand across his jaw. "I didn't say anything."

"You didn't have to."

For a second, he thought he caught the edge of hurt in her tone, but the stone-cold glare she shot him reassured him that he was sorely mistaken. It hadn't been hurt, but simply irritation. That was par for the course with them.

"Okay, so you're busy *running* the preschool. Between work and Rosie, I'm pressed for time too. But there really wasn't much of a choice."

She closed her eyes as if the very act of having a conversation with him was stressing her out beyond reason—the feeling was mutual. "I guess that's true. Not agreeing would have made us inconsiderate jerks."

He lifted a brow as soon as she met his gaze. "Careful…that almost sounds like you agree with me, which means you think I'm right."

"Ha! Don't hold your breath. We're going to end up killing each other during this whole thing, and then Caleb will be out a best man and Issa will be out a bridesmaid. How are we going to explain that to them?"

"Well, in your scenario, I'll be dead, so I probably won't say much," he said dryly.

She gritted her teeth and clenched her hands at her sides. "Are you always this irritating, or am I just special?"

"You definitely bring it out in me."

"Yeah, well, the feeling is mutual," Savannah grumbled, crossing her arms over her chest.

"Look, we're going to have to figure out a way to make this work."

"And you assume *I'm* going to need to make concessions to do so?"

"That's not what I—" He stopped, deliberately taking a deep breath and refocusing. "Can we just agree to work together to get this done. For them?"

"Fine. But I'm doing it for my brother and Issa, not because you asked."

It took all his self-restraint to keep him from rolling his eyes. "Great."

"When do you want to get started?"

It was early September, so that meant they had just over three months to make sure everything came together. He and Jess had eloped, so not only was this going to be new territory for him, but he didn't have the foggiest idea where to even start.

"Soon, probably. I don't know much about planning a wedding, but I'd assume it usually takes more than a few months."

"I don't either. Fortunately, Abby will probably have an idea of where we should start."

"Great." He widened his stance, raising an eyebrow when she didn't make a move to call her best friend.

"You want me to call her *now*?"

"Did you miss the part about us only having three months to do this?"

Savannah narrowed her eyes and tightened her lips, and he had to force himself to ignore the latter. What was his deal tonight? "*Fine.* But I'm not doing this because you bossed me into doing it. I'm doing this because *I* decided it'd be a good idea."

"Whatever you have to tell yourself."

He could actually see how much it was costing her to keep quiet and not snap back at him. Oddly, he sort of wished she would retort with something. As much as he hated her obstinate ways, he couldn't deny that he enjoyed their back-and-forth, if only a little.

Without further comment, she pulled out her phone, pressing the speaker button as she called Abby.

"Hey!" Abby answered, a smile ringing through her tone.

"Hi," Savannah grumbled, no doubt due to her irritation with him.

"What's wrong?"

Savannah blew out a deep sigh. "My brother's getting married."

"What?" Abby paused a beat. "Which one?"

Savannah huffed out a laugh. "Which do you think?"

"Caleb asked Issa?" Abby's delight could be heard even over the phone. "Oh my God, that's amazing! But wait...why aren't you excited about this?"

"I *am* excited about this."

"Then why do you sound like you're reporting a death rather than an engagement?"

"Because *someone* told Caleb and Issa that we'd plan their wedding for them."

"And by someone, you mean..."

"Me," Noah said.

"Wait— *Noah*?"

Savannah's sigh came all the way from her toes. "Yes, Noah."

He wasn't sure what kind of reaction he was expecting from Abby, but it certainly wasn't her burst of laughter.

"Oh, great." Savannah threw up her hand. "Now my best friend is laughing at me. That's awesome."

"I'm not laughing *at* you . . . I'm laughing *wi*—"

"Nope, I'm most certainly not laughing."

Abby cut off her giggles and cleared her throat. "Right. Okay, so you and . . . Noah will be working together to make this happen for them?"

"Apparently. But neither of us has done this before, and we don't even know where to begin."

"Did you forget? I've never done this before either," Abby said, sinking Noah's hopes for help before he'd even realized he'd had them.

Savannah snorted. "Since when has that ever mattered? You've never had to plan for a baby, but you're still helping Gia like a boss."

Gia, one of their girlfriends—and the weekly art teacher at the Sunshine Corner—was due fairly soon with her and her husband Marco's first child.

"We're just hoping you can guide us in the right direction. Like maybe what we should start with? We don't have a lot of time."

"Less than a year?" Abby asked.

"Try three months," Savannah said.

Abby whistled under her breath. "You certainly don't have any time to waste, do you? Okay, well, without doing any research, my gut says to find ceremony and reception sites as soon as possible, and then probably choose the photographer. Those are the most pressing and the ones that will get booked the farthest out, I would assume."

"Okay." Savannah nodded and navigated to the notes app in her phone, no doubt typing all this out so she wouldn't forget.

"Also, you'll want to keep track of your appointments and when you've booked things. And not in your notes app, Savannah. Things will fall through the cracks there, and you can't afford to have that happen with a wedding. Oh! It looks like my favorite planner company has a wedding version. I'm going to buy that so you guys have something to organize yourselves."

Savannah's lips twitched at the corners as she stared at the phone. It wasn't often he saw this side of her—the side that had an affinity for her friends. Usually when he saw her, it was in the presence of her brothers who all had a way of getting under her skin. Was it any wonder she was usually irritated around him?

"You'll stop at nothing to get a planner in my hands."

Abby laughed. "It'll help. I promise. Hey, I've gotta run. Carter just got home. But we'll talk more tomorrow, okay? I'm happy to help you guys however I can."

"Thanks, Abby," Noah said, sincerity ringing in his tone. Savannah had to know as much as he did that they would've been totally screwed if it weren't for Abby's help.

"Yeah, thanks. I'll talk to you tomorrow." Savannah hung up after saying goodbye, then slid her phone into her pocket and looked at him with a sigh. "I guess we're really doing this."

Apparently so. He only hoped they would both make it out the other side unscathed.

Chapter Five

Savannah was a week into running the new preschool, and the paramedics hadn't been called even once, so she was counting that as a win. She had all her ducks in a row—the lesson plans checked and reviewed for herself and Tori, as well as for the teachers in the three-year-old room. She also scheduled a special visit from Jackson and a few furry friends from the animal shelter, and she had a field trip in the works to a local orchard for the following month.

For the most part, the kids in her class were sweet and caring, curious and precocious. But unfortunately the problems continued with Austin Greene...and his mother. Savannah firmly believed that there was no such thing as a bad kid and that every child was full of promise and potential. But with Austin, sometimes it was really, really hard to keep that belief front and center.

It was free time at the preschool, a twenty-minute block before lunch where the kids had free choice at any of the activity centers. One group was having a tea party, while another was apparently having a blast putting things in the toy mailbox they had set up near the class library—an area they affectionately called "Fairytale Lane."

A sweet four-year-old named Jacob was at the dress-up station, donning a pair of butterfly wings to pair with his lightsaber. He was quiet to a fault and had a hard time making friends, but Savannah hoped that would turn around as the year progressed and the kids got more comfortable with each other. Savannah was on high alert when Austin strode over to him, a sneer on his face.

"Butterflies are for *girls*. Are you a girl?"

Savannah clenched her teeth and abandoned the paper scraps she was cleaning up from that morning's crafts with a single-minded focus on the two children.

"I bet your favorite color's pink."

It took Savannah less than thirty seconds to cross the space before she was next to Jacob and Austin, but Jacob was already close to tears, the wetness brimming in his downcast eyes. "*Austin.* That's not how we speak to our friends."

"He's not my friend. I'm not friends with sissies." With that statement, he shoved Jacob in the shoulder, causing Jacob's withheld tears to finally spill over.

"Hey," Savannah snapped, her patience gone in a

flash. "We don't tolerate that sort of speaking at the Sunshine Corner." She glanced up, looking for Tori, and wordlessly called her over with a jerk of her head.

Tori's mouth tightened when she saw who Savannah was dealing with.

"What can I help with?" she asked once she was in front of them.

"Could you stay with Austin in the separation room for a minute while I talk with Jacob? I'll be right in."

Tori nodded before guiding an angry Austin away. Once they were out of earshot, Savannah squatted down in front of Jacob and reached for his hand, smiling when he allowed her to take his.

"I'm sorry for what Austin said to you. Other people's words hurt sometimes, don't they?"

Jacob nodded without looking up at her, but she could still see the rivers of tears streaking his face.

"But other people's words can build us up, too, right? And I think you look so awesome with your wings and your lightsaber."

"You do?"

"I really do," Savannah said, squeezing Jacob's hand reassuringly. "I think Maddie and Gabe would think so too."

Apprehension and the tiniest bit of fear crept into Jacob's eyes, and Savannah's heart broke a little more. She couldn't perform her job to the best of her ability if she played favorites. She would just have to try extra hard to bring out the goodness in Austin.

"They're very nice, I promise," she said. "Do you remember from the first day of school? Maddie loves butterflies, and Gabe loves playing Jedis. So I bet you three will have a lot of fun together. Can I call them over?" Savannah asked, not wanting to push this on him if he wasn't ready, but at the same time, hoping desperately that he was.

After what felt like an eternity, Jacob finally gave a small nod, and Savannah smiled. "It's very brave to try again when someone's said mean things that hurt you. I'm proud of you for trying to make new friends."

Savannah's heart inflated from the small smile Jacob shot her. And it only continued to grow when Gabe and Maddie came over, and the three of them hit it off, their tales of make-believe soaring as they commingled their imaginations.

When she was satisfied Jacob was no longer distraught and instead playing animatedly with his two new friends, she firmed her shoulders, her mouth set in a thin, straight line. She marched toward the separation room and tried to figure out what, exactly, she was going to say to Austin that she hadn't already said a million times before.

When issues arose with the kids, it was her job to remain calm and unaffected. That said, she had very little patience for bullies, and she certainly wasn't going to tolerate that kind of behavior at her preschool.

The thought jolted her, her steps faltering as she strode toward where she could hear Austin's tantrum even through the closed door. It had only been a week since the preschool had opened, and she was already thinking of it as hers? Fortunately for her sanity, she came to this realization in the middle of her workday, which forced her to shove those thoughts aside and deal with the problem at hand. The problem at hand being a difficult kid who'd never received an ounce of discipline in his life and who was under the impression that the world owed him *everything*.

If things didn't change, he was going to turn into a schoolyard bully, and then a frat boy bully, and then an employer bully. The kind of man who pushed and prodded his way to success, even if it meant stepping on those beside or below him in order to do so.

She opened the door and quickly took stock of the room. Tori was attempting to talk with Austin while the child demolished the reading nook set up and designed to give kids a quiet space to calm down. Not working especially well in this case. "Thanks, Miss Tori. Can you please get the kids ready for lunch? We'll be down shortly."

"Definitely," she said. Then more quietly as she passed, "Good luck."

As soon as the door snicked shut behind Tori, Savannah turned to Austin and used her stern teacher's voice—which, coincidentally, sounded an awful lot like the voice her mom used when she or her brothers were in trouble—to gain Austin's attention. "That's enough."

The minimal but forceful words were enough to stop his actions, and he turned to look at her, a scowl on his face. "You can't keep me in here! I'm going to tell my mom!"

"We don't plan to keep you in here. This is our special room kids go when they need some time by themselves."

"I didn't do anything wrong!"

And the sad thing was, that was exactly the story he was going to feed his mother, and exactly the story his mother was going to believe.

"You and I both know that's not true. You spoke very rudely to Jacob, and we don't allow that here. We treat our friends with kindness."

Austin fisted his hand at his side and stomped his foot. "He's *not* my friend."

Savannah closed her eyes and slowly counted to ten, willing herself to remain calm and find a way to reach this child. After her breathing technique, she opened her eyes, but the pause hadn't done much to alleviate her irritation. "We're all friends here at the Sunshine Corner. And because we're all friends here, we speak to each other with kindness and respect. What Jacob does by himself has no effect on you. He wasn't asking you to dress up like him. He was doing it because he wanted to and because he enjoys it. You get a say in what you do, but you do not get a say in what others do, unless they're being hurtful or harmful to you. Do you understand that?"

Austin glared at Savannah, his mouth set in a grim line. "I don't have to listen to you! I'm telling my mom!"

Savannah blew out an exasperated breath. Yeah, she was going to tell his mom too. And she already knew exactly how the conversation would go. Megan would brush off all concerns or make it out somehow to be Jacob's fault. Because that's what parents like Megan did. Deny and deflect. It was impossible to show them their kids might need something different.

* * *

The absolute last thing Savannah wanted to do after a long day at work—especially one in which she'd had to have yet another frustrating discussion with Megan about her son's behavior—was to meet up with another person who got under her skin like no other. But after their budget and wish list talk with the happy couple the night before, all of them joining on Zoom, it was clear that time to plan Caleb and Issa's wedding was extremely limited. They needed to start immediately. And since Noah had the day off from work, today was the day.

She pulled her car into the parking lot of a local hotel and parked, glancing around for Noah's car. Like a magnet, her gaze locked on his almost immediately. His car was two over to her left, and when she found him, his eyes were already focused on her. A shiver ran through her body, her insides vibrating beneath her skin. She should have brought a coat, because apparently it was colder than she'd realized.

She grabbed the bag that housed the beautiful planner Abby had gifted her and stepped out of the car. A squeak left her lips and she stopped short when she nearly face-planted into Noah's chest.

"God, are you a cheetah? I know it's been a while since you've been in the company of the opposite sex, but you can't just sneak up on women like that, Noah."

"Sorry," he said, not sounding sorry. It appeared suspiciously like he was rolling his eyes as he plucked her bag from her shoulder without comment and turned to stride toward the door, seemingly unconcerned if she was following, "I forgot that you used to cry to your parents whenever Caleb and I would sneak up on you when we were younger."

Savannah parted her lips on a gasp, a sound of indignation escaping as she stared dumbfounded at Noah's back. "I hope you know that your and Caleb's pranks have scarred me for life. I still have to sleep with the closet light on."

A rumbling laugh came from somewhere deep in Noah's chest, and her lower belly responded with a flip. She ignored it and stormed up to him, a glower ready on her face.

As she walked through the front door, he leaned in. He probably just meant to taunt her, but he was so close that a shudder of awareness rippled through her.

"Do you need me to come check your closets for the boogeyman, Savannah?"

A Fourth of July's worth of fireworks erupted inside Savannah. It'd been too long since she'd been with a man—casually or not—and this was her body's way of saying this drought had to end. That was the only explanation for why Noah was affecting her this way.

"I'm almost thirty, Noah," she said, imbuing as much haughtiness into her tone as she was physically able. "I think I can take care of myself."

He snorted softly, a sound of pure disbelief. Like what she was saying was so utterly preposterous, he wasn't even going to acknowledge it. But he didn't have to. She knew what his unspoken words were because he'd never been shy about saying them before. *Could* she take care of herself? After all, she was twenty-nine and living above the garage at her parents' house. That wasn't exactly the pinnacle of adulthood. She could tell him why she lived at her parents' and about the ever-growing nest egg she had in her savings account in order to buy herself a cozy little cottage right on the beach, but it wasn't any of his business. Especially when he saw her as nothing more than a spoiled child in need of adult supervision.

Savannah snatched her bag back from him, her response due entirely to the one-sided argument between them that she'd had in her head. Noah glanced at her with a confused expression, but before he could open his mouth, a man appeared at their side. He wore a gray pin-striped suit and a navy polka-dotted bow tie, his gray hair coiffed just so.

"Hi, I'm Mark. You must be the happy couple here to check out the Rose Room for your reception," he said with an expectant smile.

"Oh, we're not—" Savannah glanced at Noah, whose jaw was set in a tight line, then back to Mark. "We're the best man and one of the bridesmaids. The bride and groom don't live in the area, so we're doing the legwork for them."

"How lovely of you! That's very thoughtful, and a *lot* of work."

Yeah, he didn't need to tell her that. The planner Abby had gifted her was both a blessing and a curse. It guided her through all that she needed, reminding her of what she should be doing. But in that same vein, it also reminded her of everything she hadn't yet done.

Worse, she'd had it less than forty-eight hours and had already ruined it, writing today's appointments on the wrong day... *after* setting her mug on it and leaving a ring of coffee on one of the pages. Abby had fixed her up with some washi tape and stickers and declared it as good as new. Except Savannah could still see the splotches of black ink peeking through the pale blue striped tape and the slight warp of the paper, a forever reminder that she had no idea what she was doing here. She pasted a bright smile on her face. "We're happy to help them, and we're excited to see the room. We've got a few other places we're scheduled to look at this evening, so we should get started."

And that was how she and Noah spent the next three hours, with each new venue—and each new aggravating comment from Noah—driving her closer and closer to the edge of her patience.

By the time they got to the Ocean View Inn, Heart's Hope Bay's fanciest hotel, she was having a hard time focusing on the details of the venue at all. Which was too bad, considering she'd been the one to add it to Caleb and Issa's list of places to check out. Based on the increasingly tight set to Noah's jaw, he was starting to hit a wall too.

The event coordinator, Brittany, smiled as she showed them samples of the favors they included with their deluxe package. "We can do these with Jordan almonds or custom chocolate coins."

"And how much is all of this going to run us?" Noah asked.

Savannah's stomach growled almost as loudly as her tempter. She'd gone straight from the Sunshine Corner to the first venue possibility, and then two others immediately following. It was after seven and she was starving, which would explain why she had absolutely no patience for Noah, or his cynical approach to planning a wedding.

Yes, Caleb had tasked him with keeping the wedding under budget, but did he have to be so rude about it?

"Well..." Brittany hedged.

Noah shook his head. "Stick with the basics. We don't need any of this."

"What is your deal?" Savannah finally snapped when she couldn't take it anymore.

Noah glanced over at her, lines appearing between his brows. "I don't have a deal."

"Then tell me why you're insisting on ruining your best friend and my brother's wedding by your asinine suggestions."

"*Asinine*? At least they're realistic. We can't all be floating in the clouds all the time, disconnected from reality."

She jerked back, stunned at his words. "What's that supposed to mean?"

He blew out a breath and scrubbed a hand down his face. "It means you may have been raised to expect your parents to foot the bill for a big 'dreamy, swoony' wedding, but not everyone has that luxury. Caleb and Issa set a budget, and I'm here to help them stick to it. So I'd say favors are *optional*."

Savannah shoved down the prick of hurt that flooded her. Of course Noah wouldn't keep this just about the wedding. He never missed a chance to bring up how spoiled and coddled she was.

Her hurt manifested as anger, and she squeezed her fists at her sides, clenching her jaw as she tried to get herself under control. "You've already told me you don't think they need favors, centerpieces, flowers, or even a damn cake, so please, enlighten me on what you *do* think they deserve."

"It's not about what they deserve. This place is so over the top. There's a reason it wasn't on Caleb's list." He waved a hand toward the space behind him, narrowly missing Brittany. She pretended to give them space yet stood a mere six feet away, no doubt eavesdropping on every word.

Savannah darted her gaze farther afield. They'd caught the attention of a few people in the lobby too.

Embarrassment burned her cheeks. He was probably right; the Ocean View was extravagant. But she also knew Issa would love it.

She pointedly lowered her voice. "It's a *wedding*, Noah. It's not a tax prep appointment. You think Caleb and Issa would be okay with a stripped-down wedding that only delivered on the bare minimum? You think that's what they want and why they asked us to do this?"

"What I think is that it's impractical to spend thousands of dollars on details in a room—that's going to cost even more, by the way—just to throw a party."

Savannah stared at him, breathing out a disbelieving laugh as she shook her head. "Weddings aren't *supposed* to be practical. They're supposed to be *romantic*. My brother and Issa love each other so much that they want to share that with their friends and family."

"Funny, I thought they could do that without sparklers and personalized mini champagne bottles for each guest." He crossed his arms over his chest, his jaw ticking as he stared her down.

Neither of them said anything for long minutes, each waiting for the other to back down. Well, that wasn't going to happen. He might think that she was spoiled and flighty, but she was doing her best to fulfill her promise to Issa and Caleb to help make sure their special day was perfect.

So she matched his stance and raised an eyebrow in defiance, ignoring the flip of her stomach when those whiskey-colored eyes bored into hers, the intensity enough to make her toes curl. She inhaled deeply through her nose, her lips pursed as she held on tight to her irritation instead of whatever these new sensations were that she'd developed around him.

Why the hell did Issa and Caleb think putting her and Noah together was a good idea? For the entirety of their relationship, they'd gotten along like oil and water. Planning a wedding was almost definitely only going to solidify that animosity, making it near impossible to complete the task at hand—something she already found challenging.

And now, thanks to their very public disagreement, everyone in Heart's Hope Bay was going to be privy to just exactly how poorly they worked together.

Chapter Six

Noah unlocked their front door and held it open as Rosie ran inside ahead of him, her backpack bouncing as she went. "You know the drill, squirt."

"I know, Daddy!" she called as she ran straight for her bedroom.

She *said* she knew, but there was no doubt that when he tucked her in tonight, her backpack would be tossed on her floor, still full of the day's papers and not unpacked and hung up as was the expectation. But, really, how could he have that discussion with her when his room wasn't any better? At the end of the day, he was so exhausted, he was lucky to strip down to his boxers before he fell into bed, his clothes forgotten in a pile on the floor.

"It's almost time for your call with Mommy. Put

your stuff away and get the laptop ready," he called
down the hallway toward her room.

"Yay!" Rosie tore out of her bedroom, nearly screeching to a halt in front of him as she jumped up and
down, her eyes bright and her excitement palpable.

He smiled at her, though the edges of it were brittle.
For the thousandth time, he wished things had gone
differently. For Rosie's sake.

"It's ringing, Daddy!"

"Okay. Do you remember how to answer it?"

She didn't even respond to him before she clicked to
accept the call. "Mommy!" she said, pure joy ringing in
her voice.

"Hi, sweetie." Jess's tone was pleasant but subdued.

Rosie tilted her head to the side as she regarded the
computer screen. "You look sleepy, Mommy."

Jess breathed out a laugh and shook her head. "I just
had a long day at work."

Since Rosie was set up with the video call, Noah left
them be and strode into the kitchen under the guise
of giving them privacy. When in reality, he knew if he
stayed and listened to her complaints about how busy
she was, he wouldn't be able to hold his tongue. She was
alone in Houston with only herself to worry about. She
worked a regular eight-to-five job and rarely brought
work home. Yet *she* was the one who was tired?

He and Jess were friends—as much as two people
who'd once been married could be. But the love
was gone. And he certainly wouldn't have wanted a

reconciliation even if she did still live in Heart's Hope Bay. No, what he wanted was for his daughter to have her mother around, especially when he saw firsthand what that separation did to Rosie. No matter how many times he shoved it down and reminded himself that he had this under control, he still couldn't help feeling the tiniest bit resentful of her for leaving them.

"Mommy had to go, Daddy!" Rosie called from the other room.

Noah didn't even bother to glance at his watch. He didn't have to. Their call had lasted less than ten minutes, and that resentment level that he'd buried deep inside bubbled up just a little bit more. "Okay, I'll be right there. You remember how to shut it off?"

"Yeah! When's Grandma gonna be here?"

"Any min—" Before he could get the words out, the front door opened and closed.

His mom called, "Hello?"

"Grandma!"

Noah finished putting away the dishes and made his way toward the front door.

His mom stood there, all five foot nothing of her, weighed down by what had to be at least six reusable grocery totes. "Ma," he said, admonishment clear in his tone as he took the bags from her and bent to drop a kiss on her cheek. "You don't have to keep bringing us groceries. I'm perfectly capable of going to the store."

He lifted up the bags she'd carried in—substantially

more than what she'd need to cook the single meal she'd come to prepare for them.

She lifted a shoulder. Her dark hair was cut bluntly at her shoulders, her bangs sweeping down over one eye. "What, I can't take care of my only kid and my only granddaughter?"

"That's not what I said. You know I appreciate it."

Appreciated it, but hated it all the same. He was a full-grown adult, and he should have a handle on this without his mom running interference just to keep him sane.

"Careful, there's lasagna in one of those bags," she called after him as he heaved the loot into the kitchen.

"Are we gonna have your yummy bread, too, Grandma?" Rosie asked, dragging his mom along behind her.

"Well, of course! You can't have lasagna without garlic bread."

As if on cue, Noah's stomach growled at the mere mention of his mom's cooking. "You don't have to do that either."

"What?" she asked, feigning innocence.

He rolled his eyes as he unpacked the bags before preheating the oven for the lasagna. "You know what. I can manage to feed us, you know."

"He can, Grandma," Rosie said with a nod. "But sometimes I like hot food too."

His daughter was cute, but she was a rat. "Why

don't you go grab that picture you wanted to show Grandma, squirt?"

"Okay!" Rosie dropped his mom's hand and tore off toward her bedroom.

"You're not feeding her hot food, huh?"

He blew out a breath. "You know kids—they exaggerate."

"That so?" His mom made a show of opening the fridge and glancing inside before looking at him with a raised eyebrow. So it'd been a few days since he'd gotten to the grocery store. Okay, it'd been more than a week. The pantry shelves—broken as they were— were basically empty, and they were subsisting on peanut butter and jelly sandwiches and apple slices. Which, to be fair, was one of Rosie's absolute favorite meals. And he didn't really care what he ate as long as he ate.

He knew he should've already had some sort of a routine now that it had been just the two of them for months. But he was still getting his bearings. He hated that his mom knew that. Hated that she felt like they needed her help…that he wasn't capable of doing it on his own.

Hated it, but also couldn't deny the truth of it.

"I can feed you all I want, Noah Christopher, and you can't stop me. Mom privileges and all that. Besides, I had to make some for Betty. You remember Betty, who lives down the street from me? She fell and broke her wrist, so cooking's going to be a challenge for her for a while. So I wanted to send over some meals for her to just pop into the oven."

Noah pulled out two large mason jars full of soup and glanced at her with a raised eyebrow. "Are these for her?"

She waved a dismissive hand. "It's just as easy to double the recipe, so I brought you some chicken noodle soup, enchiladas, and some taco meat. And I already picked up all the fixings for that at the store, so it should be an easy meal for you to throw together."

Before he could admonish or thank his mom—he wasn't sure which way he was leaning—Rosie came tearing out of her bedroom, a piece of paper held high above her head and flapping as she ran. "Grandma! Look what I made at school today!"

"I can't wait to see it, sugarplum." His mom squatted down and held her arms open for Rosie. She ran into them, wrapping an arm around her grandma's neck and squeezing tightly as she guided her grandma's attention to the paper in front of her. Rosie may not have her mom around, but at least she had his.

He focused on unpacking what his mom had brought, keeping one ear on Rosie and his mom's conversation in case she said anything about preschool that he needed to be aware of. Since the first day he'd picked up Rosie when she'd been crying, he'd been on high alert for any instances that bothered her. So far, though, she seemed happy enough to discuss her day when she got home, and if those conversations were anything to go by, she loved it there. But the drop-offs were still absolute hell on her. He knew why she was so upset...why she had such a hard time with it. And it all boiled down to Jess's abandonment. He hated that Rosie feared he would abandon her too.

After dinner, Noah and his mom cleaned up while Rosie was occupied with her evening TV time. He scrubbed a plate and rinsed it before passing it to his mom, who took it with a smile.

She dried the dish, focusing her attention on that. "So," she said, drawing out the word, and Noah's muscles locked down tight. Nothing good had ever come from a conversation starting with that single word, especially with his mom.

He glanced over at her with a raised eyebrow and passed her another washed dish. "So...what?"

"I hear you and Savannah have had a difficult time trying to find a reception site for Caleb and Issa's wedding."

Noah scrunched up his brow, trying to figure out where she would have gotten this information. Had Savannah called her? He couldn't fathom why—why she would or even why she'd have his mom's number.

"Oh, don't look so surprised," she said, slapping a hand against his biceps. "Everyone in town knows about it. You two weren't exactly subtle in your disagreement at the Ocean View Inn. Honestly, if you guys are going to fight, next time try not to do it at the nicest hotel in town where people look sideways if your shoes click wrong."

Noah braced his hands on the edge of the sink and hung his head, blowing out a harsh breath. He hadn't even considered who was around or what they'd heard when he and Savannah had checked out the reception site yesterday. Truth be told, he didn't pay attention to much outside of Savannah when they were together. For better or worse, she eclipsed everything when he was in her presence, and since they started this wedding business, she made him feel strange things he was still trying to process.

"It's fine, Ma. You don't have to worry about it."

She laughed lightly and grabbed the last dish from him before drying it off. "I'm not so sure that's true. But Pauline and I were discussing it this morning while I did her hair. And we agreed that it would be best if you two had some mediators there."

"And by mediators you mean babysitters," he said flatly.

She lifted a single shoulder. "If the shoe fits."

He laughed under his breath and shook his head, turning to face her. "Can I take a wild guess and say you think you two would be perfect for the job?"

She gasped, feigning surprise, and rested her hand on his forearm, turning a bright smile on him. "That's a fantastic idea! Pauline and I will go with when you scout out the next venue. Just let me know when, and we'll get it in our calendars."

Noah didn't know whether to be irritated or impressed, but he finally decided on the latter. After thirty-three years, he should have learned by now never to underestimate his mother, and never to put it past her to get exactly what she wanted. Right now, for some reason, she wanted to check out wedding venues with him and Savannah. He felt a little flip of disappointment but quickly pushed it down. Where on earth did that come from? If his mom wanted to join, who was he to stop her?

Besides, having his mom and Pauline along wasn't an issue for him. After all, it couldn't possibly be any worse than the disaster that was last night.

Chapter Seven

Usually Noah spent his days off hanging out at home with Rosie, catching up on housework, maybe trying out a new recipe, or just watching a movie. Today he was spending the day scouting reception locations, yet again, with Savannah, which was how he'd spent two out of the past three days he'd had off. Only this time, her mother and his, as well as Rosie, were in tow. They hadn't been at it long enough yet for him to tell if that was going to make it better or worse.

His mom and Pauline Lowe were good friends and had been for as long as Noah could remember. When his mom was busy working two jobs to support them, Pauline took Noah in without question and helped out his mother whenever she could. Fortunately, he and the Lowe boys had gotten on like a house on fire—unlike him and the Lowe girl, who got along like a dumpster fire. But in the end, his and Savannah's contentious relationship hadn't mattered. Their families were close enough that it wasn't out of the ordinary for them to spend holidays together. But as good friends as the two moms were, they also apparently had very differing ideas about weddings.

They were at the Bluffs, a fancy hotel in a neighboring town. While they'd stuck to Caleb and Issa's list today, this one was a stretch budget-wise, and Noah's mom was having as hard a time processing her sticker shock as Noah had at the Ocean View.

"I'm sorry...is there an extra zero on the end of this price?" his mom asked Stephanie, the event coordinator, pointing to the handout.

Stephanie made a show of glancing at the sheet, although Noah was certain that she was quite aware of exactly how much was written there, and offered a smile. "No, that looks like it's right for a Saturday wedding in December. With this short notice, unfortunately we only have the largest ballroom still available, which is also our most expensive. If you're flexible on the dates, I would be more than happy to show you something smaller that may better fit into your budget."

"No, they wanted a December wedding, so that's what they're going to get," Savannah said. She'd knocked him on his ass once again when she'd shown up in a fitted sweater and jeans that hugged every inch of her, her hair hanging in loose waves down her back. He tried to ignore her scent that wafted toward him every time she walked past him or turned her head or even breathed.

One good thing about both of their moms being there, as well as Rosie, was that he hadn't had the time or opportunity to focus on this suddenly new and very weird tension that continued to plague him.

"I see," Stephanie said. "Well, in that case, we could look at cutting corners elsewhere, if you think that it may help."

"Would you excuse us for just a minute," his mom said, not waiting before she tugged Pauline off to the side and jerking her head to get Noah and Savannah to follow.

Noah rested his hand on the back of Rosie's neck and squeezed lightly, guiding her in the direction of where Pauline and his mom stood. His phone was currently entertaining his daughter, though he knew that would be short-lived. She usually lasted about thirty minutes playing games before she got bored and wanted to do something active, her imagination kicking into high gear. And since they still had more places to visit today, he had no idea how that would shake out.

"We're being summoned," he said under his breath toward Savannah as they strode to where their moms were holding what appeared to be a lively discussion.

"Maybe we should have just let them plan it."

Noah snorted. "Are you kidding? Your mom would have swan ice sculptures at every table, and mine would give out slips of paper tied to a single Hershey's Kiss that said, *Thanks for coming, have a kiss on us.*"

Savannah's peal of laughter caught him off guard, and his gaze was drawn to her like a magnet. Without his permission, the corner of his mouth ticked up in response to her laughter. Even Rosie looked up, a smile on her face.

"You have a pretty laugh, Miss Savannah," Rosie said quietly. With Savannah around, Rosie wasn't her usual boisterous self that she was with him and his mom, but neither was she quite the timid, quiet girl that she'd been since Jess had left.

Savannah grinned down at Rosie and tucked her hair behind her ear. "Those were very kind words, Rosie. Thank you."

Rosie's smile only brightened further at the praise, and a string tied to Noah's heart gave a sharp tug. Which was stupid. All Savannah did was say a few nice words to his kid. That shouldn't have gotten to him as much as it did, but the truth was, Rosie had had a hard go of it, and any kindness shown to her was welcome.

"You can't be serious, Pauline," Noah's mom was saying as they walked up. She held up the paper that showed the quote for the reception space. "These prices are ridiculous."

"While I agree that they certainly aren't what Alan and I paid back when we got married, they're not all that outrageous now."

"I know this is your son's wedding, not mine, so my opinion doesn't hold much weight. That said, I'm merely suggesting that they look at something a little less expensive."

"Which is why we're looking at a variety of reception spaces—just like Caleb and Issa asked us to," Pauline shot back. "I'm sure we'll find something more reasonable."

"Pauline, you have a beautiful backyard. Why don't you just host the reception there? It's free, and—"

"And they'd still need to buy or rent absolutely everything, which means the price is going to be near what we'd pay at an actual venue."

"You know as well as I do that we could find deals on all those things. And we could even make some of the decorations." She looked to Noah and Savannah, her eyes wide and smile bright, as if she was encouraging them to agree with her. "That makes sense to you guys, right?"

Noah loved his mom fiercely. She was the second most important woman in his life, right behind Rosie. But even his love for her wasn't enough to get him to agree. "No, Ma, I don't think it's a good idea to have a reception in a backyard in December."

His mom scowled at him—he definitely wasn't getting lasagna again for a while—before turning a tentative smile on Savannah. "What about you, Savannah? You see the value in that, don't you?"

Savannah ran a hand through her hair, the move

sending a wave of her scent directly toward him, and he inhaled deeply before he even realized what he was doing. "I can't believe I'm saying this," she said, sliding her gaze toward Noah, "but I agree with your son."

Noah made a huge production of looking around, his mouth agape. "Has . . . has hell actually frozen over?"

Rosie gasped and stared up at Noah with wide eyes. "Daddy, you said a bad word."

He rested a hand on her head and ruffled her hair. "You're right. I guess that means ice cream after all this, huh?"

"Yes!" Rosie jumped up and down in excitement before glancing over at Savannah. "Whenever Daddy says a bad word, we get to go have ice cream."

Savannah smiled down at Rosie, fondness in her eyes, and that string tied around Noah's heart tugged a little harder. "I think that sounds like you made out pretty good on that deal."

"Well, fine." Noah's mom threw her hands up in the air before dropping them to her sides. "I'm just trying to save them some money, but if you guys don't want to hear any of that, I get it. Let your kid go into debt for a one-day event. Who am I to stop it?"

Pauline scoffed. "I think you're being a little dramatic, Cheryl, don't you? Caleb and Issa gave us a budget. They're in their thirties, so if they tell us that this is how much they have to spend on a wedding, I'm going to take them at their word that they understand the financial ramifications of doing so. If this is what they want for their wedding, I'm not going to try to talk them out of it."

"Are you insinuating that I wouldn't do the same for my son?"

"Don't be ridiculous. You're purposely twisting my words. All I'm saying is—"

Noah turned toward Savannah with raised eyebrows, attempting to transmit a *Do you believe them?* message. She matched his look and pressed her lips together as if biting back her thoughts. Who would have thought what would bring them together on common ground was their mothers bickering over a wedding they were roped into planning?

He leaned toward her, close enough so that his voice wouldn't carry, and said under his breath, "And to think they came along because of the scene *we* caused."

Savannah turned her head toward him and huffed out a laugh. Her breath blew across his lips, and their noses nearly brushed. He stood frozen for a moment, locked in her gaze. In the quiet stillness of the moment, something electric passed between them, and it felt like time stood still.

"Daddy, I'm bored," Rosie whined, tugging on his hand.

Noah blinked and glanced down at her, breaking whatever weird connection he and Savannah had shared. He cleared his throat and tried to impart some moisture into his too-dry mouth. "We're almost done, squirt. We'll head to the next one pretty soon."

"I don't *wanna* do another one. I wanna go get ice cream!"

"I know you do. And we will, but we have to do this first."

They were now walking a very thin line. When Rosie got bored, they usually had about a fifteen-minute window before she'd slowly spiral into whiny four-year-old mode. Which meant she'd be a nightmare at the remaining appointments today.

"I have an idea," Savannah said, squatting down next to Rosie so they were eye level with each other. "While we're waiting for your grandma and my mom to finish up, let's try to come up with the craziest ice cream flavors we can think of. Do you want to go first or should I?"

Rosie's face lit up. "Daddy should!"

Noah glanced down at her, his gaze distracted momentarily by Savannah as she stared up at him, one eyebrow raised, and his heart gave an unwelcome thump inside his chest.

What on earth was going on? He didn't know what was different about today. If it was that they'd finally set aside their animosity for more than five minutes and actually agreed on something, or if it was the fact that she treated his daughter with kindness and respect that showed how much she truly cared for kids. Not just for kids but for Rosie specifically. Whatever it was, there was no denying any more that he was seeing Savannah in a whole new light.

And there was also no denying just how much that simple fact was going to complicate everything going forward. The last thing he needed right now while juggling everything else was to worry about an attraction to Savannah.

Chapter Eight

This girls' night couldn't have come at a better time for Savannah. Trying to run the preschool to the best of her ability, planning this wedding to make it as perfect for Caleb and Issa as she possibly could, all while attempting to get along with the one man who drove her absolutely up the wall was an effort in futility. She was exhausted, a husk of a human, really. She just needed some time to set all that aside and not think about anything but good food and good drinks with good friends.

For the past few years, she, Gia, and Abby had had a long-standing girls' night each week. But they'd recently expanded their trio to include Rebecca, Abby's boyfriend's sister, as well as Tori, who was tentatively settling in at the Sunshine Corner. Becca was a single mom to four-year-old Sofia and in desperate need of adult interaction, and since Tori and her husband had just moved to the area from Seattle and was such a lovely fellow adventurer in the classroom, Savannah was glad she agreed to join.

Abby was prepping the food, her brand-new engagement ring glinting as she cooked, while Gia sat at the table, directing Becca on where to place the items she'd brought, her burgeoning belly becoming more and more of an obstacle each day. That meant Savannah was performing her favorite duty as the bringer of alcohol. She poured four glasses of merlot and made a virgin mimosa for Gia to help her get in on the fun.

She gathered the drinks and was about to head over to the table when Abby's grandmother Hilde swooped in out of nowhere. Hilde had a ladies' night of her own with her friends this evening, but she often joined the younger women to chat for a bit before heading out. Her gray hair was twisted into a knot at the base of her neck, and too many bracelets to count jingled on her wrist. Grabbing one of the wineglasses, she patted Savannah on the shoulder. "Thanks, dear."

That was unusually forward, even for Hilde.

"No problem." Savannah smiled and went to grab another glass.

"Actually, I heard Abby mentioning she had a headache earlier," Hilde said, a little too casual. "She might prefer one of those mimosas you made for Gia."

Savannah stopped in her tracks, narrowing her eyes at the older woman.

Hilde was known around town as the Baby Whisperer. Not only did she have the magical ability to calm even the most distressed baby simply by picking them up, she also seemed to be able to sense when a person was pregnant just by looking at them. She never came out and said it, of course. Instead she dropped weird, out-of-the-blue hints, like she had with Gia, suggesting to her that she might want to wait a bit before converting a spare room into an art studio. Lo and behold, not a week later, they'd found out they'd need it for something very different indeed—namely, a nursery.

Still, Hilde's veiled comments didn't always mean anything. Savannah furrowed her brow as she fixed an extra mocktail. Hilde shrugged and exited the kitchen, sashaying out of the way as Tori made her way in.

"Do you want some help?" Tori asked, her voice tentative.

Savannah glanced over at her and offered a smile. Her nerves had seemed to dissipate since the first day of school, but she was still a bit hesitant. Savannah only hoped this group get-together would loosen her up even more. "That'd be great, thanks."

She grabbed her glass and the two virgin mimosas, leaving the remaining two wineglasses for Tori, and made her way over to the round table in the breakfast nook where everyone was congregated. She offered Gia her faux fancy drink with a flourish. "Something a little special for the baby mama." She turned to Abby with a raised brow. "And a little birdie told me you 'had a headache'?"

Abby accepted the virgin mimosa, not quite meeting Savannah's gaze. "Yeah. Thank you—you know how wine always makes those worse."

Savannah's suspicions only rose, but she was distracted by Gia, who placed a hand over her heart, her lips turned down in an earnest expression as she regarded her drink. "This is so sweet." She took a deep breath and blinked rapidly, waving a hand in front of her face. "Oh my God, this is actually making me cry." She glanced around at the other girls sitting at the table, her eyes wide in panic. "What is *wrong* with me? Will I ever go back to how I used to be?"

Hilde's laughter joined Becca's as she lifted a single shoulder. "Maybe."

Gia's lips parted in an indignant huff. "That's not the reassurance I was hoping for, Hilde."

Becca said, "I'm not going to lie to you. Even if you *do* go back to how you used to be, it'll probably take a few years. Sofia's four, and I feel like I'm just starting to get the rest of my life back on track."

Gia groaned and dropped her forehead to the table. "Aren't you guys supposed to lie to me and tell me what I want to hear?"

Abby reached over and rubbed a soft circle on her friend's back. She bit her lip as she looked around. "I'm afraid those aren't the kinds of friends you have, G."

"Anyway, what good does it do to lie to you?"

Hilde asked, looking between Gia and her grand-daughter. "Then you'll only be disillusioned and not at all prepared."

"And we all know how much you love to be prepared," Savannah said into her wineglass.

"At least you have Marco," Becca said, dipping a tortilla chip into Gia's famous homemade guacamole. "Believe me, as someone who's been there, doing it solo is even harder."

Becca's tone was breezy, but a hint of regret lay just beneath her words. Not for Sophia—Savannah knew she loved her kid to the moon and back. But being a single parent couldn't be easy, and Becca had spoken before about how she wished she could have had a partner who stuck around.

"True...I just wish we could have been married for a few more years," Gia said, her voice shaky. "What if Marco doesn't want to stick around after he realizes the woman he married is gone? *Poof*! And in her place is a lunatic who cries at the drop of a hat and gets worked up over what shade of lavender to paint the nursery."

Was it Savannah's imagination or did Abby flinch a bit at that?

If she did, she recovered quickly. Still rubbing Gia's back, Abby asked, "Is that this week's challenge?"

"Yes," Gia practically wailed. "We agreed on purple, and he said I could pick the shade. Do you know how much pressure there is to get it perfect?"

Abby breathed out a laugh. "I know you're freaking

out about this, but can we just take a minute to appreciate how far you've come in just a couple months?"

Savannah tossed in a noise of affirmation as the other women offered nods of encouragement. Well, all except Tori, as she hadn't yet been part of their group when Gia found out she was pregnant and her world sort of imploded.

"It was only a few months ago that you and Marco weren't seeing eye to eye on anything, right?" Abby plucked a piece of Havarti from the tray and popped it in her mouth. "How's that going, by the way? I assume thanks to the paint situation that you guys have found a way to compromise without starting World War Three?"

Gia's whole body seemed to relax at Abby's question, and a small smile tugged up her lips. "Yes, thankfully. Ever since we talked and got everything out in the open, it's been so much better. And it's seriously been such a huge weight off my shoulders. We still have our fights, of course—like the fact that he suggested a camouflage paint pattern in the baby's room." She shot them a *Do you believe the audacity?* look. "I was able to sway him to my side on that. And, thankfully, we aren't fighting about the important things. We're discussing them like adults. Who knew?" She shrugged and grabbed a crostini topped with cream cheese and honey and bit into it with a hum.

"Who'd have thought we'd give such good advice," Hilde said over the rim of her wineglass, her eyes sparkling as she glanced at each woman in turn. "Let that be a lesson to all of you—there's no problem too big and complicated—or too small, for that matter— for this group."

If only…Compared to Gia's impending due date and whatever may or may not be going on with Abby, Savannah's current problems seemed pretty small indeed.

"You're so right, Hilde," Gia said. "And I appreciate it so much. You all were seriously lifesavers at the beginning of this pregnancy."

"That's what we're here for," Abby said.

"But enough about baby stuff!" Gia said with excitement, swinging her attention to Savannah, a gleam in her eyes. "I want all the juicy details on how it is planning a wedding with someone who's not your fiancé."

"Not only that," Abby said, cutting in, "but someone who you clearly have off-the-charts chemistry with."

Savannah snapped her head toward Abby on a huff, her mouth dropping open as she stared at her best friend who'd just thrown her under the bus. And what was Abby even talking about anyway? She and Noah did *not* have chemistry. Whatever bubbled between them was nothing more than irritation on the best of days, and flat-out hatred on the worst. "Excuse you."

"No, excuse *you*," Becca said, her elbow propped up on the table, chin resting in her hand as she leaned toward Savannah. Her expression was one of pure, undiluted interest. "I don't know anything about this.

Tell us all the things. *Please*. I have to live vicariously through you."

Savannah waved a hand through the air, dismissing the question. "There's not really anything to tell. My brother and his fiancée live in San Francisco, and money and time are both tight for them right now. So they asked me and Noah to plan their wedding for them here in Heart's Hope Bay."

Becca's eyebrows shot up toward her hairline. "Noah, as in your brother's hot friend?"

At the same time, Tori said, "Noah Adams, Rosie's dad?"

"Yes. That Noah."

Abby smirked at Savannah as she took a sip of her drink, one eyebrow raised.

"What?" Savannah snapped. "Why are you looking at me like that?"

Abby set her glass down on the table and plucked a sliced pepper from the charcuterie board. She lifted a shoulder, playing at nonchalance, though she and Savannah had been friends too long for that to hold any weight. "Nothing. I just think it's interesting that you agreed."

Savannah frowned. Of course she would agree—it *was* Noah she'd been roped into planning this with. "Did you think I would deny his name being mentioned?" she asked, confusion ringing in her tone. "Make you refer to him as the One Who Can't Be Named?"

"No," Abby said, drawing out the word. "But I did

think you would object to Becca's signifier of him being your brother's *hot* friend."

Savannah rolled her eyes even as she felt her face flame. God, how stupid was she? She was an adult and yet apparently embarrassed that she'd been caught finding a grown man attractive. There was no denying that fact. Noah *was* attractive—smoking hot, if you wanted to get right down to it—but his attitude and complete dismissal of her turned him unappealing in her book. "Whatever. You caught me. He's good-looking—that's not a newsflash. Also not a newsflash is the fact that we can't agree on anything for this wedding."

"Not a surprise, honey," Hilde said. "Combustible chemistry oftentimes manifests in arguments."

Savannah narrowed her eyes at Hilde. "See if I let you help yourself to our wine next time."

Hilde smirked as she took a sip of her pilfered wineglass while the rest of the ladies chuckled.

"What are you working on now?" Tori asked.

If it had been any of her other friends asking, she might have blown them off and changed the subject. But Tori had said all of twenty words that evening, so Savannah didn't want to shoot her down when she actually spoke up.

She blew out a heavy sigh and popped a chocolate-covered cashew into her mouth. "We're still scouting venues. This rushed timeline, combined with my brother and Issa's budget, is really putting us in a bind. Noah and I can't agree on *anything*. I thought we'd come to some sort of a mutual understanding after the disaster that was our moms both tagging along to 'help.' They disagreed and caused more of a scene than we did, so we finally found some common ground."

"That sounds like a good thing," Abby said, a question clear in her voice.

"You would think. Except the next day, it was like nothing had ever happened. Now he's pushing back on absolutely every suggestion I have for the combined bachelor/bachelorette party."

"Ohh..." Gia rubbed her hands together, her eyes bright with interest. "Party planning is my and Abby's jam. Maybe we can help. What ideas do you have so far?"

"You mean what has he already shot down?" At their nods, she continued. "I suggested chartering a boat. He countered with paintball or a casino night. When I suggested a wine tasting, he threw back a road trip to camp down the coast. It's like he's being intentionally argumentative just to get under my skin."

"Or to get under something else..." Hilde mumbled under her breath only loud enough for Savannah to hear—which was exactly why she ignored it. No sense in feeding the monster.

"Ohh..." Abby straightened in her seat, her eyes bright. "What if you combined some of your ideas? I bet we could find a winery halfway between here and San Francisco, so everyone in the wedding party could attend. And you could rent a bus to drive down.

You could probably even set up game tables inside to entertain everyone on the trip. It'd be so fun!"

"That sounds *amazing*!" Gia gushed.

Becca nodded. "Yeah, it does sound like a pretty good compromise."

"Too bad Noah will never go for it if I suggest it." Savannah rolled her eyes.

"That's why you should just FaceTime Issa and see what she thinks before you even bring it up to Noah," Abby said. "That way you won't have to waste your breath with him if she doesn't like it."

"Devious," Becca said, nodding as if she were impressed. "I like it."

"Before we bring it up to her, let me just check on some things real quick." Abby pulled out her phone, her thumbs already flying. "Grandma, can you grab me one of my blank notebooks and a pen, please?"

"Of course, dear." Hilde's tone was placating as she grabbed a pink notebook off a stack of what looked like at least a dozen, along with a pen. "Heaven forbid you not have a fresh, clean space to write all your notes."

"You get me." Abby smiled up at Hilde as she placed both items next to her.

Savannah felt a little strange just sitting there while Abby researched what, technically, was her job. But she'd known Abby long enough to understand that once she got into this frame of mind, little could derail her. It would be both the quickest and the easiest to just let her run with it.

Sure enough, not even five minutes later, as Savannah was pouring everyone a second round of both wine and virgin mimosas, Abby said, "Yes! I think I've got it." She turned her phone around and showed it to each woman in turn, a picture of a gorgeous inn and several wineries near it. "It's not quite halfway. It would be a little farther for you guys coming from here, but I figured that's okay, especially if you rent a bus to take you down. But this inn is small enough that you could rent out the whole thing for a discounted rate."

Savannah couldn't deny how stunning the pictures were, or how easily Abby seemed to stumble into the ideal solution. "That does look amazing."

"Perfect! Why don't you see if Issa can FaceTime and you guys can discuss it."

Savannah pulled out her phone and queued up Issa's name.

After only a couple rings, her soon-to-be sister-in-law answered with a bright smile, her curls already tucked under the bonnet she slept in to keep her hair protected. "Hey, you! How's it going?"

Savannah tilted her head to the side as she stared at Issa. "Wait...did San Francisco switch time zones without me knowing?" She glanced at the time, noting it was barely nine. "Are you already heading to bed?"

Issa's shoulders drooped, and she frowned slightly. "Yes, unfortunately. Our usual opener at the bakery is out on vacation, which means I'm the lucky one who gets to be there by four thirty a.m."

"That's rough. Do you want to chat tomorrow?"

"No, don't worry about it. What's up?"

"I'm just hanging out with Abby and some other girlfriends." A chorus of greetings sounded around her, and Issa smiled in response, calling out a hello. The couple of times Issa had been up to Heart's Hope Bay, Savannah had dragged her along to girls' night, knowing she'd need a break from the testosterone-filled Lowe house. Sure enough, she'd fit right in and had stayed in touch with all the girls online. "I was telling them about some disagreements that Noah and I have had on the bachelor/bachelorette party."

"Oh no. Are you two at each other's throats? I told Caleb I wasn't sure if this would be a good idea to ask you to plan it together."

"No, no," Savannah reassured her quickly. Though planning this with Noah wasn't particularly enjoyable, it was far more enjoyable than having another failure or a half-finished project on her hands. "It's fine. Just some stumbling blocks."

"And anyway," Abby said from her perch over Savannah's shoulder, "we found the perfect compromise." She filled Issa in on what she'd been able to find, showing Issa the same images on her phone that she'd shown the rest of them. Issa's eyes lit up as soon as she saw them, her excitement only growing when Abby mentioned the discount rate for the inn.

"It sounds amazing," Issa gushed. "Seriously, I love it. I don't care what Noah thinks. *This* is what I want."

Savannah didn't know whether to feel resentment or gratitude toward her best friend for doing in less than twenty minutes what Savannah hadn't been able to do in two weeks.

They hung up shortly after she said a quick hello to Caleb so Issa could settle in for the night. The rest of the girls gathered around Abby and her fast thumbs as she researched the party, moving on from the wineries to the bus options they were able to charter.

After all this time as Abby's best friend, Savannah was used to this flurry by now, but it sat a little differently this time. This had been Savannah's job, and while she was grateful for the help, she wasn't sure she loved being completely sidelined in the process. She'd already been feeling left out after all the baby talk— and seriously, she and Abby were going to have to have a Talk tomorrow about Hilde's numerous off-handed remarks. Watching everybody else handle her responsibility of party planning for her had only compounded the issue.

While the rest of the girls were oohing and aahing over the luxury buses available, Savannah escaped to refill her drink, needing just a bit of space. She was so focused on the task that she didn't hear anyone come up behind her until Tori spoke.

"At least that's one less thing for you and Noah to fight about."

Savannah startled, nearly sloshing the wine out of her glass.

"Oops, sorry. Didn't mean to scare you."

She laughed lightly and shrugged. "Don't worry about it. And believe me, Noah and I will find something else to argue about."

Tori glanced over at the table where everyone sat, chatting animatedly, before focusing back on Savannah. "I don't know you as well as everyone else, and I know Noah even less, but maybe things wouldn't be so rough if you just try to talk to each other. If you were able to hear each other out without getting defensive, you guys might be able to get somewhere. And it might make planning the rest of this wedding an enjoyable rather than an excruciating experience."

"Yeah, you're probably right."

That didn't mean it would be easy. Because like it or not, she and Noah had had years—decades even—of preconceived notions about each other and a not-so-secret animosity. And she had a feeling he still saw her as nothing more than his buddy's annoying little sister who was naive and spoiled and completely without any worthwhile ideas or ambitions of her own.

Chapter Nine

Savannah stood on Noah's front porch, a six-pack of his favorite beer in her hand as she stared at the door and willed herself to knock already. She'd barely waited twenty-four hours after Tori's suggestion before she made the trip over, but that was Savannah for you. She was a spontaneous, spur-of-the-moment person, and if the girls' night hadn't finished so late yesterday, she probably would have just headed straight over then because this needed to be addressed immediately. Since they would be seeing even more venues this weekend, she wanted to start off on the best foot possible.

She ran a hand down her hair and blew out a deep breath before rolling her eyes at herself. She was being ridiculous and had no idea why she was so anxious. If Noah wanted to continue to be a complete jerk about it even after her extended olive branch, well, then at least she could say she tried.

Before she could second-guess it any more, she knocked on the dark wood door, then stepped back and waited for Noah to answer. The blinds in the front window separated for only a moment, and then almost immediately, the door swung open.

Noah gawked at Savannah, darting his gaze to the space around and behind her, as if searching for an answer or trouble or both. "Savannah? Everything okay?"

Having grown up with four older brothers, she was so familiar with that particular move that she nearly rolled her eyes at him and told him where he could shove his overprotective crap. Except that, coming from him, this felt different somehow. Different and not entirely unwelcome if the swoop of her stomach was anything to go by.

"I was hoping we could talk." She held up the pack of his favorite beer. "I brought a peace offering."

He lifted his brows. "Wow. You even called Caleb to find out what my favorite was, huh?" he said, opening the door wider and tipping his head to welcome her inside as he took the pack from her. "Come on in."

No, she hadn't called Caleb, actually. She'd known that piece of trivia all on her own. She had no idea where she'd acquired the knowledge, just that it was there. Along with the fact that he hated mustard, thought pineapple on pizza was a travesty, and disliked peanut butter cookies but raved about her mom's despite that.

Rather than admit any of that to him, Savannah busied herself with glancing around at the space as Noah led them inside. She'd never been in his house before, the bulk of their interactions happening either at her parents' home or around town.

The front entry split into two different directions. She followed Noah to the right, which meant the bedrooms were probably off to the left. Family photos and framed drawings of Rosie's hung on the walls as he led them down a long hallway to the kitchen and small attached dining room. A family room anchored that end of the house just beyond it. The space was homier than she thought it'd be, the walls painted a warm, soft gray and the furniture plush and inviting, looking for all the world like an ad encouraging a movie night curled up under a blanket. It was clean and tidy—no surprise there—save for what looked like an unfinished home improvement project going on over by the pantry. Of course, there were also touches of Rosie sprinkled throughout, like her shoes discarded by the front door, her backpack hanging over the chair at the dining room table, and an array of crayons and coloring books spread out on the floor in front of the TV.

"You want one?" he asked, setting the beer on the counter before plucking a bottle from the carton. He popped the top before holding it toward her.

"Yeah, thanks." She took the proffered bottle from him, her gaze focusing on his large hands as he wrapped one around another bottle and retrieved it for himself. "Rosie in bed?"

She figured the little girl probably would be, which was why she'd come later in the evening, so they could have some privacy to talk about what had been going on between them. It hadn't ever occurred to her that maybe being alone in his house, this late at night, with alcohol greasing the wheels, may not have been in her best interest if she had any hopes of not acting like an idiot...especially considering her growing attraction to the infuriating man.

"Yeah, she just fell asleep a bit ago," he said, his voice a little weary.

"Are you tired already?" Savannah asked, not attempting to tamp down the teasing lilt to her voice. "It's only eight thirty. I knew you were old, but I didn't realize you were *that* old."

Noah huffed out a laugh as he braced his hands on the counter and glanced down, shaking his head. "I'm exhausted," he said without an ounce of joking in his tone.

Savannah took that moment to study him, really see him and read beneath the hardened exterior he showed the world. He *looked* exhausted now that she was really paying attention. Of course he was gorgeous, but there was a weight on his shoulders, his eyes pinched and mouth tight. He had the weariness of a world traveler after a solid forty-eight hours of just trying to get home. Or, more accurately, an EMT single dad whose ex-wife was basically out of the picture and who looked out for everyone else. Who looked out for Noah?

"I take it things haven't been going as well as you'd hoped?" she asked.

He glanced up at her then, an eyebrow raised. "You're going to have to be a little more specific than that."

She took a pull from her beer before setting it back on the counter. "I mean with you and Rosie...since Jess left."

"Ahh," he said, nodding and averting his gaze. "I look that bad, huh?"

Savannah snorted and slapped a hand to his arm, ignoring how hot—not to mention hard—he was beneath the thin cotton T-shirt he wore. "Oh, please. You know exactly how good-looking you are. I just meant you seem tired."

As soon as the words left her mouth, she wished she could snatch them back, cringing internally at the heyday he was going to have teasing her about her slip. Except he didn't taunt her at all.

Instead, Noah studied her for a moment, his gaze scrutinizing as it darted all over her face, finally settling on her mouth where her lips tingled at his attention. She tried to lick away the sensation, though that was her second dumbest idea in as many minutes, as Noah cleared his throat before averting his gaze.

"We're figuring it out," he said, his voice a little rough.

"I'm sure you are. After all, you're Noah Adams, and you do everything you set your mind to. But that's not what I asked."

He took a deep breath and blew it out slowly, seeming to judge her intention. Finally, he admitted, "It's hard." He took a long pull from his beer before shaking his head. He glanced at her out of the corner of his eye. "What, no ribbing?"

"Please, if I wanted to do that, I wouldn't take the low-hanging fruit."

"Fair enough," he said with a smile.

She'd been studying his smiles for what felt like a lifetime and knew them all. His *I'm about to school you* smile, and his *I'm placating you* smile, and his *you're an idiot* smile. She, too, knew his real and true smile, but this wasn't it. This was something along the lines of *I'm barely hanging on but don't you worry about me* smile.

"Do you want to talk about it?"

"Do I want to get heckled about it, you mean?"

She laughed. "I can do that, too, if you want. But, no, I was thinking something along the lines of you letting me know what's been going on and seeing if I can help at all. You know, what friends do."

"Is that what we are?"

If he'd asked her that even a month ago, she'd have said no. But she wasn't ready to give up on the glimpse of connection she'd seen last weekend. When they'd stopped hating on each other and found common ground.

"Sometimes. Let's consider this one of our on days."

He paused for only a moment before tipping his head toward the family room. Savannah sat next to him on the couch, folding one leg under her so she could face him. She waited long moments for him to say something, but instead watched him down the rest of his beer with little pause.

"Maybe I should've brought something a little harder," she said, lifting her chin toward the empty bottle in his hands. "What's going on?"

"I don't like to lean on anyone."

"What do you mean, like your mom?"

"My mom, yeah, but anyone, really. Hell, even your parents have offered to help. Your brothers, too, and the guys down at the station. But I just feel like if I take them up on it any more than is absolutely necessary, it's like admitting that I failed."

"That's a lot to put on one person's shoulders, even yours."

There was no denying his were big and broad, strong, too…Enough to withstand a tremendous amount of pressure. But even the strongest broke sometimes, and there was no denying the cracks in his facade that he'd finally allowed her to see.

"Maybe, but I learned when I was pretty young that I needed to figure things out on my own."

While the two of them had never actually discussed

this, the details surrounding his dad's departure from his life hadn't been a secret. Nothing ever was in Heart's Hope Bay. "You mean...after your dad left you and your mom?"

"Yeah," he said, scrubbing a hand down his weary face. "But that was only one aspect of it. She had to work so much just to support us that I had no choice but to figure out how to get by on my own. I guess it sort of stuck."

Savannah's heart broke for the little boy he'd been—his dad left them when he was only around ten, if she remembered right. Those kinds of expectations were a lot to put on anyone's shoulders, let alone a little kid. She'd known Noah's mom, Cheryl, her whole life and knew this pressure wouldn't have come from her. She'd also known Noah her whole life, and she had little doubt it was anything but self-imposed.

"It's normal for everyone to need help once in a while," she said.

"For everyone else, maybe. I don't like to rely on anyone but myself. It kills me that I even have to ask my mom for help watching Rosie when I have to work and she's not in school. Or setting up something with Abby so Rosie can stay past the normal day-care hours just so I can pick her up after work. They've already moved my schedule around to let me work four twelves instead of two twenty-fours just so I can get all this figured out. But it's been a few months now, and I don't feel like I've gotten anywhere. Pretty soon, they're going to tell me my time's up and I need to figure something else out. And I have no goddamn idea what I'll do then."

God, the defeat in his voice tugged on every one of her heartstrings, and she had to fight the urge to reach out and comfort him, unsure of how he'd react. Even more so worried about how *she* would. "I think you need to cut yourself some slack, Noah."

"Yeah? I think I need to get my act together."

She made a show of looking around at this house that was a place to call his own. "I don't know—you seem pretty put together to me. Someone who doesn't have their act together wouldn't be living your life. Just ask me."

He turned his gaze on her, his brow furrowed. "What's that supposed to mean?"

"Don't sound so surprised. You don't have to play dumb. I know you think I'm a spoiled brat who still lives off her parents' dime." In fact, she was pretty sure everyone in Heart's Hope Bay thought the same thing.

"I don't—"

"You do," she said, her voice firm but kind. She lifted a single shoulder and focused all her attention on peeling off the label of her now-empty bottle. "Most people do. But sometimes the lives we lead are the lives we're dealt, you know?"

"How do you mean?"

She breathed out a humorless laugh. "You don't want

to count on anyone and just want to forge your own path. But being the baby of the family—not to mention having four overbearing older brothers—means I've never been allowed to do anything on my own. Someone was always there to hold me up or catch me before I could ever actually fall. I never learned how to pick myself up because I never had to."

"And you don't like that?" he asked, confusion ringing clearly in his tone.

She shrugged. "I never knew any better. But as I got older...let's just say it's left me uncertain about my abilities in, well, everything."

He hummed as he studied her, and she waited for a taunt that never came. Finally, he set his empty bottle on the coffee table before mirroring her position, his leg tucked under him as he faced her. "Looks like we're quite the pair."

He rested his arm over the top of the couch, the tips of his fingers near enough to her shoulder that he could touch it if he wanted to. She had no idea why that thought sent shivers racing down her spine, her stomach flipping with nerves or anticipation or both. And, God, did she actually *want* him to reach out and touch her?

She totally did.

And the thing was, she wasn't even that surprised by it. She thought back to all the remarks Abby had made about the two of them, at the undeniable chemistry she and Noah shared. She'd thought it was hatred, but that hadn't been right at all. It'd been attraction this entire time. And now...she was in trouble. While she'd known Noah her entire life, they'd never talked— truly talked—about things that mattered. And they'd certainly never opened up to each other about anything personal. Tonight, they'd done both.

"That we are," she said, willing her voice to be steady. "So how about we cut each other some slack?"

He lifted an eyebrow. "What do you propose?"

"Well, we're going to be spending a lot of time together in the next few months while we plan this wedding. Maybe we can be less judgy toward each other for the duration. And leave our mothers out of it."

"That's reasonable."

"Do we have a deal, then?" She held out her hand, pinky extended, waiting for him to swear on it.

He glanced down at her hand before meeting her eyes, his gaze boring into her so deep she felt it straight to her toes.

She'd been so busy helping Abby get everything set up for the preschool this spring and summer that she'd scarcely had time to date. There was also the small matter of watching Abby fall head over heels in love with Carter that had made her question her own casual approach to relationships. Combine the two, and she was in the midst of quite the dry spell. Still, she couldn't remember the last time her stomach had flipped—over and over and over again—merely from eye contact. If this was what it felt like when only his eyes caressed her, what would it be like to have his hands on her skin?

Hooking his pinky with hers, he said, "I'm in." His voice was low and rough, his eyes darkened to a deep chocolate, and she curled her fingers into the couch cushion just to keep herself still.

Dear God, what had she gotten herself into?

Chapter Ten

Noah drove to Savannah's house to pick her up for their packed evening of looking at a few more venues. He didn't know if it was the seed that the guys at the station had planted in his head as they'd taunted him about his *dates*, or his and Savannah's conversation at his place the other night—or maybe a combination of both—but somewhere along the way, he'd started to think of Savannah as someone a man would aspire to go out with.

On some level, he'd always found her attractive, of course, but something had shifted in his thinking of late. It was getting harder and harder to ignore the prick of jealousy that burned in his gut at the thought of anybody else taking her out. It was stupid. What on earth did he have to be jealous about? She wasn't his.

Never mind that the thought alone made the fire flare hotter; it didn't make it any less true.

They were getting down to the wire to choose a venue for Caleb and Issa's December wedding. As it was, their pickings were slim to none. They'd almost run through the list of places Caleb and Issa had asked them to scope out—plus a few Savannah had found herself—and they were all unworkable, out of budget, or already booked. He and Savannah had the appointments this evening, and then another several set up for Saturday. If they didn't find something during one of those viewings, they were going to have to get creative.

He pulled into the Lowes' driveway, feeling off as he walked around the garage to the entrance of the carriage house. The only time he had been in this space had been when they'd moved Savannah in after her parents had completely rebuilt the garage in order for her to have a place of her own. He ignored the prick of envy that fluttered in the back of his mind, reminding him just how very different their lives were. When he was growing up, he and his mom could barely afford a two-bedroom apartment, and Savannah came from the kind of family who built her an apartment above the garage, just because.

Shaking those thoughts from his head, he knocked and heard rumbled footfalls on the stairs beyond the door. It opened and Savannah stood there, looking for all the world like a siren sent to Earth for the sole purpose of driving him crazy in both the best and worst ways. Her blond hair was down, hanging in loose waves around her shoulders. Her blue eyes were bright—something he didn't usually get to see as they were generally filled with fury whenever he was around. He couldn't deny how much he enjoyed having them turned on him now.

"Hey," she said, a little breathlessly.

His gaze dropped to her lips, then lower still as he catalogued the soft-looking, fitted sweater she wore, before he snapped it back up to her eyes and silently berated himself for checking her out. "Hi. You ready?"

"As I'll ever be." She stepped out of her apartment and directly into his space as she closed the door behind her. "I hope we find something that works so we can cancel our appointments this weekend."

"Getting sick of me already, so soon after our truce?"

Her tinkling laugh erupted into the otherwise quiet night, and his lips tugged up in response. "Not yet. Though I wouldn't place bets on us staying civil. We'll see how it is at the end of the night."

"Probably a good call, given our history." He opened the passenger door for her, feeling absurdly pleased at her look of surprise. "What? You didn't think I was a gentleman?"

She lifted a single shoulder. "In general, maybe. For me? Not so much."

If she had a window into his thoughts that starred

her, she'd know just how true that statement was. It seemed the last thing he was when he was around her was a gentleman.

He cleared his throat. "I do love to keep you on your toes."

Noah didn't stick around to see if the smile lifting one corner of her mouth spread across the whole thing before he shut the door and walked around his car, willing himself to get his mind in the game. He clearly had been without female companionship for far too long, though that was hardly a surprise. Jess had been gone for months, and they hadn't been intimate since they'd started the separation process over a year ago. It was no wonder that spark of attraction arced between him and Savannah.

After sliding into his seat and starting the car, he pulled out of the driveway and directed them to their first stop, a restaurant right on the beach. It had a rental space just large enough for the number of guests Caleb and Issa were planning to invite.

Savannah glanced into the back seat before resting her attention on him. "No Rosie tonight?" A thread of disappointment was present in her tone that managed to somehow get under his skin even more. It was one thing to be nice to him, but when it was clear she genuinely would've enjoyed his daughter's company for the evening, he was a goner.

"She has ballet class on Tuesdays. That's why my mom picks her up from school early. They spend the evening together, usually go out to dinner, and my mom spoils her way more than necessary."

"That's sweet," Savannah said. "And look at you, allowing your mom to do that without freaking out."

Noah shot her a glance out of the corner of his eye. "To be fair, I didn't ask for this help. My mom signed Rosie up for the classes and then informed me that she'd be going to them, that my mom would be taking her, and that they would be having a girls' night every week. I could either suck it up and get over myself or I could 'throw a mantrum'—that's a man tantrum, her words—because she was doing it regardless."

Savannah's peal of laughter drew his gaze, and he stared for a beat too long, grateful they were currently stopped at a red light. "I see. So really the people in your life just need to be mind readers and offer the help before you can ask for it."

He exaggerated a scowl as he regarded her before turning his attention back to the road and driving through the green light. "I could have sworn we pinky promised that we'd cut each other some slack. This feels like you're ribbing me."

She reached over and rested her hand on his forearm, the thin material of his Henley not nearly enough to keep out the heat of her touch. Dormant parts of his body stirred—the kind that a woman hadn't been able to get a rise from in far too long. "You're right. I'm sorry. I know how sensitive you are and how you can't take a joke." Her voice was heavy with a teasing taunt, but he couldn't focus on the words. Not when she'd rested her elbow on the console between them and leaned even closer, her thumb mindlessly rubbing against his arm. "Do you think you can forgive me?"

Jesus. Was it getting hot in here? Sudden, unwelcome warmth flooded his veins. He fumbled with the temperature controls, switching the air from warm to cool.

Dropping her hand from his arm, she sat back in her seat and laughed. "I can't believe I got you so mad you had to turn on the air-conditioning. We've only been together for five minutes. I think that might be a new record."

He could have told her that his reaction had absolutely nothing to do with anger and everything to do with the casual way she'd been touching him. But that definitely wasn't the best course of action. Not when he considered the fact at hand, which was that they were stuck together planning this wedding for the next couple months. Not to mention that she was his best friend's baby sister. He had absolutely no business thinking about touching her right back.

So he let her think it was anger that was burning him up inside, and not that, somehow, a switch had been flipped, making him suddenly want her in the worst way. He was in a whole hell of a lot of trouble if he couldn't figure out how to flip that switch back.

* * *

Noah managed to get through their non-date-date without incident. And by *incident*, he meant that he didn't push her up against a wall, press his body to hers, and kiss her within an inch of her life. Unfortunately, that was the only good news that had come out of the evening. Well, that and the fact that he and Savannah had managed to get along for a record three hours. They'd even grabbed a quick dinner at their first stop. They had never gone that long without being at each other's throats. And he couldn't lie—he'd actually enjoyed it.

Their relationship had always been volatile—matches and gunpowder stored in a too-small space—and while there was still the underlying ribbing between them that he'd always secretly enjoyed, it was now accompanied by flirty grins and soft words instead of the biting remarks he'd gotten so used to not only giving but also receiving.

Unfortunately, they hadn't found the right space for the reception, which meant that they still had one more day of searching. One more day where they would hopefully find what they were looking for. He diligently ignored the part of himself that was secretly pleased at this turn of events. Recognizing how much he was looking forward to spending more uninterrupted time with her could only lead to madness.

He pushed all thoughts of Savannah out of his head

as he finished reading the last few lines of Rosie's favorite story to her. He closed the book and set it aside.

"All right, squirt, it's time for bed." He and Rosie lay squished together on her twin-size bed, his back up against her headboard, an arm around her as she snuggled into his side.

"Aw, Daddy, please? Just one more?" Rosie pleaded, her big brown eyes staring up at him.

He breathed out a laugh and pressed a kiss to her forehead before sliding his arm out from around her and slipping out of her bed. "Nice try, but this was book five. You've already gotten three more than you were supposed to."

She pulled her covers up, burying half her face beneath them, but he could see from the crinkle in the corner of her eyes that she was smiling. And yeah, he'd read her five stories every night if it would put that look on her face. Especially when she hadn't been having the easiest time lately.

"I'll see you in the morning." He braced himself on her bed as he pressed another kiss to her forehead. "Now, get to sleep. You've got school in the morning."

She snapped her covers down and grinned widely up at him, her eyes bright. "Yeah! Miss Savannah said we're making zoo maminals tomorrow. I can't wait to show you what one I'm doing, Daddy!"

"I'm glad you're excited," he said, his voice a little rough with emotion. It had only been four weeks since the tumultuous start at the beginning of the school year, but he was more relieved than he could say that Rosie had found her footing with not a little help from Savannah. "I could guess right now. Is it a—"

"No, Daddy!" she yelled, clamping her hands directly over his mouth. "No cheating. You can't guess till tomorrow."

He chuckled, pressing a kiss to her palm. "All right, tomorrow, then. I love you." Standing in her doorway, he flipped off her overhead light. "Good night."

"I love you, too, Daddy. Night! Don't let the bedbugs bite."

He made it only three steps out of Rosie's room before his phone buzzed in his back pocket. He lifted it out, saw Caleb's photo flashing on the screen, and swiped to answer. "Hello?"

"Hey, man, what's going on?" Caleb asked.

"Not much. Just got Rosie into bed, and I was going to fall asleep watching *Schitt's Creek*. You know, the usual."

"Ah, yes, living that glamorous, single life I see."

With a chuckle, he grabbed a beer leftover from Savannah's peace offering and popped the top on his way to the family room. He dropped down onto the couch and took a long pull. "Something like that. Although it feels pretty weird living the single life while planning a wedding."

"Yeah, I bet. Hey, I want to thank you again for agreeing to do that. You don't know what a relief it's been for me and Issa that we've got trusted people there to help us out. I can actually focus on this project that's been taking every second of my spare time so I can, you know, keep my job."

"Don't mention it." It was a lot easier for Noah to say the words now than it had been even just a few weeks prior when he'd been blindsided with the request. True, he was even more exhausted and had fallen behind on household duties—he'd need to do laundry soon, or he and Rosie were going to be in trouble—but there was no denying the relief in Caleb's voice. Noah was only too happy to be able to finally repay the favor.

"How's that going anyway?" Caleb asked.

Noah figured it wasn't the wisest plan to fill Caleb in on his newfound friendship, not to mention attraction, with his little sister. So he stuck to strictly the facts. "Savannah and I checked out a few places tonight, actually. Savannah was going to send you the pictures."

"Oh yeah? Any contenders?"

"Not unless you want the reception in an actual barn—like with animals—or what amounts to an oversized storage garage." He recounted the details of the venues Caleb and Issa had pointed them at, namely a farm-to-table restaurant that had ended up being heavy on the farm, and the hotel that was apparently renting out a storage locker on the back of the property, *not* their ballroom.

Caleb laughed, a thick, hearty sound. "See? This is

why we needed you guys to check everything out in person."

"We've got appointments with two more on Saturday." He left off the part where they needed to find a place this weekend, or they were going to be out of options, not wanting to put any more stress on Caleb when his job was apparently already providing him plenty.

"How're things with Savannah, by the way?" Caleb asked. "You and my sister at each other's throats every second?"

For some unknown reason, Caleb's words sparked images in Noah's mind, where he and Savannah weren't at each other's throats so much as he nuzzled against hers. In this dream sequence, his lips ran up the smooth column of her neck to the underside of her jaw before kissing a path to her lips where he hovered, their breaths intermingling as she stared at him with hooded eyes.

He shook his head and cleared his throat, shifting in his seat and willing his body's reaction to subside. "We called a truce the other night, actually."

"No kidding? I never thought I'd live to see the day. How'd you talk her into that?"

"It was her idea. She stopped by with my favorite beer. She didn't tell you?" Hadn't that been what she'd said when she'd shown up on his doorstep, peace offering in hand—that she'd asked Caleb what Noah's favorite was?

"Nope, she didn't say a word to me. Otherwise I would have talked her out of it. You two are like feral cats when you get in the same space."

He finished the rest of the call on autopilot, trying to pay attention to what Caleb was saying and reassure him that he and Issa didn't have anything to worry about because Noah and Savannah would make sure the wedding was perfect. In reality, all he could focus on was the tiny fact that Savannah had brought over his favorite beer, and she'd somehow known that detail all on her own.

Chapter Eleven

Savannah had no idea when she'd gone from dreading these outings with Noah to actually looking forward to them. But somewhere along the way over the past month that they'd been doing this, something had shifted between them. And she couldn't say she was sorry for the switch. Not only had it made planning this wedding a hell of a lot easier, but she also found that when she and Noah retracted their claws and met on mutual ground, she actually sort of enjoyed his company. Okay, there wasn't any *sort of* about it. She feared she liked it a little too much, because there was no way he was feeling the same as she was.

So far, they'd spent the entire day scoping out venues in Whiteport, a nearby town they'd had to expand their search to because all the best locations in Heart's Hope Bay had been snatched up. The trouble was, Whiteport hadn't had any better options. Nothing fit. Nothing was just right. And Savannah feared they were going to have to lower some of their standards; otherwise Issa and Caleb would be getting married at the courthouse and forgoing a reception altogether.

Noah drove them back toward Heart's Hope Bay, his demeanor relaxed, though she couldn't understand why. As much as she enjoyed his company, there was still a knot in her stomach over what this would mean for the wedding. "I know this was kind of a bust, but you want to grab a bite to eat? When I asked my mom to watch Rosie today, she told me not to pick her up until tomorrow, so I'm a free agent."

She turned her head toward him with a smile. "I love your mom. She doesn't beat around the bush, does she?"

"Not even a little. She thinks I need to get out more and isn't afraid to tell me so."

"Well, she's probably right. And I could eat. But I'm warning you, I'm not sure I can relax enough to be any fun."

He glanced over at her, concern written on his face. "Why not?"

Huffing out a breath, she shifted in her seat, turning toward him as she tucked her leg beneath her. "We're out of options. You realize that, right?" she said. She couldn't control the panic seeping into her voice. Didn't even try to. It was stupid to get worked up about this when it wasn't even her wedding. She just really wanted to get this right for Caleb and Issa. They'd entrusted her with such a huge responsibility. After years of feeling like her family thought she was the helpless baby of the lot, she wanted to prove that she could do this.

Noah gripped the steering wheel with one hand as he reached out with his other and placed it over hers, giving her a reassuring squeeze. "We'll figure something out. Maybe there's another place in town that Caleb and Issa hadn't considered."

At his touch, Savannah ignored the tsunami of butterflies in her stomach and the wave of goose bumps that erupted over her skin. She swallowed thickly and cleared her throat, hoping she didn't sound breathless when she spoke. "There's not—"

Her phone ringing cut her off, and she pulled it from her purse, glancing at the screen with furrowed brows. She didn't recognize the number, but she answered anyway, grateful for a distraction. "Hello?"

"Can I speak with Savannah, please?"

"This is she."

"Hi there, this is Judy down at the Sage Sanctuary. We spoke a couple weeks ago about your brother's wedding, I believe?"

"We did, yes . . ." Savannah said, the question ringing clearly in her voice. She'd found the Sanctuary herself and added it to Caleb and Issa's list as a top choice, but when she'd reached out to set up a viewing appointment, Judy had informed her that they were booked out eighteen months.

"I had your name here on our waiting list for a

December wedding, and I wanted to let you know that we had a cancellation for the date that you were looking at. I wondered if you'd like to come and view the property to see if it'd be a good fit for your needs?"

"Oh my God, seriously? Yes, we'd love to! Can we swing by today?"

"Sure, I'd be happy to show you around. Do you think you'll be able to get here before five?"

"Definitely. We're on our way now and should be there in twenty minutes."

"Perfect. I'll see you then."

Savannah hung up and beamed at Noah, reaching out to grip his forearm. "Okay, quick change of plans."

Chuckling, he darted a quick glance at her. "What've you gotten us into now?"

She ignored the dance her insides did over his use of the word *us*. She also ignored his warm, hard muscles as she squeezed his arm. "That was Judy at the Sage Sanctuary. They had a cancellation for the weekend we're looking at."

"You're kidding."

"I know, right? Do you believe our luck?"

"Well, let's hope the saying is true, and we actually saved the best for last."

* * *

Savannah was all smiles as she introduced herself and Noah to Judy and explained the situation with the long-distance bride and groom. The tour around the property was just a formality, because she fell in love as soon as she stepped through the front doors. The space was bright and airy, with the kind of whimsical touches that Issa would absolutely adore. Even still, they dutifully followed Judy as she walked them through the area, spouting off amenities and optional add-ons in hopes of enticing them to book the space.

"And, of course," Judy said, "your party would have uninhibited access to the building and surrounding two acres of land. Many of our couples like having the majority of their photos taken outdoors to take advantage of our extensive grounds. Of course, in December, the flower gardens will be dormant, but we take great measures to make sure it's a treat year-round. It's gorgeous even at night, given the hundreds of thousands of lights we have strung up on every tree on the property. And the skylights in the building will allow for plenty of natural light for inside shots as well."

"That's great," Savannah said, proud of how her voice remained calm and steady and not at all like she was practically jumping out of her skin. "Would you mind if we walked the property a little on our own before we made a decision?"

"Not at all. Take your time," Judy said with a smile. "I'll be in my office whenever you're ready."

Savannah looped her arm through Noah's and tugged him out through the back doors to the acreage the Sanctuary sat on. While it was a beautiful fall evening tonight, it would no doubt be too cool in December to take advantage of much of the outdoor space. But the possibilities just for outdoor photos would be breathtaking, and her brother and Issa would be so pleased.

As soon as the door shut behind them, Noah chuckled under his breath. "We still need to make a decision?" he asked wryly. "I'm surprised you didn't do a cartwheel in the atrium."

She squeezed his biceps and shot him a wide grin. "Do you believe this place? It's *perfect*."

"It is pretty amazing."

"And I can't believe it's in their budget."

"I'd say we definitely lucked out with this one." He glanced at her with a raised eyebrow. "I take it this was just a ruse to see more of the grounds, and you already know you want to book this place?"

"Obviously. Unless you've been holding out on me and know of something better."

"I know nothing."

Savannah snorted. "Anyway, even if you did have another place, I doubt there's anything that would come even close to this. I mean, who else has their trees wrapped in *hundreds of thousands* of lights? Not to mention the fresh flowered arch that they provide at no cost for the ceremony and the indoor garden and the twinkling fairy lights throughout the interior. Issa's going to *love* it."

Noah chuckled under his breath. "Sounds like it's more than just Issa who loves it."

"Am I that transparent?"

"Either that or I've just known you a really long time."

They turned their heads toward each other, their eyes locking, and Savannah's stomach dropped as if she were on a roller coaster, all excitement and nerves. Without her permission, her gaze lowered to his lips, full and parted, and she had the strongest urge to push up on tiptoes and press her mouth against his. But she didn't feel like making a fool out of herself today, so she averted her gaze as they continued walking through the grounds.

"Did you ever think you'd be doing this again?" Savannah asked.

"What? Walking around with a pretty girl?"

"Smooth," she said on a laugh, pretending that him calling her pretty was no big deal and didn't send a flurry of butterflies loose inside her. "No, I meant planning a wedding. Obviously it's not yours, but you know what I mean. Do you ever think you'll get to this place again?"

Noah was silent for so long, she worried she'd made a mistake by asking. He didn't talk much about his relationship with Jess, and she shouldn't have assumed he'd be ready and willing to do it now, with her.

Just when she was ready to take back her words, he said, "Honestly? No. Not even a little."

"Really? That's too bad."

"Why? Because you think I'm such a great catch?" he asked, his tone heavy with sarcasm.

She bumped his hip with hers. "Oh, please. Don't pretend like you don't know you are."

He glanced down at her with a raised brow. "I guess I'll claim stupidity, then, because there's no pretending here."

"Wait...you seriously don't—" She huffed out a disbelieving breath as she stared at him, slack jawed. If this had been even a month ago, she'd assume he was playing at this strictly in order to get compliments—although he'd never been one to fish for them before. But that wasn't what was happening here. He actually had no idea of his appeal.

"I'm not sure I should tell you this because who knows if it will go to your head," she said, "but you're kind of a catch."

He snorted. "Yeah, I hear single dads who don't even have time to do the laundry or fix a broken shelf, let alone go out on a date are in high demand around here."

"That's downplaying yourself quite a bit, don't you think? You don't give yourself enough credit. Besides, you not having time for much else besides work and your daughter proves what a good guy you are. Seriously, Noah, take my word on this. I've gone out with my share of some not-so-fine specimens."

"Maybe that has less to do with the men you're finding and more to do with the fact that you've only been interested in flings..."

She flinched. "How do you—"

"Oh, come on, Savannah. You've never hid it very well—not that I've thought you tried to. Besides that, I had to listen to your brothers complain about it one too many times. If they had it their way, I think they'd have you married off just so they could stop worrying about you."

"Yeah right—those fools will worry about me for the rest of their lives. And if they had it their way, they'd have me locked in a tower with no way for anyone to get inside except climbing up my hair."

He chuckled low under his breath. "I guess that's probably true enough."

She lifted a shoulder. "It may not be what they'd want, but flings have always worked for me."

"So no major relationships in your books?"

"There are hardly even any *minor* relationships in my books." Her family had always joked that she treated boys like hobbies. She picked them up and dropped them. Few had ever captured her interest for long before she was off to the next. Abby put it more kindly, assuring her she just hadn't met the right person yet. She wanted to believe that her best friend was correct, but who knew? She sighed heavily, stepping closer to him as the evening's chill began taking over, her thin jacket not enough to keep her warm. "Don't get me wrong—it's not that I don't want that some-day. I do."

"Yeah? Tell me about it."

"About what?"

"What you want. What you like." As soon as the words were out of his mouth, he cleared his throat. "In a relationship, I mean."

Savannah swallowed deeply, the intimate tone of his voice making it hard to focus. "I guess I haven't really thought about it much."

That wasn't exactly true. Watching Abby find her happily-ever-after with Carter that spring had given Savannah plenty of food for thought. It was part of why she'd slowed her dating life to a screeching halt. But while she'd realized that casual flings weren't as fun as they used to be, she hadn't deeply considered what she might be looking for instead.

"Well, think about it now. What would you want from your boyfriend or husband? What would make you happy?"

She thought for a long moment, allowing herself to imagine a time in the future when she might have someone like that. Unsurprisingly, the images that flashed in her mind featured one tall, dark, and handsome man, and this time, she didn't force them out or tamp them down. Instead, she let them play out, a series of fantasy snippets she hadn't ever allowed herself to explore.

"It'd be the little things for me, I think. The tiny instances that show how much someone loves you just by being aware of your everyday needs. Like, I'd love to be greeted at the end of a long day at school with a kiss and a glass of wine by someone who understands me well enough to know when to order in for dinner and who would send me off after to a candlelit bath strewn with rose petals."

"Rose petals?" he asked, surprise in his voice. "Wow...I never took you for a romantic."

She laughed. "Don't let the flings fool you. Just because I haven't had romance doesn't mean I don't want it."

"I'm getting that," he said, his voice a low rumble that shot straight to her belly...and even lower still.

Her reaction was just thanks to this place and their proximity strolling through the grounds. It had to be. There wasn't another logical explanation for why she was suddenly so entranced by him. She'd always been able to ignore the connection between them before. Though maybe that wasn't exactly true. She'd just mistaken the friction between them for disdain rather than what she was beginning to understand it truly was—pure, undiluted attraction. The more time they spent together, the more impossible it was becoming to dismiss.

Desperate for a subject change, lest she jump him amid the trees lit with burnished leaves, she asked, "What about you? Have you dated much?"

"You mean since the divorce?"

"Yeah."

"Not at all, actually." He blew out a heavy breath, and she sensed there was more he had to say, so she stayed silent. "I, uh...I haven't been in that much of a hurry to get back out there, considering the past year."

"I can imagine it's been difficult. Especially if . . . Well, if you still felt—" She couldn't bring herself to voice the thoughts that had been pinging in the back of her head. That the year had been rough because he hadn't wanted the divorce. That he'd still loved Jess when she'd left. Maybe even still did now.

"I didn't," he said, conviction ringing soundly. "Jess and I had been in the process of separating for a while before she decided to take the job in Texas. It was a lot more sudden of an end than I was expecting, but I wasn't devastated or anything. Hell, I wasn't even sad— for myself, anyway. I was for Rosie, obviously, but me? Not so much." He shrugged. "We were never really a house on fire, if I'm being honest. And after Rosie was born, we grew apart. I don't know when it happened, but at some point we stopped taking care of each other. Stopped touching each other, even. We never talked about anything except work and parenting. And she . . . well, she was never much for candlelit dinners and rose-petal-strewn baths . . ." He smiled down at Savannah, one side of his mouth curved higher than the other. "I wouldn't even know where to start with giving someone those things."

"I don't know about that. You're a smart guy. I bet you could figure it out."

She bit her lip to trap the words inside her . . . words that would beg him to figure it out *with her*. Except trapping them caused her body to act out in other ways. To force her hand more than she expected. That was the only excuse she had for sliding even closer to him, her side now pressed against his as they walked, arm in arm, through the sprawling acreage.

"Cold?" he asked.

The sound of his voice, all husky and rough, shook something loose inside her. The restraint that she'd been holding on to by a frayed thread snapped, and she nodded. He slipped his arm from hers and wrapped it around her shoulders instead. She didn't waste any time curling her own around his waist beneath his jacket, her other hand resting against his rigid abs as she inhaled deeply, breathing in the scent of him.

He smelled of ocean air and sunshine—a scent, she realized, she'd associated with him for as long as she could remember. Except this time, her mouth watered at it, imagining his taste on her tongue. Desperately, she wanted to slide her hand into the back pocket of his jeans and tug him to her. Feel the length of his body pressed against hers and his breath against her lips as they met that close together for the first time. As she satiated her curiosity and finally... finally tasted him.

She didn't know who stopped walking first, but suddenly they stood still in the middle of the path, their eyes locked. She breathed his name as she stared up into his deep, brown eyes, and silently pleaded with him to lower his head and kiss her already. He must've heard her silent plea because suddenly he was there, whispering her name against her lips, their eyes still locked, just before hers fluttered shut as he pressed their mouths together.

Before the first swipe of his tongue against hers, fireworks erupted behind her closed eyelids. Savannah had been kissed before. Many times. By men and boys alike, some who knew what they were doing, and some who weren't much more than a fumbling mass of hormones. But in all those times, it'd never felt like this. Like her insides were too big for her body. Like she was lit on fire from within, an inferno raging and desperate for release.

On a moan, she pressed higher on tiptoes and delved her fingers into his hair, tugging hard as his tongue swirled with hers. She got lost in his taste and the feel of his hands gripping her hips, fingers digging into her flesh as he tugged her closer, closer, closer, until there wasn't even a hair's breadth between them. She ached to somehow move closer still, even though it was an impossible wish. At least out here, in the open.

He must've had the same thought, because after minutes or hours, he pulled back, his breaths coming hot and hard against her lips. His eyes were molten, dark pools of chocolate as he stared at her as if she were his last meal. "My place?" he said, his voice like gravel.

She inhaled deeply, not taking a second to consider if this was a mistake. It didn't matter. At this point she just didn't care. She nodded quickly. "Yes."

Chapter Twelve

The drive back to Noah's house was a blur—much like confirming they wanted the venue with Judy and grabbing the contract on their way out of the Sanctuary—but he didn't regret it. He wouldn't have regretted getting a speeding ticket for clocking in twenty above the speed limit, either. Not if it meant getting Savannah back to his place and having her in his bed all that much sooner.

Something had snapped in him, and he wanted—no, *needed*—to act on it immediately. That wasn't him. He didn't do spur of the moment. He was a planner. A deliberate kind of man who always thought things through. His sudden ability to throw caution to the wind where Savannah was concerned may have something to do with their history, or their newfound friendship, or simply because it'd been too long since he'd slept with someone. Regardless of the reasons, he was desperate to be with Savannah. To strip her of every stitch of clothing, kiss along each inch of her body, until he settled between her legs and took them both out of their minds with pleasure.

And now that whatever had snapped, he had no intention of ignoring those needs unless she told him otherwise.

He pulled into his garage, shut off the engine, and closed the automatic door behind them. It threw them into darkness, a heavy silence filling the air. Why hadn't she said anything? Was she having second thoughts about this? About them? It'd taken them less than five minutes to drive to his house, thanks to his speeding, but five minutes without their lips fused together may very well have been enough time for worries to creep in.

Turning toward her, he reached out and swept her hair back over her shoulder, trailing his thumb down the smooth skin of her jaw. "We can just watch a movie, if you want?" His throat was full of gravel, and his voice came out low and rough, threaded with a need he was no longer interested in hiding.

"Instead of what I'm hoping we'll do?" She nipped his palm before opening her door, and the harsh overhead light shone down, illuminating her flushed cheeks and kiss-swollen lips. Swollen from *him*. "Not a chance. Besides, you never gave me a tour of your bedroom the other night. It's definitely something I should see."

He was already out of the car before she'd finished speaking and around to her side before she could even shut her door. Gripping her rear, he hauled her up against him and kissed her with a frenzy he was tired of questioning. It'd never been like this for him. Even in the early days with Jess, there hadn't been a sea raging beneath his skin merely at the thought of touching her. But with Savannah, there was no denying its existence.

She wrapped her legs around his hips as he walked them blindly toward the side door, fumbling in the dark for the knob until, after several long, excruciating seconds, they poured into his kitchen.

Laughing into his mouth, she cupped his face and pulled back only enough to say, "I promise I'm still going to want this in fifteen minutes. Actually, I'm still going to want this in an hour."

"That's good to hear."

"Why's that?"

"Because I plan on this taking a hell of a lot longer than fifteen minutes."

"Promises, promises," she teased.

Without caring much where they landed, he tossed his keys in the general direction of the counter, not caring in the least as they clanked to the floor, because his mouth was already back on hers and he was striding toward his bedroom. He'd never been so grateful that he'd spent the morning catching up on laundry, his bed made with fresh sheets and his room free of the scattered remains of late-night exhaustion.

He didn't stop until he sat on his bed with her in his lap, her legs still wrapped around him, the heat of her pressing into him and driving him insane. One way or another, it seemed that was exactly what this woman was put on earth to do—make him lose his mind.

Breaking away from her lips briefly to reach back and tug the neck of his shirt, he rid himself of the material keeping his skin from Savannah's. But it wasn't enough. He needed her flesh on his. Needed her free of every stitch of fabric more than he needed his next breath.

He gripped the outside of her thighs and slid his hands up and over her hips until he slipped them beneath her thin jacket and the hem of her shirt. "May I?"

She huffed out a laugh before shrugging out of her coat and tossing it behind her. "I already said I was in, Noah. As far as I'm concerned, the faster you get me naked, the better."

He wasn't one to look a gift horse in the mouth, and having a blonde bombshell perched in his lap, ready for a mind-blowing night was the gift horse to end all gift horses. So he did as she suggested, stripping them both in record time until there was nothing at all between them. Nothing keeping Noah's gaze from Savannah's pure, naked perfection.

She was more than he'd even imagined, all long, golden limbs and soft curves just begging for his hands or his mouth or both.

He attempted to impart some moisture in his mouth as he stared at her openly, without shame. "You're gorgeous."

She held out an arm toward him from where she was sprawled out on his bed, her blond hair a tousled mess on his pillow. "And you're too far away."

"I better fix that, then." He crawled over her, allowing his lips to guide his path up her body. Allowing them to take any detours they so desired. They had the whole night, and he intended to take every single bit of it. He kissed across the soft curve of her stomach, the underside of her full breasts, and then each pebbled nipple, until she was nothing but incoherent pleas.

"Noah," she said on a moan. "I want you inside me."

Jesus, had he ever heard five more beautiful words? He fumbled through the nightstand for a condom and didn't waste any time sheathing himself. Settling between her legs, he hitched one up over his hip as he fused their mouths together, found her entrance, and slowly sank inside.

Savannah sucked in a breath, pressing her head back into the pillows, as Noah nearly spiraled out of his damn mind. She was hot and wet around him, and felt so good, he worried he'd never come back from this. Never come back from *her*. More than how good she felt, though, was how right. Somehow, sliding inside her had been like a puzzle piece clicking into place...a connection he hadn't yet experienced before in his life.

And as they rocked together, their panting breaths and whispered words a rhythmic cadence in the room as he guided them higher until they came apart together, her nails digging into his back while he groaned her name, he wasn't sure he ever wanted it to end.

* * *

It had been so long since Noah had woken with a soft, warm body pressed against him that it took him a while to remember what had led to this.

Savannah. Hot, hungry kisses and wandering hands and frenzied, exploratory touches. And, oh, had he explored. Hours' worth of journeys mapped out on her skin with nothing more than his mouth and hands. He couldn't get enough of her, and it seemed she couldn't either. Neither of them had been satisfied with one and done, which meant they'd been up half the night, entertaining themselves with unexplored territories and newfound reactions.

True, he'd known her nearly her whole life. But he'd never known the sound of her breathy moans, or the shape of the birthmark under her navel, or how sweet she tasted. And truth be told, he wasn't so sure he *should* know those things now.

He untangled their limbs, careful not to wake her, and threw his legs over the side of the bed, turning his back to her sleeping form. He squeezed his eyes shut and scrubbed a hand over his face. What the hell was he supposed to do now? Was this a one-night stand? Or something more?

No way one night sounded like enough to him. But if this was going to turn into a regular thing, how would he handle it with Rosie? He couldn't keep her in the dark forever. She was still devastated over her mom leaving, and she was already so attached to Savannah as her teacher.

And Noah's mom? He didn't even want to think about her response to him dating Savannah. It would go one of two ways. Either she would be thrilled and pushing for marriage as soon as possible, or she'd be horrified at how irresponsible Noah was being by taking this risk with Rosie's teacher while his daughter was in this delicate state.

That was to say nothing of Savannah's brothers. He'd borne witness to enough of their reactions to her previous flings that he didn't have to guess at how they'd respond. They'd want his head on a pike, no matter that he was a surrogate Lowe.

He still didn't understand how this had even happened. It had just been a little more than a week ago when he didn't even particularly like her. And now he could still smell her on his skin. Could still taste her on his tongue. Could still feel the full, lush curves of her as she'd sat astride him last night, his name on her lips.

"Morning." Her voice was thick with sleep, a sexy sort of rasp he'd never heard from her before. Just another first for the books. The bedsheets rustled behind him, and then her warm and very naked body pressed up against his back, her arms wrapped around his shoulders. "You're thinking awfully hard considering it's not even eight in the morning, and we kept each other up most of the night. Are you having a mini freak-out?"

Noah huffed out a breath and turned his head toward her. She had pillow creases on her cheek, her makeup was smeared, her hair a little wild...and she'd never looked more beautiful to him. "Just a little."

She smiled and walked her fingers down his bare chest. "Let's see if I can get to the bottom of this. Are you worried about what my brothers will think, or that you have somehow stolen sweet little Savannah's virtue, or are you worried about Rosie?"

"Yes."

She breathed out a laugh and slipped out of bed, not an ounce of self-consciousness as she stood before him, completely bare. Though she certainly didn't have any need to be. She was gorgeous, all golden soft skin, her long blond hair just kissing the tips of her breasts. Tips *he'd* been kissing only last night.

Placing her hands on his shoulders, she dug her thumbs into his muscles and pulled a groan from deep in his chest. "I think I can probably set your mind at ease with all of these."

"Is that so?" he said, attempting to keep his voice steady and failing miserably.

"Mmm-hmm. First, I had my virtue stolen a long time ago, so I think we can both agree to take that one right off the list."

"Fair enough."

She smiled and stepped closer, and it was second nature for Noah to place his hands on her hips, his thumb brushing soft strokes along her skin, as if they'd done this hundreds of times before. "Second, my brothers don't have to know anything about this. Despite what they've led you to believe, it's none of their business who I date or who I sleep with."

He could see that, too. Except that one of her brothers was his best friend, and he didn't particularly relish the idea of keeping this from him. But instead of voicing that, he kept his mouth shut and let her continue.

"And lastly, Rosie doesn't have to know anything either. This doesn't have to be a big deal, Noah. We can keep this casual, if you want to keep doing it at all."

He could hear the question in her words, and he swallowed down the unease that had crept up at the idea that last night would be their only night together. He didn't know what the hell was going on. Why he was suddenly so drawn to her, or why they had off-the-charts chemistry, or why he'd had the best sex of his life last night with someone he'd once considered an annoying, unshakable thorn in his side. But he could wonder all he wanted...it still didn't stop any of it from being true.

"We don't have to decide anything now," Savannah said, a gleam in her eye. "As far as I'm concerned, the morning after is technically still part of a single night." With that, she placed her hand flat on his chest and pushed until he fell back onto the bed. She climbed atop him, straddling his hips and sliding against where he was already achingly hard for her.

She was warm and wet against him, a siren call that pulled a groan straight from the depths of his soul. This might have been their fourth time, but each one had been just as powerful as the first. He wanted to sink inside her and never leave. Wanted to lose himself in her body and forget everything else.

With one hand, he gripped her hip tightly, guiding her movements against his length. He slid his other hand up her back and under her hair until he reached her neck, tugging her toward him. He captured her lips, their tongues brushing against each other's immediately, and their groans mingled in the space between them. He reveled in the sensations of having her on top of him, of the soft glide of her hair against his chest, her puffs of air against his lips, her warm wetness sliding over where he was aching with a desperate need. Not for sex, but for *her*.

Noah didn't know what this was, how long it would it last, or if it was a good idea to pursue. All he knew was that as of right now, he didn't want it to end.

Chapter Thirteen

Savannah glided into the Sunshine Corner on Monday morning, her smile way too bright for 7:30 a.m., but she couldn't help it. She'd been gliding and smiling her way through the entire weekend. Yesterday, she'd left Noah with a lingering kiss and a promise that what had happened between them didn't need to be any more complicated than they wanted it to be.

The trouble was, she was a little worried that she wanted it to be slightly more complicated than she was used to. Her usual MO might have been as the queen of casual. With most men, she was out the door as soon as the action was over. But things were different with Noah. Last night, after they'd slept together, she'd wanted nothing more than to stay right where she was. It wasn't just their physical connection, which had left her little more than a heap of tingles on the bed. There'd also been this...longing, which she'd been wholly un-prepared for. Longing to stay close to him. Tuck into his side while his fingers trailed soft paths down her arm and laugh until evening had turned to morning, and their talking turned to breathless whispers and urgent pleas.

She could lie and say that it was their compatibility in bed that made her intrigued about exploring some-thing more with him, but that didn't feel quite right either, despite the truth of it.

"Why do you look like you ate a seven-layer chocolate cake for breakfast?" Abby asked with narrowed eyes.

"I don't know what you mean." But even as she said the words, she was smiling. It seemed she couldn't wipe it from her face today.

"What I mean," Abby said, stepping into Savannah's path, "is that you're *never* this chipper in the morning, least of all before your first cup of coffee."

"Which I was on my way to get before you so rudely blocked me."

"And," she said, drawing out the word, "you didn't call me back this weekend, which never happens unless you're occupied with a gentleman friend."

Savannah snorted. "'A gentleman friend'? Really?"

"Little ears and all that." Abby tipped her head toward the breakfast nook where their early morn-ing charges—only half a dozen kids—sat, eating their breakfasts.

Savannah waved to them before she sniffed, side-stepping her best friend as she poured herself a mug of coffee. "Fine. I... may have had some companionship, and it may be putting a slight spring in my step today."

"I knew it! Who is it and when did you have time to meet him? I thought you were spending Saturday with Noah looking at—" Abby cut off on a gasp, her hand pressed over her mouth and eyes wide. "Oh my God."

"What?" Savannah asked over the rim of her mug.

Abby hissed, "*Noah* is your gentleman friend?"

Rather than answering her outright, Savannah dodged the accusation altogether. "I can't tell if you sound horrified or excited at that prospect."

Abby gripped Savannah's forearm and squeezed, her eyes bright. "You're not denying it. Holy crap. *Noah*? I can't believe this. Tell me everything."

This time it was Savannah who raised her brow and gestured to the children animatedly chattering a mere ten feet from them. "How about I don't?"

Abby huffed and tucked her hair behind her ear. "I'm not looking for an explicit play by play—I can get that in real time with Carter, thank you very much. I just want to know what this all means? Are you guys a couple now?"

Savannah blew out a deep sigh and brought the coffee to her lips, taking a long drink to buy herself time. Honestly, she had no idea. The little she and Noah had talked about it had been when she'd woken up to find him sitting on the side of the bed, his back to her, shoulders rigid and head bowed. He'd obviously been battling some sort of inner war, and it hadn't taken her much to guess what that war had been about. But then she'd distracted them both for the next hour, and by the time they'd come up for air, his mom was on her way with Rosie, and their time was over.

With resignation, she said, "I don't know."

"What do you mean you don't know?"

"I *mean*, I don't know." Savannah grabbed a freshly baked blueberry muffin from the basket before turning around and leaning back against the counter. She picked it apart—top first, like a heathen, Abby always said—and popped the morsel in her mouth. "It's probably nothing."

Abby sidled closer, concern radiating off her as she tentatively touched Savannah's arm. "Why do you say that?"

Savannah lifted a shoulder, keeping her gaze locked on the muffin she was demolishing. "I'm the first one since...you know."

Abby lifted her brows. "Since Jess?"

"Yeah. I was surprised too. It's not like our little town is booming with eligible men, let alone drop-dead gorgeous ones. He's probably had to beat the women off with a stick."

"Hmm..."

Savannah narrowed her eyes on her best friend. "What's the *hmm* for?"

"Nothing."

Normally, she'd try to tease this out of Abby with pleas and subtle coercion, but it was already nearing the start of the school day, and the rest of the kids would begin showing up any minute. She didn't have time for beating around the bush. So she did what she had to, and pinched the tender skin at the back of Abby's arm. "Tell me."

"Ow!" Abby slapped Savannah's hand away before rubbing her skin. "You're such a brat."

"The kids are going to be here any minute. So spill already."

"Fine. I just find it interesting is all."

When Abby didn't elaborate, Savannah groaned long and low. "Oh my God, would you just spit it out? *What* is interesting?"

"That he'd beat off all the other women in town, yet open his arms wide to you."

"He didn't—" She couldn't finish that statement because…yeah, he kind of had. One minute they were looking at the wedding location, and the next they were in a mad dash back to his house. "Maybe it was just because I was available when he was finally ready."

"Peculiar timing, don't you think? Besides, I'm completely certain every other interested woman in town has made it clear they're wide open for him, any time, any place. And yet…"

And yet, he chose Savannah.

For the night, she reminded herself. Or maybe for

a few nights. Which was great. She'd always preferred casual and uncomplicated.

So why did the idea of casual and uncomplicated with Noah feel like the most complicated option of all?

* * *

Savannah and Noah had run out of the Sage Sanctuary so fast on Saturday evening, they'd only managed to grab the contract from Judy before fleeing. Savannah called yesterday and left a voice mail letting Judy know that they were very interested in booking the space and that she'd drop the contract and check in the mail. Mail pickup was at two, and it was imperative she got it sent off today. With the wedding only a couple of months away, they didn't have the luxury of time, nor did she think they were the only people in the area who would be interested in such an amazing property.

While the kids were occupied eating lunch, she sat at her desk and filled out the contract, her years working with children allowing her the ability to block out the sounds of them laughing and chatting among themselves as she focused. She folded the paper, then slipped it, along with a check for the deposit, into an envelope and sealed it before filling out the address and verifying that it was correct. It was just her luck that she'd write the wrong information on the envelope and have it returned too late to do anything about it. With careful precision, she skimmed it all over one last time as she pulled a book of stamps from her drawer.

"Ow!" Jacob cried. "Miss Savannah, he *bit* me!"

Savannah snapped her head up and narrowed in on the problem. Austin. Of freaking course. That child was going to be the death of her. She'd already had two conversations with his mom, and they were only little more than a month into school. She had no idea how she was going to last the remainder of the year while keeping a cool head. Tossing the stamped envelope into the outbox on her desk, she made a beeline toward the children, eyes narrowed on the troublemaker.

"Austin," she said, her voice firm. "We do *not* bite our friends. We've had this discussion before."

"He started it!" Austin said, pointing an accusatory finger at Jacob.

"Pack up your lunch and stand right here." She gestured toward a wall only a couple feet from where she was—close enough that she could still keep an eye on him while far enough away as to give the little boy he'd injured some space.

She squatted down next to Jacob and pulled his sleeve up to inspect the bite. The area was red, but thankfully the wannabe vampire hadn't broken the skin. "Are you okay, sweetie?" She slid his sleeve back into place and rubbed a gentle hand over the injury.

The little boy looked at her with wide eyes, fat tears spilling over his thick lashes, his bottom lip pushed out in a pout. "Yeah, I think so," he said, his voice cracking.

She hugged him tight. "You're so brave. I think you deserve a trip to the treasure chest."

His eyes lit up, his injury forgotten, and he pushed back from his seat as a smile replaced his frown. "Right now?"

Savannah laughed. "Yes, right now. Go ahead and pick out *two* treasures."

"Okay!" He took off at a run, his arms pumping as he dashed to the back corner near her desk where she kept the chest.

"What about me?" Austin whined.

"Oh, don't worry, I didn't forget about you." Savannah walked over to him and laid a hand on his shoulder, guiding him toward the door. "You'll be eating your lunch in the separation room with Miss Tori. And after school, I'll be discussing this instance with your mother." *Again*, she added silently.

When she'd accepted this job, she hadn't had the faintest clue how many conflict-charged conversations she'd be having with the kids' parents. Well, okay, it was really only *one* kid and one parent—but dealing with the pair of them left her drained as if she'd fought with a pack of rabid wolves.

The rest of the day was a blur of activities, including cooking hour with Abby's grandmother, Hilde. Savannah had been so distracted keeping an eye on Austin all afternoon to make sure he didn't unleash his teeth on any other poor, unsuspecting children that she completely forgot about the check and contract to be mailed until after three.

In a panic, she looked in the outbox she'd dropped it in, relieved to find it empty. As part of Tori's daily duties, she took outgoing mail down shortly after lunch. But Savannah was feeling exceptionally paranoid with this particular piece of mail, so she figured it was in her best interest to double-check, especially when her brother and soon-to-be sister-in-law's perfect wedding location was on the line.

"Tori?" Savannah called, poking her head into the communal area where her assistant sat in the middle of the circle rug surrounded by children, a cow puppet on one hand and a horse on the other.

She glanced over her shoulder. "Yeah?"

"Did you take the outgoing mail downstairs to the mailbox?"

"Um…" Tori tried to meet Savannah's eyes, but the kids, all attempting to gain Tori's attention with their own puppets, made that difficult. On a laugh, she finally gave up and turned back around, focusing on the puppet theater. "Um…" she said again between an Oscar-worthy performance as two different farm animals. "Yeah, I think so."

Normally, *I think so* would suffice, but this wasn't a normal circumstance.

"I'm just going to run down and make sure. Can you handle this okay?"

"*Moo*," Tori called, barely audible over the various other farm animal sounds coming from the children.

With a laugh, Savannah jogged down the stairs and to the front door. Loretta, their mail carrier, always came inside to pick up their outgoing mail—well, that and to snag whatever freshly baked muffin Abby had made that day—and, thankfully, the bin was empty.

Savannah breathed a sigh of relief. That was one less thing she had to worry about today. Now she could focus on the matter at hand—figuring out how to broach the biting incident with Austin's mom, as well as the defensiveness, the callous words, and the thinly veiled insults about her capabilities as a teacher that she'd come to expect from Megan.

Savannah also needed to figure out when, exactly, this evolved from merely a preschool problem to a Sunshine Corner problem, and thus, when she'd need to involve Abby if she couldn't get this handled on her own.

Chapter Fourteen

If Savannah didn't love her brother so much, she might actually kill him. To be fair, she felt that way about all of her brothers. But this time, in particular, it was Caleb who was on her list. The little weasel had spilled the beans to their mom about Savannah and Noah booking the wedding venue, which meant she had to field an early morning phone call in which her mom accused her of not wanting her help. In order to placate her, Savannah had had to compromise and allow both her and Cheryl to come along to the caterer and baker appointments with her and Noah.

The only reason she'd finally relented and agreed that they could both attend was because her mom had assured Savannah that she and Cheryl wouldn't be there for mediating, but rather merely for the delicious free food.

Today was packed with appointments, and, to be fair, both Savannah's and Noah's moms had behaved fairly well thus far. Unless one was deducting points for embarrassment, in which case that *fairly well* would plummet to the depths of the earth, considering the amount of extra canapes they'd asked for, not to mention the second—and third—helpings of specific cake flavors to try.

"Apparently, all we needed to do was get some food in them," Savannah said under her breath, while their moms were distracted with all of the possible fondant decoration options for the cake.

Noah glanced over at her with a smile, one that managed to melt her insides and make her swoon, as well as set her entire body aflame. "I bet alcohol would make this run even smoother."

"I'm just glad they didn't put up a fuss about the caterer we selected earlier. Although I wouldn't put it past my mom to set up appointments on the sly."

Noah laughed loud enough that it drew Rosie's attention from where she sat at a table, surrounded by her own samples.

"I don't think I've ever seen a kid eat as deliberately as she does." Savannah tipped her head toward Rosie, where she was currently lining up each sample in rainbow color. "Most of the kids at the preschool would have inhaled those in fifteen seconds flat, with the only evidence being the crumbs in their hair."

He chuckled lowly and glanced over at Rosie. "She's

always been a bit methodical," he said, a fondness seeping into his tone that he only ever really got when he was talking about his daughter. "I think she probably got it from Jess."

"Oh, I don't know. I've found you to be pretty methodical with some things. Certainly enough to get the job done."

He met her gaze, hunger glinting in his own. It was enough to throw her back to the week prior, when she'd seen that same glint as he'd stalked toward her across the bedroom. "I've been known to take my time when I'm exceptionally hungry for something."

Bubbles erupted in Savannah's stomach, as if someone had popped a bottle of champagne in there. It had been like this all day between them, seemingly innocent words twisted in her mind until they were laced with innuendo. She'd wondered if it was just her riding the train to dirty town. But with the glances Noah had shot her and the lifted brows, she knew she wasn't a solo passenger. They hadn't been able to find another time together since she'd spent the night at his place, and she'd wondered if they ever would again.

That was, at least, until one highly charged moment with some spilled icing and Savannah licking it off her finger. He'd gripped her arm and leaned over, whispering that he wanted her at his house that evening after Rosie was in bed, no ifs ands or buts about it.

As if she would voice any of the three. As far as she was concerned, it couldn't get here fast enough.

But, even with Noah's demands, she still didn't know where they stood. Didn't know if he was feeling this unrelenting tug toward her, a mirror of what she was feeling for him, but she was desperate to find out.

"Come here, you two! You've got to try this. It's absolutely delicious," Cheryl called, waving them over.

"What flavor did you say this was, Louise?" Savannah's mom passed over two mini plates to Noah and Savannah.

"That's our chocolate Guinness cake topped with caramel buttercream."

Savannah took a bite at the same time Noah bit into his, his gaze locked on hers.

"Well?" Cheryl asked, eyebrows raised and eyes bright. "Isn't it divine?"

Noah licked his lips, the move drawing Savannah's attention and sending a flurry of memories in its wake. With how her body was responding to him, you'd think she hadn't had sex in months or even years, let alone the *days* that it actually was. But she couldn't be held accountable for her reaction. Not when he stood there, looking devilishly handsome and taunting her with his closeness the entire day.

"Well," he said, drawing out the word, "it's not the best thing I've ever had in my mouth, but it is delicious."

Savannah's face flamed as she snapped her gaze to his. His eyes sparked with humor, secrets dancing in their depths.

She sucked in a breath to try and get herself together, only she ended up inhaling cake crumbs as she did so, and promptly fell into a coughing fit. Noah, ever the gentleman, set a hand on her back, rubbing and patting gently. To everyone else, he no doubt looked like he was merely offering her assistance, when in fact, he was stoking the fire burning inside her.

Once she got her coughing under control, he trailed his fingers up until he brushed them lightly across the nape of her neck before letting his hand drop to his side. He'd taken every opportunity today to touch her, even in the most innocent ways. The trouble was, however innocent it seemed didn't matter, because she knew all too well exactly how sinful that touch could be. Had been dreaming about it for days.

"Here you go, sweetheart," Savannah's mom said, handing her a glass of water.

"Thanks," she managed through a tight throat, whether from her near choking or pure undiluted desire, there was no telling which.

"You'll all be joining us for Thanksgiving as usual, right?" Savannah's mom asked—well, demanded, really.

Starting decades prior, it had been tradition for Noah and Cheryl to join the Lowes for Thanksgiving each year. The Lowes had a habit of picking up strays; Abby and her mom and grandmother had been semi-regular attendees as well. Even when he'd been married to Jess, the two of them, his mom, and Rosie had all been made welcome at their table.

"Of course we'll be there," Cheryl said with a nod. "I'll bring the pies as usual."

"I don't know why you bother yourself with that. I'm the one with the football team of men in my house."

Cheryl laughed. "Five is hardly a football team."

"Well, they eat as much as one," Savannah's mom said.

"She's not wrong," Savannah interjected wryly. When they'd been teenagers and eating everything in sight, she was lucky she hadn't had a hand bitten off as she'd reached to dish up.

"Nonsense. I'm happy to bake as many pies as your boys will go through. Besides, mine isn't exactly a lightweight when it comes to devouring tasty things."

Savannah made the mistake of glancing at Noah, only to find his eyes already on hers. He stared at her as if *she* were a tasty thing he wanted to devour, and she couldn't wait until tonight. When he'd suggested— demanded, really—that she come over, she'd probably embarrassed herself with how quickly she'd agreed, but the trouble was, she couldn't muster up any embarrassment. Not for this, with him. Not when she'd spent the past six nights thinking about the next time she'd be in his bed, pinned by his weight and covered in his scent. She didn't know how she'd wait now, as he continued to steal touches, brushing a finger down the outside of her hand, pressing his fingers lightly to the small of her back, as if she were his in the truest sense of the word.

As their moms grabbed one final sample and popped them into their mouths, Savannah turned to Noah and whispered, "You're driving me crazy. Why are you taunting me so much?"

He chuckled low under his breath and appraised her, his eyes taking a slow perusal of her from head to toe and back again. "You show up looking for all the world like you're good enough to eat, and you think *I'm* the one who's taunting?

"You can't be serious. It's just—"

"What's in this?" Savannah's mom asked, her voice tinged with the slightest hint of panic.

Savannah snapped her gaze in her mom's direction, cataloguing every inch of her face.

"It's our lemon with white chocolate buttercream."

"Are there nuts in it?"

"No, ma'am, it's just—" The baker's assistant's face paled. "Not whole nuts, but there is almond extract."

"What?" Savannah nearly shouted.

For as long as she could remember, her mom had had a severe allergy to almonds, so much so that she carried an EpiPen with her everywhere she went. Even though Savannah had been prepped on the steps enough times as to have it drilled into her head, she was still rooted in place, frozen and unsure of what to do next. First, she needed to...she needed to...*what*? What did she need to do?

But it didn't matter, because Noah didn't hesitate even for a second before he leaped into action, striding straight to her mom's side. "Pauline, do you have your EpiPen with you?" he asked, his voice calm and clear.

Pauline's eyes went wide, and she fluttered her hand uselessly around her throat. She nodded quickly, and Noah didn't waste any time before rooting through her purse. He found the EpiPen quickly, unpacked it, and administered it to her thigh, without pausing so much as to tell her mom not to panic. She sort of wished he'd tell *her* not to panic because she could hardly catch her breath, her eyes filling as she watched her mom nearly faint with relief.

Noah scooped Savannah's mom up and calmly but firmly ordered the baker's assistant to call for an ambulance. "You're going to be fine, Pauline. It was sixty seconds, tops, before I administered the EpiPen. The ambulance is just a precaution. I'd lose a whole lot of cred at the station if my second mom up and died on me when I had the ability to save her."

It wasn't until Pauline breathed out a laugh, her voice scratchy as she teased Noah about his heroic ways, that Savannah finally took a deep breath for the first time in what felt like an hour but that had, apparently, been less than two minutes.

Cheryl fluttered around Savannah's mom, her hands flapping in the air as if she didn't quite know what to do with herself but wanted to appear useful. She knew the feeling.

Savannah glanced over at Rosie, who stared on with wide eyes, and decided that that was where she would be the most helpful. Her mom was in good hands. Noah had seen to that—something over which she would swoon later. But right now, Rosie was scared and worried over the commotion. While Savannah wasn't great at a whole lot of things, one thing she could always count on was her ability to distract a child.

"How's your cake, Rosie?" She was proud that her voice only wavered the slightest bit as she knelt in front of the little girl, eyeing the array of desserts lined up in front of her. "Do you have a favorite?"

Rosie glanced over Savannah's shoulder toward her dad and her grandma, where Cheryl barked nonsensical orders at the bakery staff, none of which would help Savannah's mom, but it no doubt made her feel useful all the same.

"I liked the strawberries and cream best," Savannah tried again, "but I think I'm going to get outvoted. Unless you can help me? Which did you like the most?"

Finally, she'd managed to say the right words, because Rosie tore her gaze away from the excitement behind Savannah, her eyes bright as she met Savannah's gaze. "That's my favorite too! Do you think that's the cake Uncle Caleb is gonna pick?"

Savannah smiled and squeezed the little girl into her side. "Maybe if you and I team up, we can get him to agree to that before the others even have a chance to sway him otherwise. What do you say? Want to be my partner?"

Rosie grinned and nodded quickly, and Savannah

breathed a sigh of relief that she'd been able to distract the little girl from the issue at hand. She glanced over her shoulder to where Noah squatted in front of her mom, his eyes intent, fingers pressed to her mom's wrist, completely laser-focused. If she hadn't already been ready for tonight, his utter calm and take-charge attitude in what could've been a life-threatening situation certainly cinched it. Her body was pumped full of adrenaline, and there was no one she wanted to experience the crash with more than Noah.

Chapter Fifteen

A few weeks later, after Rosie was fast asleep for the night, a now-familiar knock sounded on the front door. He pulled it open, his blood already pumping, expecting to tug Savannah in by the hand and carry her straight to bed.

Ever since the evening her mom had been accidentally dosed with almonds, Savannah had started coming over to his place a few nights a week. Those visits always started the same—animalistic urgency as soon as he opened the door, so much so they sometimes didn't even make it to his bedroom before their lips were fused together—but the minutes and hours that followed never seemed to adhere to any sort of script.

Sometimes they'd lie in his bed for hours, just talking until well past midnight. Not great when they both had to be up early for their jobs, but neither of them complained. Other times, they'd be famished and order pizza or scavenge in the kitchen before bingeing some Netflix. Once in a while, she'd challenge him to a wrestling match or a tickle fight—those usually led to even more bedroom shenanigans.

The only issue was that tonight, instead of standing there, cheeks flushed, full lips parted, arms ready to wrap around his neck, she was burdened down with what looked like the better part of a hardware store.

"Uh…"

"Hear me out," she said from behind a roll of wallpaper sticking out of the top of a precariously balanced milk crate.

Remembering himself, he swooped in and grabbed the boxes from her. They were surprisingly heavy, crammed full of nails, boards, paint, and who even knew what else. "I'm listening."

Savannah came inside and closed the door behind her. "So, Abby decided we needed to reorganize the crafts closet at the Sunshine Corner."

"Didn't she just do that this summer?"

Savannah waved a hand. "This is Abby we're talking about."

"Right."

Setting down her bag, she led him toward the kitchen, and he followed behind, hardware store sampler crates in tow.

"Anyway, you know how she is. She did a ton of

research, then still ordered about ten times more stuff than we needed. After we were done, I looked at it all, and it struck me." She turned around to face him, a nervous glint to her eyes that he didn't like. "Noah keeps complaining about never having time or energy to redo his pantry. What if I just bring all the leftover stuff over here and we can bang it out tonight?"

He blinked at her, completely caught off guard. First, had he really been complaining about it that much? Yeah, having the unfinished—let's be honest, barely started—project hanging over his head had been bringing him down. He used to pride himself on taking care of things around the house, back before Jess left and his domestic skills basically took a nosedive off a cliff. But he'd thought he'd kept his frustration with himself and the project more or less to himself.

Secondly, wait—what? She really thought they could pick up this job that had been hanging over his head for months and just "bang it out"?

He set down the crates. "Uh..."

"Crap. I overstepped, didn't I?" She bit her lip, that anxious look growing. "I just thought maybe it would help to have everything you could possibly need right here to get it done. I don't know a lot about home improvement, though I did take a furniture restoration class a couple of years ago..."

He laughed, a low rumble in his chest. Of course

she had. Her family always made fun of her for picking up hobbies and discarding them. Hell, he used to make fun of her for it too. How weird was it that now he found it endearing?

First things first, though. He crossed the space to her and pulled her into his arms. "You didn't overstep." He brushed his nose against hers before planting a soft kiss on her mouth. "It was actually really thoughtful of you."

Impulsive, probably barely thought out. All the things he would have once considered to be negative qualities, but all of a sudden, they seemed anything but.

The nervousness in her expression finally faded away. "Really?"

"Absolutely." He kissed her again. As always, the heat between them flared to life, and for a second he was tempted to let himself get carried away by it.

She was the one to pull away. He noted with pride that she did so with reluctance, though, her eyes dark and her lips red from his kisses. "Should we get started, then?"

"With what?" Getting her clothes off?

Rolling her eyes, she playfully swatted at his chest. "Fixing your ridiculous half-disassembled pantry."

Oh. Right.

Pulling away, he opened up said pantry. He was greeted by the same sad sight he'd been disgusted with for months now. The whole interior was a dingy white, the paint scuffed in places, with a set of wire rack shelving that had given up the ghost under the strain of a few too many boxes of cereal—and maybe one ill-advised effort on the part of Rosie to try to climb it and get to the cookies he'd stashed out of her reach. As soon as he'd recognized it as a safety hazard, he'd given his daughter a good talking to about it, then ripped out the bottom shelves.

And that had been about the end of his energy for the project. Every day, he'd open the door to get something off one of the two remaining functional shelves, and every day, he'd promise to get to it tomorrow. But getting to it tomorrow meant researching his options, shopping for the right equipment, setting aside the time to tackle it when Rosie wouldn't be underfoot. There was no point doing a job like this halfway. All the shelves had to get taken down, the interior cleaned and repainted. And between long days at work and all the responsibilities of being a single dad, he was exhausted. At night, he wanted to have a beer, maybe watch a little Netflix, and fall into bed.

Preferably with Savannah by his side.

But now here she was, tools and paint and all the other materials he could need at the ready.

He surveyed the task in front of him. This wasn't his normal way of tackling something like this.

But he had to admit. His normal approach hadn't

been working. As much as he'd been irritated by
Savannah's free-spirited way of doing things prior to
their falling into bed together, maybe taking a page out
of her book wouldn't be such a bad idea.

He turned to her and found her gazing at him, hands
clasped in front of her as she played with one of her
rings. He smiled, and she met him with an answering
smile of her own.

"Okay," he said. "Let's see if we can bang this
one out."

Thus began three of the most fun, satisfying, and
surprisingly productive hours of his life.

It turned out all his going around in circles, trying
to come up with the perfect plan had been a complete waste. In the end, all he needed was a little
time cleared off his schedule and a firm kick in the
ass from a woman who wasn't afraid to try something new.

Together, they'd gotten the pantry completely
cleaned out and what was left of the old shelves
removed. He'd spackled the holes left behind while
she scrubbed the back of the area, the two of them
working seamlessly as a team. When he lamented
that with how long it took for paint to dry, they'd
have to finish the project tomorrow, she just pulled
out one of the rolls of peel and stick wallpaper she'd
grabbed from the Sunshine Corner and asked, "Why
not try this?"

The white and rainbow stripe pattern wasn't what

he would have selected for himself, but she assured him that Rosie would love it, and considering it would be behind a closed door 90 percent of the time, how could he say no? They had that up in no time. Then it was just a matter of screwing in new brackets, cutting boards to size, and sanding the edges down. Sure, the shelves themselves would need a coat of paint and the night to dry, but that was nothing compared to the amount of work he'd thought this would involve.

"I can't believe we actually got this done," he said with a huff, setting the last of the boards down in the garage.

Savannah put the finishing touches on the shelf she'd been painting, then glanced up at him before moving on to the one he'd just delivered. "I had complete faith."

"Really?"

"No," she laughed, and God, he was crazy for that sound. It was practically the middle of the night. In the morning he'd be exhausted, but her energy had made him feel like he could conquer the world.

Usually, it was only a few rounds of hot, sweaty adult time with her that could leave him feeling this way. More and more, though, he was coming to find that their bedroom activities were only one piece of the puzzle.

"Well, maybe I should have." His voice dropped, going suddenly serious. "Had faith in you," he clarified.

It was a quiet apology for all the ways he'd

underestimated her in the past. A thank-you for the way she'd prodded him tonight.

Despite Noah having known Savannah for most of her life, she still managed to surprise him. She was so much more than he'd ever given her credit for—than *anyone* ever gave her credit for. She reminded him to have fun, made him try new things—last week's focus had been knitting because she'd always wanted to learn—and gave him more grace than he probably deserved. Jess always used to say he didn't have a spontaneous bone in his body, but with Savannah, he was starting to come around. Maybe there was something to just diving in and giving things a shot, long-term consequences and endless plans be damned.

"I'm glad it worked out," she said, not looking at him.

He moved to sit beside her, waiting until she lifted her gaze. She had a dot of paint on her nose, and it was somehow the most adorable thing he'd ever seen. Reaching out, he cupped her face in his hand. With his thumb, he wiped the speck of paint away.

"It worked out *great*. And it wouldn't have even gotten started without you." He leaned in and kissed her softly. "Thank you."

"You're welcome." She finally met his eyes. Gone was the nervousness and the anxiety. In their place was a pride he was happy to finally see in her. One he hoped she showed more often.

One he was sorry he hadn't helped her to feel more often in the first place.

* * *

A few days later, Savannah's brothers came over to Noah's house for a long-overdue video game tournament. They usually tried to have at least one a month, but he'd been so busy of late that it'd been hard to commit to a full evening of drinking beer and shooting things.

Of course, one of the reasons he'd been so busy was all the time he'd been spending with their little sister. The night after the pantry renovation, she'd come over again to see the finished product, shelves and all. His verbal thank-you had been well received, but the one he offered her with his hands and mouth had been even more so.

Not that he could ever, ever, ever tell the Lowe boys about that.

"Are you going to play, man, or keep daydreaming over there?" Aaron asked as he nudged Noah with his elbow.

"Not that any of us are complaining about these freebie kills you keep handing us." Spencer didn't even bother with a glance in Noah's direction, his gaze laser focused on the TV.

"Why'd you have to say anything, dude?" Jackson scowled at Aaron. "Maybe Noah likes it when we hand

him his ass." He shoved a handful of chips in his
mouth and shot Noah a grin as he chewed loudly. The
youngest Lowe brother had never been one for pesky
things like manners.

Irritated at himself for letting his thoughts drift to
these guys' little sister, Noah cleared his throat and
focused back on the four-person split screen where he
was, indeed, having his ass handed to him. "Thought
I'd give you guys a break. Figured you could use it."

He was lying through his teeth, of course. They were
playing one of their favorite first-person shooters, and
five of them—Noah and Savannah's three brothers at
his place, plus Caleb long distance—were playing in
a private lobby, player-versus-player free-for-all. Who-
ever collected the most kills among them won bragging
rights and trash talking—a truly priceless prize with
this crew—until the next tournament, whenever that
may be. Noah wasn't the least bit shocked to see he was
in last place. Not when he'd spent the last who knew
how long with his head in the clouds, daydreaming
about Savannah.

Caleb snorted from the laptop. "Still with the excuses, I see. So what you're telling me is not much has
changed since I've moved?"

Most of the time, it sucked not having his best friend
around to do things like this—to hang out or even just
swing by for a beer on his way home from work like
they'd done a hundred times before Caleb had moved
to San Francisco. But, thankfully, technology had

softened that particular blow. Having him on a laptop screen on the coffee table wasn't exactly the same, but it was better than nothing. And it certainly didn't impair the taunts.

"Everyone's got jokes, huh?" Noah mumbled, his focus now entirely on the game as he attempted to snag some more kills and even the playing field a bit.

It was a losing battle, though, considering how far behind he'd allowed himself to fall, and he came out as the loser of the bunch when the game ended. And, good friends that they were, every single one of Savannah's brothers had no qualms about letting him know just how badly he'd ate it.

"So," Jackson said conversationally, "I'm curious."

"About what?" Noah asked.

"Well, I mean, did you wake up this morning and just decide you were going to suck today, or did you really have to work at it? You know, focus on it and not let anything else—least of all winning—get in your way?"

Noah attempted a scowl, but the look Jackson gave him, one eyebrow high as he shoveled chips in his mouth, had him cracking in five seconds flat. He laughed and shoved Jackson hard enough to topple him on the couch. "Screw you. I've got a lot on my mind."

Spencer eyed him with a raised brow. "A lot on your mind, as in a woman?"

"What?" Noah asked, too fast. "Uh, no, why?"

Caleb eyed him with a curious expression, but before he could voice anything, Aaron cut in.

"Should've taken the out, man." Aaron shook his head as he grabbed a slice of pizza from the communal boxes on the coffee table. "Would've at least given you a plausible excuse."

"For what?" Noah asked.

"Sucking so bad," Jackson said without missing a beat.

All of them laughed, including his traitor of a best friend. Noah glared at Caleb and gave him a one-fingered salute. "Yeah, yeah, laugh it up. This is your fault, you know."

Caleb's eyebrows lifted. "*Mine*? How do you figure that?"

"Well, I'm certainly not over here planning my own wedding."

On the screen, Caleb cringed and rubbed a hand over his jaw. "Got it. Stop being an ass when you're doing me a favor. Point taken."

"How's that all going, by the way?" Spencer asked. "It's coming up quick."

"Not bad, actually," Noah said, surprised by the truth of his words. He'd been dreading this whole ordeal from the moment he'd agreed to it, but it hadn't turned out to be half as bad as he'd been expecting. "But I'm not going to lie—it absolutely sucked in the beginning, and I wanted to kill Caleb a dozen times for strong-arming me into it."

"I didn't—" Caleb cut off at Noah's mere lifted brow and laughed softly, holding up his hands in surrender. "Fair enough. I totally strong-armed you. Next time we get together, expect a bottle of Bowmore as a thank-you."

"That'll suffice."

"Has Savannah at least been pulling her weight?" Spencer asked, grabbing the last slice of pepperoni.

"Are you kidding? She's the one steering the whole damn ship."

"Wait…Savannah is?" Jackson said, his brows furrowed. "*Savannah*…as in our baby sister. The one who can't commit to anything and is flighty as all get-out? *That* Savannah?"

"Yes, that Savannah. Is that so hard to believe?" Noah asked, his words unintentionally biting. "She's done the majority of the research, booked nearly every appointment, and has kept track of all the comings and goings. I just show up when and where she tells me to. Actually, Caleb, if you want to get someone a bottle of liquor as a thank-you, you should buy her some Double Eagle Red."

Silence descended on the room for long moments before Caleb said, "Since when do you know what her favorite wine is?"

Noah froze for half a second, realizing his error. The reason he knew what her favorite was had been thanks to a night in…wherein he'd tasted the wine directly from her lips. He cleared his throat, willing away the images from that night and shifting in his seat. "Um, she mentioned it when we were sampling caterers, I think."

"Wait—you two actually speak to each other on these outings?" Jackson said.

Noah snorted and rolled his eyes. "Uh, yeah. That's how adulting works, Jackson. We actually speak when we're in the presence of each other."

"I know how to adult. I'm just surprised is all."

"Me too," Spencer said. "Considering you two don't usually speak as much as yell when you're conversing."

Aaron nodded. "Yeah, all these years have been pretty clear in one fact."

"What's that?" Noah asked.

"You two don't get along."

Noah shrugged, forcing himself to play this off like it was no big deal. Like he hadn't had Savannah in his bed just last night. Like his sheets didn't still smell of her. "We get along fine. Besides, it's not like we have a choice since this one"—he jerked his head toward Caleb—"shoved this whole planning thing in our laps. We were kind of forced to figure it out."

Noah finally took a deep breath when the focus shifted from him and his relationship with Savannah to the good-natured ribbing of Caleb. And he couldn't find it in himself to be the least bit sorry he'd thrown his best friend under the bus just to get some breathing room from their scrutiny.

Why hadn't he anticipated this line of questioning?

Better yet, why hadn't he been prepared for it? In all the evenings he and Savannah had spent together, laughing and talking for hours, putting up shelves, or making love until they were both breathless, they'd never managed to actually discuss *them*. Or just what the hell they were doing together. Besides the obvious, of course.

He still didn't have the foggiest idea what they were doing. All he knew for certain was that he sure wasn't going to let her incredibly overprotective brothers in on any of it. Or stop it from continuing.

Chapter Sixteen

Savannah had hoped she would be able to find a way to handle the situation at the preschool with Austin without involving Abby. However, today, at Austin's third instance of biting another child, she knew she couldn't keep it from her any longer. Preschool had released a couple hours prior, but several of the kids stayed for after-school care, Austin among them. His mother would be here soon, and Savannah had finally admitted that she needed to bring in some backup.

"I'm sorry I didn't tell you right away," Savannah said as she met with Abby in the sitting room on the main floor, which had become a sort of makeshift office for her. She had a particularly fussy baby balanced on her lap—one who only settled when attached to someone willing to bounce her for hours on end, which Abby was usually more than willing to do. Unfortunately, they had some serious business to attend to at the moment.

As if she could magically sense that she was needed, Hilde chose that moment to wander by. "Oh, sweetie," she cooed, and the fussy baby lit up. "Do you mind?" she asked Abby.

"Not at all." Abby held the little one out, and Hilde scooped her up. In a flash, the baby's mouth spread into a wide grin.

"Baby Whisperer," Abby and Savannah silently mouthed at each other in unison, before both laughing.

Hilde took her now-cheerful charge back to the infant area. Abby let out a sigh of relief, but Savannah found her tension only rising.

Returning to the matter at hand—namely, the need to take more significant action with regards to the little vampire in Savannah's class—Abby said, "I'm not mad that you didn't bring it to my attention right away. I'm just curious why."

Savannah heaved a sigh and crossed her arms as she glanced down at her tapping foot. "I just...I guess I just didn't want to disappoint you quite so early in the school year." Savannah forced out a laugh and met Abby's eyes. "I thought I'd at least have until the New Year before that would happen."

Except it didn't matter how much luster or bravado Savannah injected into her words because she and Abby had been friends for a long time. Long enough, certainly, for them to see through the other's facades, and Abby had absolutely no problem doing so now.

"You know I asked you to head this up not because you're my best friend but because I thought you were the best person for the job, right?"

On one level, yeah, sure, Savannah knew that. And the reason she knew that was because she also knew that the Sunshine Corner was Abby's baby, and there was no way she would do anything to jeopardize its standing in the community. But on another level...a lower level, the kind that held insecurities and years of feeling like she just never quite had her head on straight, she wasn't so sure. The whispered words of her subconscious—that not so surprisingly sounded a heck of a lot like the people in her past, who, whether meaning to or not, talked down to her about her ability to stand on her own—wondered otherwise.

"I know." But Savannah could hear the uncertainty in her voice, and she knew Abby could too.

Abby huffed and walked straight up to Savannah, her gaze set like a woman on a mission. She stopped directly in front of Savannah and set her hands on Savannah's shoulders, giving them a gentle shake. "I love you, but I do not love you enough to throw my business into the gutter just to make you feel better. I hired you because I know what you can do. I know what you're capable of. And you've proven that in the time that you've been leading the preschool."

Savannah ignored the way her heart melted at Abby's

words as she allowed herself to believe them. "Even though we've got a biter on our hands?"

Abby breathed out a laugh and squeezed Savannah's shoulders before she gathered up the documentation Savannah had assembled about Austin's aggressive behavior. "That doesn't fall on you. That's all him. And his mother," she said, the second sentence muttered slightly under her breath.

"Well I, for one, can't wait for Cruella de Vil to arrive. I'm *really* looking forward to another conversation with her," Savannah said, her voice dripping with sarcasm.

She'd had countless interactions with Megan, the majority of which happened during pickup and drop-off. However, there were a handful of times when she'd had to discuss Austin's behavioral problems. And while their daily conversations left something to be desired, they had nothing on the outright hostility Megan showed anytime her precious son was accused of anything less than perfection.

"Speak of the devil," Abby said under her breath.

Savannah turned to see Megan stomping toward them, her face set in anger.

"Hi, Megan," Abby said, just friendly enough to pass as professional. "Thanks for coming a bit early so we could chat about the situation we find ourselves in."

Megan huffed out an indignant sound and rolled her eyes. "The situation is, quite frankly, ridiculous. And I don't have time for this. I am a *very* busy woman."

Savannah barely kept the snort lodged inside her. Megan certainly thought a lot of herself, didn't she? Although perhaps her inflated sense of self explained a great deal about the son she was raising.

"Yes, well, I'm sure you agree that the situation demands attention and is worth any amount of time necessary in order to come to a solution that works best for all parties involved." Abby handed over a copy of the school rules each parent had signed off on at the beginning of the school year, not allowing Megan a second to respond. "As you can see here, a third instance of a physical attack on another child necessitates that the offending child be removed from school for three days."

"You cannot be serious," Megan said with disbelief.

"I'm afraid I'm quite serious."

"And just what has he done that is so atrocious that he needs to be removed from school?"

Savannah cleared her throat. "As we've discussed multiple times, Megan, he has problems with aggression that manifests in yelling, hitting, and most recently, biting. This is the third instance of the latter, and I can't allow it to continue to affect the rest of my students."

"Well, perhaps if you were a better teacher and kept the children engaged and entertained, my son wouldn't feel the need to lash out."

Savannah clenched her teeth to keep the scathing remarks that sat perched on the tip of her tongue from leaping out. On any other day, Megan's words might have landed like daggers in Savannah's chest, her insecurities reflected back on her from one of her students' parents. The worst kind of confirmation of exactly what she feared most. But right now, she was still riding high on Abby's words. And on the fact that her best friend hadn't doubted her for a second when Savannah had brought the concern to her. She'd simply nodded in agreement and backed Savannah up on whatever path she deemed necessary.

And that path happened to be Austin, out of school, for three days.

Savannah straightened her shoulders and met Megan's glare head-on. "The only problem with that line of thinking is that none of the other students have issues with aggressive behavior. I took some time today to call a friend in the area who is a behavioral specialist. His schedule is packed, but he's agreed to see Austin if you—"

"I will *not* be sending my son to any shrink," Megan cut in, her face red and blotchy. "He doesn't need that. All he needs is a *good* teacher, and apparently, I'll be taking the next week to find him one."

Megan turned and stormed off, her fist clutching the paper denoting every rule her son had broken thus far in the school year. Savannah had worried Megan would respond negatively to the suggestion of a specialist, but she'd hoped it would be different.

Savannah turned to Abby, uncertainty hanging heavy

in her heart. "Did I push it too far when I brought up the specialist? Maybe I shouldn't have even called."

Abby shook her head. "No. This was her reacting to news she didn't want to hear. You did the right thing, all around."

Savannah knew her friend wouldn't lie to her, especially not about something like this. She also knew, deep in her gut, that she was doing the right thing. True, Austin stretched her patience to its limits some days, but she wanted him to get the help he very obviously needed.

Still, she couldn't help but worry that this was what it was going to be like as a preschool teacher. Butting heads with uncooperative or ignorant parents who refused to see anything but the absolute best in their kids? To hear anything but glowing praise?

Abby's words may have been a balm to her heart and allowed her to stand tall when facing Megan. But now that she was facing nothing but herself, her own insecurities, and her uncertainties over whether this path was right for her, well, they weren't so easily silenced.

* * *

After a quick detour home to change into leggings and an oversized sweater, Savannah walked back into Abby's house, more than ready for this girls' night. After the day she'd had, she needed it. The funny thing was, after she'd gone home, the first person she wanted to call to vent to was Noah.

She had no idea where things stood with them, only that in the past few weeks, she'd spent an equal number of evenings with him as she did without him. If you'd asked her even a couple months ago if this would have been possible between her and Noah, she would have laughed in your face.

But now, after spending so much uninterrupted, one-on-one time with him, she was beginning to realize that she'd had him pegged all wrong. True, he was unyielding and stubborn, but he was also sweet, especially when it came to Rosie. And he was appeasing, especially when it came to her random whims. And that didn't even speak anything of how they were between the sheets. Or on top of the sheets. Or in the shower.

Actually, they hadn't yet found a surface where their connection didn't singe the air around them.

"I love that idea!" a voice said from the breakfast nook. A voice that sounded an awful lot like her soon-to-be sister-in-law.

Savannah pinched her brows together and rounded the corner, stopping short at the scene that greeted her. Abby, Gia, Becca, and Tori all sat around the table, focused on the laptop screen where Issa smiled back at them.

"There you are! I was about to send out a search party," Abby said, beaming up at Savannah.

She glanced at her watch. It was only five minutes past the time that they'd agreed to meet...or so she thought. Had she gotten the time wrong? Maybe she should've made more of an effort to use that stupid planner Abby had bought her.

"If I'd known you were going to start the party without me, I wouldn't have stopped to pick up these," she said, holding up the bottle of merlot and the sparkling juice she'd grabbed for Gia—and maybe Abby, now that she thought about it again. She'd tried to corner her best friend about her grandmother's ambiguous comments a few times over the past few weeks, but Abby had been evasive every time. She dropped into a chair, tucking the long wisps of hair that had escaped her ponytail behind her ear. "What's going on?"

"I was just telling Issa about the estate tour at that winery I found," Abby said. "I'm seriously in love with this area all these wineries are in."

"Me too! I've been obsessed with it since we started researching." Gia leaned back in the chair, placing one hand on her baby bump. "There's so much to do there. I'm super jealous of all the fun you guys are going to have!" Gia handed Savannah a list in her handwriting with no fewer than fifteen tourist sites and activities in the area.

Issa gasped and covered her mouth with her hands. "We should make it a whole weekend!"

Abby whipped her head toward the laptop screen,

her eyes dancing. "I love that idea! You guys will be able to do so many more of these activities."

"Oh, there's no 'you guys' in this situation. You're coming, too, aren't you? Actually, you *all* should come. It'd be so much fun!"

Becca grinned, lifting her glass in a toast. "This single mom will gladly take a weekend away, as long as I can sweet-talk my brother into babysitting."

"Well, if you can't, I certainly can," Abby said. "I'd love to check out this place to see if we'd like to do something there for our wedding too."

"Yes!" Becca agreed. "It looks so romantic." There was a wistfulness to her voice that reminded Savannah that between her kid and her job, she'd had way too little time in her life for romance.

"What about you, Tori? Will you come too? We'd love to have you!"

Tori's eyes widened in surprise before a soft smile swept over her mouth. "That sounds really fun. Thank you for inviting me."

It didn't slip past Savannah that that wasn't exactly agreement, but none of the other girls seemed to notice as they fell into a flurry of discussion over the smallest of details. Things, no doubt, that Savannah should have already had figured out. Things she should have anticipated, considering she'd been tasked with this. Not Abby or Gia. They weren't even bridesmaids, and now they'd forged ahead and planned what sounded like the perfect bachelor/bachelorette parties.

"It seriously sounds *so* amazing. Thank you guys for all that you're doing for this," Issa said, sincerity ringing in her tone. "Savannah, I appreciate it *so* much."

Savannah smiled even as her stomach twisted. Had she really even done that much? She'd basically lucked into the ceremony and reception site. Her mom, as well as Noah's, kept tagging along on all their appointments, nominally because they just wanted more free catering samples, but she couldn't shake the feeling that they didn't trust her. Hell, Abby had taken over planning the entire bachelor/bachelorette party at this point.

"Send me all the details, will you?" Issa said, although Savannah knew she was speaking to Abby and Gia, not her. "I've got to run, but I'll see you guys in a couple weeks!"

A chorus of goodbyes went up around the room, and Savannah kept her pasted-on smile present as she stood and strode into the kitchen, intent on pouring herself a very large helping of wine.

"Hey," Abby said quietly, sounding unsure. "You're not mad, are you?"

"About what?" Savannah asked, forcing brightness into her voice.

Abby glanced back at the table where Becca, Gia, and Tori all laughed, before meeting Savannah's eyes again. "The party. I totally did my Abby thing and completely took over."

Savannah smiled and waved a hand through the air as she poured herself a glass of wine. "No, don't worry about it. It's a relief, honestly. Between running the preschool and planning everything else, I didn't know how I'd get it done. Besides, watching you do this is giving me a lot of fodder for when I have to plan yours. So thanks."

"Are you sure?"

Savannah nodded, keeping her smile bright, though it was slipping. After the weight of the day, her veneer was cracking. If she didn't sneak away soon, she would make a fool of herself in front of everyone. She blinked rapidly before squeezing one eye shut. "Ouch—I think I've got an eyelash in my contact. I'll be right back."

She slipped out of the room and into the half bath down the hall, resting her shoulders against the shut door and closing her eyes. Why couldn't she be as confident and on top of things as the rest of her friends?

Was she just doomed to always be the baby of the family, struggling to keep up? Never quite able to do the same things as the people around her did? Always needing help?

Faking it in the hopes of someday making it had served her well for most of her life thus far. But for some reason her confidence was failing her now. Maybe it was because she had so many responsibilities all of a sudden. Maybe it was watching all her friends get married and successfully parent their kids.

Meanwhile, here she was, in relationship limbo with a guy who—up until a couple of months ago— thought she was flighty and annoying, and who used to basically hate her guts. Add that to her leaning on her best-friend-slash-boss to both plan her brother and future sister-in-law's party for her *and* to mediate her toughest situation at work.

Was it any wonder she always felt like she was never quite measuring up?

Chapter Seventeen

It had been a hell of a day for Noah. It had started out innocuously enough, but when Noah and his partner had already been on three emergency calls before 9:00 a.m., he knew he was in for a rough one. And it shouldn't have surprised him. Full moons were always completely nuts. He didn't believe there were werewolves running around, but even ordinary humans lost their minds a little bit this time of the month and did some completely inane things, and Noah was the lucky one who got to patch them up.

By the time six o'clock rolled around, he was exhausted. All he wanted to do was pick up Rosie, maybe order in a pizza, because the thought of cooking anything nutritious was insurmountable to him, and spend a nice evening with her. And then, once Rosie was in bed, invite Savannah over so he could lose himself in her, for even just a few hours.

He hauled his bag over his shoulder and lifted a hand in goodbye toward the crew surrounding the dining table.

"See you tomorrow, slacker," Grant called, a wide grin stretching his face.

Noah barely hid the grimace the word caused. Deep down, he knew he wasn't a slacker. He worked as many hours as the other guys—he just did them in a different structure. But it was that difference that made him feel, well, different. Doted on. Like people were bending over backward to throw him a bone, and he hated it.

"Adams," his shift captain barked as Noah's hand settled on the door. "Can I see you for a second before you leave?"

He glanced at his watch and cringed, hoping that Abby would be lenient with him. Again. Because when his captain asked if he could see him, it certainly wasn't a question.

Noah strode into his office, clutching his bag over his shoulder. "What's up?"

Chuck settled himself in his chair and folded his hands on top of his desk. "Shut the door, will you?"

Nothing good ever started that way, but Noah did as the man asked, trying not to read too much into it. "Sure thing, boss."

"I won't keep you too long," Chuck said, his mustache twitching. "I know you've got to get Rosie."

"It's all right," Noah lied. "What did you need to talk about?"

The older man sighed heavily and leaned back in his chair, resting his folded hands over his round belly. "We're coming up on six months, Adams. We're all a family here, and we all want to help out as much as we can. Which is why we've been flexible with your schedule to give you a little breathing room. Some time to figure things out, what with Jess moving out of the state and all."

"I know you have, and I appreciate it."

"No one thinks you don't. And if there was a way to make this work where we could do this indefinitely, we would. But the truth is, it just doesn't. We take care of our own, which is why we've allowed this leniency. But we're coming up on the better part of a year here. I think it might be time for you to make some tough choices."

"What do you mean by tough choices?"

But Noah didn't need him to say the words. Not when he already knew what was coming. He'd been waiting for this day since the moment Chuck had agreed to an altered schedule in the first place.

Chuck cleared his throat and met Noah's eyes. "We're going to need to move you back to twenty-fours to be in line with the rest of the guys. They've got families, too, who'd love to have them home every night for dinner."

He knew they had families. It had been that detail

that had eaten him the most since he'd needed to ask for a schedule accommodation. Why should he get this allowance when the others didn't?

Chuck must've read the look on Noah's face wrong, because he was quick to clarify, "Now, I don't want you to get the wrong idea. No one's brought a formal complaint to me. But you hear whispers, you know? I'm looking out for you as much as I am for the unit. I don't want those whispers to turn into resentment."

"I understand," Noah said through a throat filled with glass. But he didn't. Didn't have the foggiest idea how the hell he was going to make this work.

"All you need to do is find some additional childcare. That should take care of this, shouldn't it?"

Oh, yeah. Just some additional childcare was all he needed. Additional childcare he couldn't afford—especially not when it'd be an overnight rate if he was working twenty-fours. He was barely scraping by now with what he paid for Rosie's preschool and after-school care. Some of the latter cost would go down, since he could pick her up early on his off days, but that would barely touch the overnights. He didn't know how he'd make ends meet. Though his mom was available for watching Rosie almost anytime he asked, she also had a job to contend with. And he couldn't ask her to work her schedule around his.

"I'll get it figured out."

Chuck slapped a hand on his desk, a smile blooming

under the overgrown mustache. "Good, I'm glad to hear it. But, Adams, listen, if you can't…" He pressed his lips together as if he didn't want to say the words, but they were necessary all the same. "There's no shame in finding something else. Doesn't mean you couldn't hack it. It just means this career didn't fit quite right in your life, right now."

Noah left the station with a hollow ache in his chest, the thought of not being an EMT weighing him down. He couldn't remember a time when this wasn't exactly what he wanted to do. Who would he be, anyway, if not this? He had no other training…no other skills that would allow him to obtain a nine-to-five job somewhere else.

He'd known this day would come at some point. Yet, though it had been nearly six months, he still hadn't expected it to come quite so soon. And he certainly hadn't been ready for it.

* * *

Later, after Noah had picked up Rosie from Sunshine Corner and they'd arrived at home, he and Rosie had, indeed, feasted on pizza before her weekly video chat with her mom. They sat on the couch, Rosie tucked into his side, as she regaled Jess with her week's adventures.

"I can even write my name now, Mommy! And I'm getting really good at scissors. But Daddy says I can't play with them by myself, because that's how accidents happen."

"By accident, did he mean you *accidentally* cutting your hair?" Jess asked.

Rosie pressed her hands to her mouth and giggled, shooting a glance over her shoulder toward Noah before focusing once again on the laptop. She leaned close and dropped her voice to a whisper. "He got really mad at me when I did that."

"I don't blame him."

"Thankfully Grandma could fix it, huh?" Noah said. He had no idea how long they'd been talking—five minutes or fifty—it was all the same to him. He had so much weighing on his mind that he was there but not. Present, but not *present*.

"I'm gonna go color your picture! Bye, Mommy!"

"Bye, sweetie, love you!" Jess called, though Rosie was already halfway down the hallway to her bedroom.

Noah sat up, exhaling a deep sigh and rubbing a hand through his hair. "I guess she's had enough of that."

Jess hummed and regarded him with narrowed eyes. "And what have *you* had enough of?"

Noah's brow furrowed and he stared at his ex-wife. "What do you mean?"

"Oh, please." She rolled her eyes. "We might not be married anymore, but we *were* married for seven years. I can still read your cues pretty well, even through a computer screen. So spill. What's going on?"

The last thing he wanted to do was lay this all out

for his ex-wife, but the truth was, Jess was more than just that. She was also the mother to his kid. And while things didn't work out between them, their split had been amicable, and neither of them held any animosity toward the other. Sometimes relationships just fizzled without any big cataclysmic event to cause it. And that was exactly what had happened with theirs.

He heaved out a deep sigh. "It's work."

After a long beat of silence, she made a *continue on* gesture with her hand. "Yes, and?"

"You know how they switched my schedule to better accommodate me taking care of Rosie on my own?"

"Yeah."

"Well, Chuck called me into his office today to tell me that I need to get it figured out."

"Get what figured out?"

"I need to either find more childcare for Rosie, or I need to find a different job."

Jess was quiet for long moments, her gaze boring into him even through the screen. Finally, she said, "You know, I got a two-bedroom specifically so Rosie could come visit."

"Yeah, I know," Noah said, not quite understanding where she was headed with this. A two-week visit over the summer wasn't exactly going to help with the situation he found himself in now.

"Maybe...maybe Rosie should come live with me for a while."

Noah's entire body jerked at the mere suggestion, a

pit forming in his stomach at the idea of his daughter moving away from him. There was no way. No. Way. He wouldn't be able to stand not seeing her every day. Not hugging her and listening to her talk about her day, not watching her grow and change in the tiny, daily ways that happened at this age.

"You know that's not what we agreed," he said, his voice firmer than necessary.

Jess had hated leaving Rosie behind, but they'd both been on the same page that Heart's Hope Bay was her home. She had stability, friends, and family here. She had *him*. And yes, a kid needed her mom, but she needed her dad, too, and her dad was the one who had been here, holding things together all this time.

"I know," Jess said, her tone much softer than the one he'd used on her. "I'm just saying it's an option. We might not still be married, but you don't have to do this all on your own."

Except that he did. He would. He'd figure this out, one way or another, without anyone's help. He could take care of himself and Rosie. After all, he'd been doing it for the past six months. It was him who'd finally gotten them back on track following the sharp decline when Jess left. Rosie had been better in the past couple months. She'd become less clingy, less anxious. He realized, too, that that had happened in no small part thanks to Savannah and her influence at the preschool.

Jess was the one who had fled. Rosie was already

dealing with one parent abandoning her. He'd be damned if he shipped her off and made her go through that all over again. Hell would freeze over before he forced his daughter through that. Before he'd give her up.

Somehow, he'd figure out a way to make this work.

* * *

Noah opened the front door to the sight of Savannah on the other side, a wide smile stretched across her face. One that slowly melted away when she got a good look at him.

"Hey," she said. "What's going on?"

But Noah didn't answer. Instead, he hooked his finger through one of her belt loops and tugged her inside, straight into his waiting embrace. He wrapped his arms around her and took a deep breath for the first time in what felt like days, inhaling her scent and setting his body at ease. Which wasn't all that hard to believe, considering the past three hours had felt like a lifetime in and of themselves. Had it only been three hours ago when Chuck had told him, basically, to shape up or ship out?

As soon as he'd hung up with Jess, he'd texted Savannah and asked her to come over early. Rosie had only been in bed for fifteen minutes, and he knew he was playing with fire, but he'd wanted to eke out as much time with Savannah as he possibly could. He didn't know when she'd suddenly turned into the person he went to for comfort. But somewhere in the past few weeks, it'd happened, whether she realized it or not.

"What's wrong?" she asked, pulling back to look up at him, her fingers threaded through the hair at the base of his head.

But he didn't want to talk about it. Not right now, anyway. Before he discussed this again, he needed to process through it on his own. He shook his head and met her eyes. "Just a long day at work."

"Are you sure that's all it is?" Her gaze darted all over his face, and he knew she could read it. Every pained, frustrated inch of it.

"Yeah."

After several long moments where she continued to study him, she finally nodded. "Okay."

And that was it. She didn't push. Didn't press to get him to open up to her and spill all his secrets, even though she could very obviously still tell something was bothering him. And that small act only attracted him to her more.

"You want to watch a movie?" He was throwing her all sorts of curveballs tonight. With the exception of the DIY project she'd instigated, movie watching and other extracurriculars always came *after* the bedroom activities.

But instead of calling him on it or pressing him for more details, she smiled and nodded. "Girl's choice?"

He laughed low under his breath and allowed her to

drag him into the family room, their hands connected between them. "Depends on what you pick."

"You know I have excellent taste in movies."

"Are we basing this off of your love for Nicholas Sparks movies?"

"Not movies. *Movie*, okay? And *The Notebook* is an amazing theatrical masterpiece that demonstrates a lifetime love any of us would be lucky to have, I'll tell you that much."

Noah snorted and settled into the corner of the couch, tugging Savannah down next to him and tucking her into his side. "If you say so."

She glanced over at him. "Have you even seen it?"

He raised his eyebrows at her. "Pretty sure you already know the answer to that."

"Then you can't talk trash about it. And you just bought yourself an evening with Ryan Gosling and Rachel McAdams," she said, grabbing the remote and burrowing into his side.

The funny thing was, as long as that evening consisted of Savannah, too, it could be filled with just about anything else, and he wouldn't have minded in the least. Their relationship was growing far more serious than he'd ever intended it to. Outside of the woman he married, he'd never called a girlfriend—and Savannah couldn't even technically be classified as such—when he'd needed support. And yet he'd reached out to her automatically, as if going by nothing more than instinct.

But the last thing he wanted to do after the day he'd

had was to examine that particular instinct too closely tonight. Not when the whole reason he'd needed Savannah's comfort in the first place—*comfort*, just her being there; not sex, but intimacy—was all thanks to his last failed relationship.

Later, he might worry that he was traversing down a slippery slope. That asking Savannah over for something other than to satiate their physical need for each other was opening up Pandora's box. But for now, tonight, he was content to lie with her on the couch, breathe in her scent, and find comfort in the silence.

Chapter Eighteen

Savannah was being ridiculous. She knew she was, and yet she couldn't stop her mind from spiraling to thoughts of how, even though this Thanksgiving was going to be similar to a dozen previous, it really wasn't.

The Lowe family had always been big and welcoming, and Savannah's mom was notorious for inviting anyone who so much as hinted that they might be considering keeping the holiday small to join them. Abby and Hilde had been feasting on turkey and her mom's famous buttery mashed potatoes with them for years. Abby's boyfriend, Carter, was new, sure, though his sister Becca and her daughter Sofia had joined them a time or two, back before Carter returned to Heart's Hope Bay. Becca and Savannah's younger brother Jackson had been friends forever, not that Savannah would ever understand it, considering Becca was a responsible human being while Jackson was a surfing-addicted man-child.

Noah, however, had been a fixture at their family's house during the holidays for actual decades. But in all those prior years, never once could she have recalled, at any point during a meal, exactly what he'd done to her the night before. Exactly how many times he'd made her bite her lip or moan. How many times he'd pulled her back as she was trying to leave, just to get one more kiss.

She'd also never been able to sit across from him and picture him naked with any sort of accuracy. And now she could paint a mural of his bare chest in her sleep, not to say anything of his backside.

"You okay there?" Abby said, poking her elbow into Savannah's side.

Savannah jolted and glanced over at her best friend, who sat next to her at the behemoth of a dining room table her mom had insisted on when they'd built the house. "What? Yeah, fine, why?"

Her dad boomed out a laugh. "Then pass the potatoes already. I've been asking for ten minutes."

"Oh, you have not," Savannah's mom chided. "Leave the poor girl alone." But her mom eyed her with curiosity and just a little concern.

"Sorry, just, um, thinking about, uhh...the preschool," Savannah said, passing over the potatoes and hoping no one noticed her stumbled words.

"How's that going, by the way?" Aaron asked in between bites.

"Good. Mostly," Savannah said. "I think, anyway."

"She's not taking enough credit." Abby beamed at Savannah before regarding the rest of the table. "She has done such a fantastic job of developing this preschool to be exactly what I envisioned it to be, and in such a short time."

"And believe me, that's a tall order to meet Abby's expectations." Carter chuckled, his arm resting on the back of Abby's chair, his thumb grazing her shoulder blades.

Abby shot him a smile and rolled her eyes. "I'm not that bad."

A wave of laughter rippled around the table. Every single one of them had been affected in one way or another by Abby's high standards.

"What? I'm *not* that bad."

"You kind of are," Savannah said.

Abby sniffed. "Well, regardless, what I said is true."

"You're my best friend—you have to say that."

Before Abby could respond, Becca cut in. "Well, I don't. And I'm not exaggerating when I say every day I'm shocked at what this one"—she gestured to Sofia—"has learned in the short time since school started." She smiled softly at the little girl and ran a finger through a strand of her hair. "It's always hard to let your kid out of your sight, especially when you're a mama bear like me, but I know she couldn't be in better hands."

Savannah's face flamed, and she ducked her head, so unused to that sort of praise, especially in the presence of her family. She had no idea how to handle it without turning into a tomato.

"Yeah?" Jackson asked, at the same time Aaron said, "No kidding?" Both their eyebrows were raised as if they couldn't quite believe their baby sister was capable of such things. And, yep, that brought her right back down to earth again.

"Don't sound so shocked," Hilde said, pinning Savannah's brothers with narrowed eyes. Her savior to the rescue. "When it comes to taking care of those children, she could run circles around you boys, even with her hands tied."

"That so?" Spencer asked. "What about you, Noah? Are you happy with what Savannah does, even with her hands tied?"

Noah choked on the sip of water he'd just taken, and his mom regarded him with worried eyes, reaching over to pat his back.

"Oh, honey, you okay? Did you swallow wrong?"

Noah lifted his eyes to meet Savannah's across the table, and she'd swear she felt them as sure as if they were his fingers trailing up her spine. She shuddered but tried to disguise it by shifting in her seat. From the look Abby shot her, she wasn't so successful.

Noah took another drink before clearing his throat. "I completely agree. Savannah's abilities are far beyond what I anticipated or even hoped for."

He was talking about her abilities as a teacher. A *teacher*. She knew that...logically, anyway. But there was no stopping the illogical swoop of her stomach, like she was riding a roller coaster, her insides a mix of nerves and exhilaration. Especially when he met her eyes after the conversation had switched to something else entirely. Conversations she tried to keep up with so that she wouldn't be caught off guard again and wouldn't look like an idiot. But it was hard to focus on that when she had more important things to contend with. Like how anytime she glanced across the table toward Noah, his eyes were already locked on her, his gaze hot and hungry. Needy in a way that had shifted some time over the past couple of weeks, as their evenings had started to include as many home improvement projects and movie nights as anything else.

Not that she was complaining. For the most part, she loved this change. Loved how it made her feel wanted and needed in a way she hadn't felt, well...maybe ever. But her heart? Her heart wasn't so sure because it feared just how badly this could all end if things went sideways.

* * *

Later, after everyone had finished moaning their way through the afternoon, their stomachs too full to do anything but veg in the family room and watch the football game, Savannah was curled into the couch. She was pretending to watch a game she wasn't at all interested in, when in reality, she'd spent the past who knew how long actually watching Noah. More specifically, watching Noah watching her in a way that said he couldn't wait until tonight. Couldn't wait to hold her in his arms again. Couldn't wait to get her behind closed doors. Couldn't wait for his lips to finally be on hers once more.

Because she was so engrossed in this silent exchange, she startled when someone plopped onto the cushion next to her and cleared their throat. She whipped her head in that direction, startling like a kid caught with their hand in the cookie jar.

Abby regarded her with an amused expression, a single eyebrow raised. "Jumpy, huh?" she said, with a teasing lilt to her voice.

Savannah cleared her throat and tucked her hair behind her ear. "No, why?"

Abby turned toward Savannah, tucking her legs under herself, and regarded her fully. "That might pass with, say, Becca, who doesn't know you very well. Or even one of your brothers, who are so oblivious to absolutely anything that they wouldn't notice a fly, even if someone smacked a newspaper to their forehead.

But this is *me* we're talking about. Your best friend for decades. Remember her?"

"I remember how irritating you can be."

Abby smiled and rested her elbow on the back of the couch, leaning even closer toward Savannah. "Irritating enough to press you on telling me what's really going on here?"

Savannah paused. That was rich, considering how squirrelly Abby had been acting about some parts of her own life just of late. It hadn't escaped Savannah's attention that her best friend had yet again opted for water instead of wine with dinner.

But unlike Abby, Savannah could give people space when they clearly needed it.

"I'm watching a football game I am not the least bit interested in because the Seahawks aren't playing," Savannah said, embedding as much confidence in her answer as she possibly could.

"I didn't mean with the game," Abby said with an eye roll. "I meant with you and—" She tipped her head toward Noah and raised her eyebrows.

"I don't know what you're talking about," Savannah lied, completely unconvincingly.

"No?" Abby raised a single eyebrow. "Like I said, everyone else might be too preoccupied to pay attention to what's been going on, but don't think that I haven't noticed exactly how cozy you and Noah have been today, or how you've been undressing each other from across the room."

"Oh my God, would you shut up?" Savannah hissed, her gaze darting around, though no one was paying them any mind. Even Noah's attention had shifted elsewhere as he'd been pulled into a lively debate between her brothers, Carter, and her dad of who had the best quarterback in the league.

Sofia and Rosie were coloring in a corner, their whispers and giggles enough to warm Savannah's heart. Her mom, Cheryl, Hilde, and Becca were playing cards, their laughter washing over the room every so often. Which meant there was no one around to hear their conversation. Or to save her from it.

"You don't give me enough credit," Abby said, narrowing her eyes at Savannah. "I wouldn't have sprung this on you now if we had any eyes on us."

"Sometimes I'm not so sure."

Abby reached out and gripped Savannah's wrist, shaking it slightly. "Spill."

With one final look around the space to verify no one was paying them any attention, Savannah breathed out a heavy sigh. "Fine. Our one night after looking at venues has... continued."

Abby squealed, drawing questioning glances from several people, Noah and her brothers included. Somehow, Abby managed to turn her squeal into a gasp. "I cannot believe Megan said that to you," she said, faster on her feet than Savannah had ever before given her credit for. "What did you say to her?"

The second part of the sentence was unnecessary, because almost immediately, everyone's gazes had flitted away from them. Though she could have sworn she felt Noah's on her for a beat longer than necessary.

"I'm not going to tell you anything anymore if you can't keep your reactions in check," Savannah hissed.

"Well, what do you expect me to do?"

"Maybe not ambush me after Thanksgiving dinner with my entire family and yours in attendance."

"Well, *someone* didn't give me much of a choice, now, did she?"

Savannah cringed, properly chastised. "You're right. I'm sorry I've been keeping this to myself."

"Why?" Abby asked, the tiniest flicker of hurt seeping into her voice.

That flicker of hurt killed Savannah. She'd never been one to keep things from Abby—she'd never needed to. They told each other everything and were each other's sounding boards, or at least that was how it had always been in the past. "It's not really a big deal. We're just...hanging out. Friends who sometimes do super friendly things with each other."

Abby laughed, but Savannah could barely call up a smile, the words ringing hollow in her heart. Just as she'd never kept things from Abby, neither had she ever outright lied to her, but apparently there was a first for everything. Whatever was happening between Savannah and Noah *was* a big deal. It may not have started out that way, and she may have assured him it could be as casual as he wanted, but somewhere along the way, things had shifted between them.

More than ready to take the focus off herself and her feelings, Savannah nudged Abby with her elbow. "By the way, don't think I haven't noticed that you've been keeping some things to yourself too."

Now it was Abby's turn to look guarded. "Oh?"

"Your grandmother made a few interesting comments to me several weeks ago, and you've been squirrelly as hell any time I've tried to ask you about them."

"Oh." Abby sat up straighter, her cheeks going pink. "Well…"

Ha! Savannah knew it. Her sense of vindication nearly eclipsed her own hurt about having been left in the dark about something going on in her best friend's life. "So?" She poked Abby again. "Spill."

"I will," Abby promised. But she nodded, looking across the room toward Carter. "But can you wait? Just a little bit longer."

Savannah opened her mouth, ready to needle her harder. But then she stopped herself. Cautiously, she said, "Okay. If it's that important to you."

"It is," Abby assured her. For the first time, her own frustration with keeping this secret of hers to herself shone through.

"But I'll be the first one you tell?" Savannah made her promise. "When you're ready?"

"Of course."

That made Savannah feel a little better. She hated to think Abby didn't trust her with whatever this information was. She had her suspicions, of course, and if they panned out, she understood why Abby was holding her tongue. She had to trust that her best friend would tell her what was going on in her own time.

Something big happened in the game they were all pretending to watch, and mixed shouts of excitement and disappointment went up from the other side of the room. With that, she and Abby drifted back to talking about more everyday things. Becca eventually joined them, which was great.

Because as they talked, her gaze kept drifting to one particular spot in the room. And if that spot in the room just happened to be where Noah was sitting...well, that was just an interesting coincidence, wasn't it?

Or at least that's what she'd tell Abby if she called her on it.

In reality, she couldn't stop thinking about him, or about the half-truths she'd told her best friend when she'd been prodded about her not-quite-relationship with him, or about why she'd been keeping these developments to herself.

Which was a problem.

She and Noah had said that they were casual, but more and more, her feelings about him were becoming anything but.

When had it happened that the person she wanted

to call when she had a bad day had slowly started to morph from her best friend to Noah? He was the last thing she thought about before she fell asleep, and the first thing she thought about when she woke up. She'd never before been with someone who she could see being with long-term. But now it physically pained her to think of a time in the future when Noah wouldn't be part of her life.

She'd never before been able to picture a future with anyone else. Could never visualize bringing someone home for the holidays, because it had felt strange to insert another person into their already-overflowing group. But what if she didn't have to insert another person? Noah was already settled into her life and had always been a part of the family. But what if he were *her* family? Her person? The one she could go to for anything. The one who had her back when it seemed like no one else did.

Thoughts of a future Thanksgiving played out in her mind as clear as if they were happening in real time and not mere fantasies. Noah standing by her side, Rosie between them, holding their hands, and a baby snuggled against Noah's chest. *Their* baby. She'd never really given that much thought to having kids of her own—she'd never felt like she was at a place in her life to consider it before, and she wasn't exactly one to plan too far ahead. But now that glimpse of a possible future with him felt so real, she nearly ached with the desire to have it.

She turned her gaze to Noah, and, almost as if he felt

the weight of her stare, he turned and glanced in her direction, offering a small, secretive smile that spoke of all that was to come for them.

She could only hope that his daydreams looked even a glimmer like hers.

Chapter Nineteen

As much as Noah wanted to see Caleb this weekend for the bachelor/bachelorette party and celebrate his upcoming nuptials, there was this niggling sense in the pit of his stomach that he was being a bad father for leaving Rosie for the weekend. Noah's mom, of course, had been thrilled when he'd asked her if she could watch Rosie while he, Savannah, her brothers, and a few of Savannah's friends traveled the five hours to Mendocino County to meet up with Caleb, Issa, and the rest of the bridesmaids.

Last he talked to his mom, she'd already had the entire weekend planned out, filled with more activities than he managed to do with Rosie in several months, let alone a couple days. That, of course, only made his guilt gnaw at him more. Maybe Rosie would get a more enriching childhood if he *did* call in help once in a while.

He hadn't even been able to enjoy the luxury party bus they were currently cruising down I-5 in. The inside looked like something straight out of a movie, black leather seats with neon lights illuminating the space. There were enough seats for twenty, but since only nine of them were there, everyone had been able to spread out.

Savannah's brothers plus Becca were up near the front, sitting in the captain's chairs surrounding one of the tables, playing poker. Gia and Tori were huddled on one of the leather benches, their heads close together as they flipped through what looked like a sketchbook. And Savannah and Abby spoke in hushed tones from across the aisle, their laughter echoing through the bus.

And there he sat, separated from the group, unable to enjoy himself, and worried about his daughter. He closed his eyes and leaned his head back, resting it on the plush leather seat. He wasn't sure how long he'd been sitting like that before Savannah dropped into the space next to him. Even with his eyes closed, he knew it was her.

"Hey," she said.

He opened his eyes and glanced at her before lifting his gaze toward her brothers, worry creasing his brow. He might have been sitting in the back of the bus, away from all the other passengers, but you couldn't be too careful.

"They're not paying attention," Savannah said. "They're too busy making sure Becca doesn't kick their asses again."

He breathed out a laugh. Considering how many times he'd lost to the Lowe brothers over the years, he'd pay good money to watch Becca wipe the floor with them.

Savannah leaned in closer, the light, floral scent of her washing over him as his body responded to her nearness. "Besides, it's not illegal for us to talk. We *do* have a wedding to plan. They'd be none the wiser if I decided, instead, to talk about what we did last night."

Noah whipped his head toward Savannah and met her gaze, her eyes dancing with mischief. "You're a troublemaker."

She lifted a single shoulder in a shrug and pursed her lips to the side. "Sometimes." She leaned into him, knocking his shoulder with hers. "Seriously, what's up? If anyone needs a vacation, it's you, and yet you look like someone just ran over your dog."

Noah sighed and ran a hand through his hair. "Just worried about Rosie."

"Why? Was she upset when you left?"

"Yeah. I just don't know how much of that is to be expected and how much of it is specifically because of her fears that popped up after Jess left."

"Ahh," Savannah said with a nod. "Well, she's been doing much better at school. She hasn't had a meltdown after drop-off in more than a month. She knows that you'll be there, Noah."

"She knows I'll be there after a day at preschool. But this is a weekend trip away where I can't run home if there's an issue."

"You know, your mom *did* raise one kid already. I think she'll be okay."

"It's not my mom I'm worried about," he said with a humorless laugh. "She's gonna keep the two of them so busy, Rosie hopefully won't even have time to miss me."

"Then what has you concerned?"

"I'm just..." He heaved out a near groan and leaned forward, resting his folded hands between his knees. "She's come so far since school started. I just don't want her to regress." He glanced back at Savannah, not even trying to hide the worry in his expression.

She leaned forward, too, and rested her fingers on his forearm, lightly brushing them over his skin. "And that right there is why she's gonna be fine. You're a great dad, Noah. You care so much about your daughter and making sure she has everything she needs. But what she needs is a dad who's a hundred percent, and sometimes, in order to get that, *you* need some time away to recharge. And you shouldn't feel guilty about it."

Relief washed over him at Savannah's words, something no amount of internal pep talks could provide. He met her eyes, then dropped his gaze to her lips.

Goddamn, the things he wanted to do to them. The things he'd *already* done...

He sat back, shifting in his seat to hide his body's reaction, and cleared his throat, though it didn't help much. When he spoke, his voice still came out rough and ragged, as if they'd already passed the finish line rather than him being desperate to start. "Jesus, I want to kiss you." He pitched his voice low to ensure no one else could hear them. Thankfully, a fairly easy feat, considering the laughter and conversation going on around them.

"I want that too," Savannah said on a whisper, just before she licked her lips, sending a flurry of more fantasies erupting in his mind. "Maybe we can sneak in some time this weekend."

"Yeah, just enough to drive me crazy with want." He allowed his gaze to trace the delicate lines of her face, down the slope of her neck to her collarbones, and to the hollow that drove her wild with need.

And then lower still.

What he wouldn't give to lean over and press his lips to her throat, trail his mouth along the V-neck of her sweater. Go slow and drive her absolutely crazy until she was as desperate for him as he was for her.

"Maybe we'll be able to do more than that?" Savannah said, her voice breathless but hopeful.

"I don't know how that's going to work when I'm rooming with Caleb. Sneaking you in wouldn't exactly be inconspicuous."

Savannah's shoulders slumped. "Damn, I forgot about that." She regarded him with raised eyebrows. "You could pretend like you met someone and are staying with her?"

"The only *her* I'm interested in staying with also has a roommate." Noah glanced toward the front of the bus, to where Abby now sat with Gia and Tori. But instead of meeting her eyes, he met those of Savannah's oldest brother, who was watching them intently. Noah froze for half a second until Jackson pulled Spencer's attention away, and Noah breathed a sigh of relief.

He hated that he had to keep this from his closest friends. True, he and Savannah were just talking. *Now*. But that most certainly wasn't all the two of them had been getting up to this past month and a half. Even though he didn't like keeping this a secret, he also knew exactly how protective her brothers were of her.

He'd never been one to openly share about relationship troubles, but if ever there was a time that he could use some advice from his friends, it was now. Normally, he'd go to Caleb to discuss what was happening in his love life, but there was no way in hell he could do that. For one thing, Caleb had enough on his plate. He was so busy with work, he couldn't even plan his own wedding. But besides that, how could Noah even begin to start this conversation?

Hey, I'm sleeping with your sister. No, it's nothing serious, but I just thought you should know.

That was laughable. For now, as much as guilt ate at

him for keeping this a secret, that was exactly what he intended to do.

* * *

Riding in a bus, no matter how luxurious it was, with three out of four of her brothers was Savannah's idea of a nightmare. The only thing that made the trip bearable was laughing with her girlfriends and the quiet, stolen conversations with Noah. She was making it her mission to see to it that he enjoyed himself this weekend. He was an amazing dad, and that was one of the things she loved most about him, but he deserved a break too. He'd been the sole provider for months. And she'd heard enough from Becca to know just how taxing that could be on a person. So she was going to get Noah's mind off of his little girl if it was the last thing she did.

"Oh my God, this is even more gorgeous than the pictures!" Abby said, twisting around in her seat to peer outside.

The heavily tinted windows of the bus made it hard to really take in the scenery, but the views were nonetheless breathtaking. Clusters of soaring redwoods sprawled out along one side of the road and the crashing waves of Mendocino Bay greeted them along the other. The inn they were staying at was small, but luckily, it was just large enough for the wedding party, plus the stowaways Issa had invited. The building, made of eco salvaged redwoods dating back to the early 1900s, sat hidden away, nestled in ten acres of lush meadows and trees.

"It really is," Savannah said, her gaze fixed on the view. "You've outdone yourself with this one."

Abby waved a hand as if to dismiss Savannah's words. "I just helped with the details. This was all you."

That statement was so utterly absurd, Savannah nearly snorted, but before she could rebuke it, the bus came to a complete stop, and the restless passengers stood, their voices rising with excitement.

After their talk, Noah had slipped up to the front of the bus to play a game of poker with her brothers. And though he didn't say it out loud, she assumed it had something to do with the look Spencer had shot them, quizzical and searching, when they'd been probably closer than was wise in mixed company. Now, Noah followed her brothers out of the bus, shooting a quick glance in her direction before he stepped down. Their eye contact didn't last more than a couple seconds, but Savannah felt it straight to her toes.

"I saw that," Abby whispered, leaning in toward Savannah.

Savannah sniffed. "I don't know what you're talking about."

"Sure you don't," Abby said on a laugh. "So, what's the plan for tonight? Are you two counting down the hours until you can be alone?"

Savannah's shoulders slumped. "I would be if we

had any hope of actually being alone. Caleb's staying with him, which means even if we did have a room to go to, Noah's absence would most definitely be noticed."

Abby pursed her lips, her brows crinkling. The look of a woman attempting to solve a puzzle.

"I know that look on you," Savannah said.

Abby wiped the expression clean from her face and straightened up. "What look?"

With a laugh, Savannah climbed down the bus stairs and into the bright sunshine of the California coast. "Don't even try it. We've been friends way too long for you to pull that over on me."

"All I'm saying is, don't you worry about a thing."

"What do you mean? Abby, what—"

"There she is," Caleb boomed.

Suddenly, Savannah was being smothered by the too-tight arms of her over-exuberant brother, her arms pinned to her sides as he squeezed the life out of her. "Hrmph," she said into the fabric of his sweater.

Caleb pulled back, rested his hands on her shoulders, and grinned down at her. "You're losing your touch. I used to be able to smother you for a lot longer than that before you called uncle."

Without missing a beat, she snapped her hand out and punched him in the stomach, smiling widely when he doubled over with a loud "*Ooof*."

"I see some things never change," Issa said, her smile wide, her gold shimmer eyeshadow glinting in the sun. Her future sister-in-law looked like she'd stepped off a runway, and Savannah looked like she stepped straight out of a Target. Issa wrapped her arms around Savannah, this hug far less painful than the one she'd received from her brother.

"No fair, you look gorgeous already! What time are we leaving for the winery?" Savannah asked, and then shook herself. "Right, I'm supposed to know that. The time that we are leaving is—"

"Ninety minutes," Abby cut in.

Right. Of course Abby would know the time more than Savannah would. After all, her best friend was the one who'd planned nearly the entire thing.

"Thank you so much for inviting me!" Abby hooked her arm through Issa's and strode toward the entrance of the inn. "We're going to have such an amazing time."

"You hear that, Vanny?" Caleb hooked his around Savannah's neck and tugged her along without her permission. "We're going to have a great time."

She reached out and jabbed him in the side, fixing a glare up at him. She hated the nickname he'd given her and had refused to stop using. "I doubt it, unless you stop treating me like a rag doll. Lighten up a little, would you? If you're feeling the need to roughhouse, the other Lowe boys are around here somewhere, and so, by the way, is your best friend."

"Yeah, but they don't get mad about it like you do, so where's the fun in that?"

Savannah rolled her eyes but finally gave in to the embrace, wrapping an arm around Caleb's waist as they strolled toward the inn. As much as he drove her crazy, she couldn't deny how good it was to see him and actually hug him. It'd been far too long since they'd talked on more than screens.

The lobby of the inn somehow managed to be even more gorgeous than the pictures they'd seen online. Making it even better were the couple bottles of bubbly waiting for them.

"Now that everyone's finally here..." Issa said.

Caleb released Savannah to do the honors. As the cork popped, the whole group cheered. He poured, and Savannah snagged a few of the first flutes to pass out to Issa and the rest of the girls. When she got to Abby, she raised a brow.

Abby squirmed. "Actually..." She glanced around meaningfully.

Then, at long last, she put her hands on her stomach.

Savannah just barely managed not to drop the flutes—or to jump up and down screaming.

"I knew it!" Ever since Hilde had first hinted that Abby might not want a drink over a month ago now. Silently, she mouthed, "You're pregnant!"

"Shh! It's still super early. And I don't want to steal any of Issa and Caleb's thunder, okay?"

"We are going to celebrate this so big when we get home." Savannah passed the flute she'd planned to give to Abby to one of Issa's San Francisco bridesmaids before enveloping her best friend in a hug. "I'm so happy for you."

And if there was a teeny tiny twinge in the back of her mind, reminding her that this was one more way her friend was moving on into the wild world of true adulthood without her? Well. At least it was a tiny twinge, and completely dwarfed by the tidal wave of joy she felt.

Abby clutched her back. "Thanks. It's such a relief to finally have somebody else besides Carter and my grandmother know."

"I'm sure." Savannah gave Abby one last squeeze before letting go. "And don't worry—I've got you covered this weekend. Grape juice shall magically flow whenever I'm in your presence."

Abby's eyes shone. "What would I do without you?"

Caleb and Issa came over to join the conversation, fortunately unaware of the revelation that had begun this line of discussion.

"And what would I do without all of you?" Issa asked. She gestured around at their surroundings. "This place is perfect."

"You're happy with it?" Abby swabbed at her eyes but otherwise changed subjects without a hitch.

"Thrilled."

Savannah followed up, significantly less smoothly, "Are you all checked in already? How's your room?"

"Amazing," Issa said. "They gave me the Meadowland Suite. The biggest one in the entire inn—which makes me feel like a bit of a diva, considering I'm going to be in there all by myself."

"Why in the world would you be staying there all by yourself?" Abby asked, glancing back at Savannah, a glint in her eye that she couldn't read.

Issa blew out a heavy sigh. "My other bridesmaids talked me into this two-week intimacy challenge before the wedding."

"What does that mean?"

"It means no sex," Caleb groused.

"Seriously?" Savannah asked, glancing up at her brother.

"We're never speaking to any of them again," he muttered. But then he smiled at Issa with hearts in his eyes. "Whatever my lovely bride-to-be wants."

"Ugh, gross," Savannah said under her breath, to which Caleb shrugged, like he thought it was funny to scar her for life.

Issa smiled back at the two of them before looking to Abby. "I know it's silly, but they showed me an article that said it was great for deepened intimacy on your wedding night."

"I could get plenty de—"

Savannah pinched her brother as hard as she could. "Don't even think about finishing that sentence."

"Ow," he said, rubbing where she'd abused. "You've gotten cruel since I've been gone."

"Nope, you've just grown soft. Ask the other boys—I'm as cruel as ever."

"That's true," Jackson called back from where he was walking with Issa's maid of honor.

"Well, you're stronger than me. It's so romantic here, I know if my fiancé was around, there's no way I'd be able to keep my hands off him, impending nuptials or not," Abby said on a laugh. "But if you two want to be in separate rooms, then who am I to interfere?"

Savannah narrowed her eyes at Abby, who tossed a grin over her shoulder. She had underestimated her best friend. Even with everything else she had going on, that little devil was planting the seed to remove the barriers—namely, her brother who currently had her in a headlock—so that Savannah and Noah would have free rein of his suite.

She didn't know whether to kiss or—gently—kick her. That all depended on how the evening went.

Chapter Twenty

Y ou understand, don't you?" Caleb asked, shoving a few things in his bag. "I can't think about anything but my fiancée right next door. Not to mention that text she sent me. I'd show you but...ah, no. Not going there."

Noah chuckled, resting back against the headboard, his legs stretched out in front of him. "Hey, man, you don't have to justify it to me. Do what you gotta do."

Even though he'd had a grand total of *maybe* twenty minutes with Caleb since they'd arrived, Noah couldn't begrudge his best friend in the least for wanting to spend the night with his fiancée. Especially when said fiancée had spent the entire night torturing her husband-to-be, according to Caleb, anyway.

Well, they weren't the only ones who'd been tortured. It'd been damn hard to keep up the facade of merely a tentative friendship with Savannah, especially when she tended to get a little flirtatious and handsy when she was tipsy. And after spending three hours at a gorgeous winery about fifteen minutes away, she was well past tipsy and teetering on drunk. He'd caught her staring at him more than once, her lip caught between her teeth. And he hadn't been any better. While the bridesmaids laughed uproariously and Caleb filled his brothers and Noah in on what had been happening in his life, Noah had struggled not to turn and meet Savannah's gaze when he felt it on him.

"We'll hang out tomorrow, I promise." Caleb tossed his duffel bag over his shoulder. "You'd understand if you heard what she whispered in my ear before she slunk off to her room."

Noah chuckled under his breath and held up his hands. "Seriously. Say no more. Go enjoy yourself. I'll see you tomorrow. If you can make it out of bed."

"We'll see . . ." With a grin that stretched wide across his face, Caleb spun around and booked it out of their suite without a backward glance.

Now what the hell should Noah do? It was late—nearly eleven. Maybe he should just call it a night and get some rest . . . especially considering what he'd *like* to do. But he didn't think Savannah would appreciate a booty call. Besides, it wasn't as if they could act on it. Whether or not his room was open, she was still sharing with Abby, and that threw a wrench into the whole thing.

He picked up his phone half a dozen times, hovering over her name, before eventually tossing it to the side. He'd been doing that for the past fifteen minutes, and it was getting ridiculous now. Just as he reached for it again, a knock sounded at the door.

Striding toward it, Noah glanced over and saw Caleb's shaving kit still perched on the side table. He must have forgotten it in his haste to leave. "You lose your key already?" he asked as he opened the door.

Only it wasn't Caleb on the other side. Instead, Savannah stood there, looking like temptation personified, her hair a little mussed and her eyes a little glassy from the wine they'd consumed tonight. She bit her lip, no doubt to attempt to stop the smile that was working hard to peek out. Eventually, she gave up and met his eyes, an unspoken question in hers.

Noah poked his head out and looked in both directions down the hallway, before grabbing a handful of her shirt and tugging her inside. He slammed the door behind them, having just enough sense to lock it before he cupped her face in his hands and crashed his lips down on hers. She matched his excitement, her soft moan echoing in his ears as he swept his tongue into her mouth.

How was it always like this? How was it *still* like this? On paper, he and Savannah didn't make sense. They were the furthest from compatible. But there was no denying the electricity that arced between them, no denying the ache he had just to get closer to her whenever she was near. It had only been a couple days since they'd last slept together, but it felt like a lifetime. The more time they spent together, the less he could stand to stay away from her.

Never breaking their kiss, he reached down and gripped her rear, hauling her up against him, completely uninterested in keeping up any sort of facade of disinterest. Not when it was the furthest thing from the truth.

She giggled into his mouth as he lifted her up so she could wrap her legs around him. "Hasty, are you?"

"*Hungry*," he corrected, nipping at her lip as he turned them toward the bed, passing the bathroom along the way.

Savannah turned away on a gasp and pointed in that direction. "Oh my God, you have a clawfoot tub! I'm so jealous."

"Later." He tossed her on the bed and climbed over her. He'd spend an hour in there with her if she wanted, but first he needed to satiate a need that had been burning inside him the entire day. And, in doing so, he intended to make her forget all about that tub in two seconds flat.

* * *

After Noah had satisfied them both...twice...they sat in the tub, Savannah nestled between his thighs, her back resting against his chest. He couldn't remember ever doing this even with Jess, let alone any other girl-friend. He'd never thought he'd want to, to be honest. But the look of pure glee in Savannah's eyes when she'd surveyed the bathroom had lured him to her side.

That and the fact that there was no way he was going to miss an opportunity to be naked with Savannah rather than just watching on from the side like some kind of chump.

"So, what was the front desk thinking when they made sure *that* ended up in your room?" Savannah pointed to the bottle of local bubble bath they'd used to get the fluffy excess of bubbles in the tub.

"What makes you think we didn't ask for it specif-ically?"

She laughed and tipped her head back to look up at him. "Now I know you're lying. There's no way Caleb would do that."

"What about me? Maybe I like bubble baths."

She narrowed her eyes at him, no doubt trying to read his expression, but he refused to give anything away. "Do you?" she asked, skepticism heavy in her voice.

He wrapped his arms around her, keeping his hands just below the swells of her breasts. "No. But I'm beginning to think they're not all bad."

That was a lie if he'd ever heard one. If all baths with Savannah were like this—her nestled up against him as he stroked her baby-soft skin beneath the water, slipping his hands to some extremely fun places once in a while—well, they weren't even a *little* bad.

"Maybe by the time you're done with me, I'll even have you softening to pedicures."

Noah forced himself to laugh along with Savannah, but really, his mind was stuck on her words. He didn't want to be done with her. Not yet. He wasn't ready. And the truth was, he had no idea when he would be. Just because it wasn't serious didn't mean that he was ready to lose her company entirely. Now that they'd stopped fighting, he'd begun to crave their flirtatious banter. Especially when she shot him that smirk that said she was about to deliver a good one.

"Speaking of pedicures," Savannah said. "How was your mom and Rosie's spa day? Did you get a chance to talk to her?"

"Not for too long, but yeah," he said, tracing a line through the bubbles along Savannah's chest. "Rosie was having a blast. Luckily, she was so busy trying to tell me about every second of her day that she didn't even have a chance to cry."

"See? I told you it'd be okay. Your mom's got it handled."

"Yeah, you're right."

"I'm always right," she said, that mischievous gleam in her eye.

"I don't know if I'd go that far. But you have done pretty good with the wedding and this party. Caleb and Issa are going to love what you've planned for them."

Savannah's face fell the tiniest fraction, something he probably wouldn't have noticed if they weren't so close. She laughed, though it sounded forced. "You mean what Abby and Gia planned for them."

He lowered his head and brushed his lips along the slope of her neck as she tilted her head to the side to give him more room. "No. I mean, what *you* planned for them. You were the one who'd had the idea of a winery in the first place, weren't you?"

Savannah rested her head back on Noah's shoulder and hummed, whether from what she was thinking, or what he was doing to her, he wasn't sure. "I guess. That feels like a lifetime ago, back when you were an insufferable jerk twenty-four-seven."

He laughed lowly and scraped his teeth against her skin before sinking them gently into her neck. "I seem to remember we were a pair of jerks."

"That's fair."

But her voice was still off, something ringing in it that he couldn't quite pinpoint. He reached up and massaged his thumb between her pinched brow, trying to ease away the tension. "I must be losing my touch if what I'm doing to you is causing this."

She breathed out a laugh and gripped his hand, pressing a kiss to his palm. "It's not you, it's me."

"Uh-oh. The *it's not you, it's me* speech. I didn't think we were quite there yet."

"You know what I mean."

"Is this about Abby and Gia helping?"

"Yes. I mean, no. I mean, maybe?" Savannah heaved a deep sigh. "I love them to death. It's just hard to feel anything but completely inadequate whenever those two are involved. They both just have everything together, all the time. And I'm over here, barely hanging on. I mean, Abby's planning her *own* wedding right now, for God's sake, not to mention..." She trailed off, but before he could prod her, she continued. "And she's able to also throw this together on a whim? Who wouldn't feel inadequate when faced with that?"

"I guess I can see that. But I think you're only focusing on your shortcomings and not everything else you're capable of."

Savannah rolled her eyes. "Yeah, like what?"

"Well, like this wedding for one thing. This has been all you. If anybody's been inadequate, it's me. You've done the research, made the appointments, and booked what was needed. You've handled everything, and I've just shown up. There's no way I'd be able to do this without you. I'd be lost."

Savannah bit her lower lip, a smile slowly spreading across her mouth as she glanced up at him. "I *have* noticed you've been a little inadequate lately." She inched her fingers down his inner thigh toward where she could feel exactly how not inadequate he was.

"Would you like to file a formal complaint, Ms. Lowe?"

"I do believe I would. I think I could probably have more fun with a battery-operated—"

He didn't even allow her to get her full sentence out before he growled and crashed his lips down on hers, uncaring of the water sloshing over the side of the tub. "Take that back."

"I'll do no such thing."

"What if I promise you'll have no complaints at the end of the night?"

"Well, in that case . . . I might be able to be persuaded."

"Then I'd better get to work."

In the end, he didn't care how much water ended up on the floor by the time he was done, so long as they both upheld their promises.

Chapter Twenty-One

How much do you love me?" Abby said, hooking her arm through Savannah's as they strolled through the redwood grove at their first estate tour of the day.

"I love you a lot. Is there something in particular I should be loving you extra for?" Savannah asked, though she already knew the answer to that.

After all this time having to sneak out of his house before his daughter got up, she'd luxuriated in the chance to sleep next to him the whole night through. She'd woken up before him, and he'd looked so peaceful, the tension in his face that was usually present suddenly gone. He was relaxed and happy, and though it probably had more to do with the fact that he was not yet aware of the world, she liked to think it had a little something to do with her.

"No, nothing else in particular." Abby smirked at

her. "Just thought you might have been able to pass on some lovin' considering all that you got last night."

"Oh my God, shut up," Savannah said on a laugh, glancing around to make sure the others were far enough back so as not to overhear their conversation.

"Nobody's paying any attention to us. Besides, they're all already halfway to tipsy, and after the rest of our scheduled stops today, I don't think anybody's going to be remembering anything tomorrow."

"You really did outdo yourself with this whole trip. Thank you again for all your help with it. Without your interference, Noah and I would still probably be bickering about where to have it."

"You don't have to thank me for this. I should thank you for letting me. I live for this sort of thing!"

Savannah shook her head. "I know. But I still can't believe you planned an entire winery expedition, fully aware that you wouldn't be able to actually drink any of the wine."

"I'll admit I've been a little envious." Abby shot her a grin. "As fabulous as all the grape juice has been…"

"I'd say I'd make it up to you at your bachelorette party, but apparently that's going to be a dry event, huh?"

"I guess so." With no one looking, Abby put a hand on her belly. She practically beamed as she did so. "Can't say I'm upset about that, though."

"You could always postpone the wedding until after you pop out your and Carter's little love child."

Abby made a shocked face that was only part joking. "I would never!"

"I know, I know. I guess that does put some pressure on you to set a date."

"It really does."

A wave of guilt swept over Savannah. She'd been so preoccupied with getting things together for Caleb and Issa's wedding—not to mention her extracurricular activities with Noah—that she and Abby hadn't even discussed much of anything regarding her upcoming nuptials. All she knew was that she was going to be maid of honor and that she'd done absolutely nothing to fulfill that role so far. She winced, feeling like she was dropping the ball all over again. "I'm sorry I haven't been a very good wing woman with planning your wedding. After the New Year and all this"—she gestured around as if to encompass all the things—"is done, I'm all yours. And you can work me as much as you need."

Abby laughed and shook her head. "Don't worry about it. Besides, I don't want to waste this time talking about my wedding." She raised her brows pointedly. "Or any of my other stuff, exciting as it is. For now, I want to focus on this weekend—and I want to make sure that *you two* are using every bit of this time to your advantage."

"Us two...who?"

Abby rolled her eyes. "You and Noah, obviously," she said on a whisper. "I'm not sure if Caleb's going to be staying in Issa's room again tonight, so you and Noah need to take advantage of every minute you've got while we're doing these tours. Sneak off any chance you get. And if anybody asks, I've got a list of excuses as long as my arm to cover for you."

While Abby's planning tendencies could drive Savannah up a wall sometimes—mostly because they made her feel like an inferior adult who didn't have her life together—now that those planning skills were being put to good use, she couldn't have loved them, or Abby, more.

"What are you two whispering about over here?" Jackson strolled up between them, breaking them apart, and tossed an arm over each of their shoulders.

"They're always plotting something, these two," Becca agreed. She shot Jackson a meaningful look as she threaded a hand through the crook of Abby's elbow.

Becca and Jackson had always been close, but they'd been thick as thieves this weekend, enjoying a rare bit of time off from both work and parenting for Becca. With no waves for Jackson to catch, he'd apparently been left with nothing to do but pal around with Becca—and gang up on Savannah with the rest of her brothers, of course.

"Yeah," Caleb said, coming up on Savannah's other side. "What's the meaning of this? You see each other every day, and you haven't seen me for months. What gives?"

"I see Abby every day, yes, but she's never once put me in a headlock upon greeting."

Caleb huffed and rolled his eyes. "It was hardly a headlock. What, now I can't even say hi to you?"

"I noticed you didn't say hi to Abby like that."

"And I appreciate that," Abby said with a grin.

"You really shouldn't be so mean to your sister." Issa slid into step on the other side of Caleb, curling an arm around his waist.

Caleb pressed a hand to his chest as if in pain. "I can't believe it's starting already."

"What's starting already?" Savannah asked.

"My soon-to-be wife is ganging up against me with my sister. I thought we'd have at least a couple months, and here it's starting even before the wedding."

Issa laughed brightly. "I hate to tell you this, honey, but when you're wrong, you're wrong. Sister agreement or not."

"I seem to recall you telling me just how right I was last night," Caleb said, capturing Issa in his arms and spinning her around, nuzzling his face into her neck.

Tossing her head back, she laughed as pure joy and contentment radiated from her. And for the first time in her life, Savannah's heart ached for that. She'd always figured she'd get married eventually, with a big romantic proposal and a happily-ever-after plucked straight out of one of her favorite rom-coms. But now, that imagined destiny of loving someone for the rest of her life was no longer a faceless entity by her side as her lifelong partner. Now he had a face, and a name, and a dozen different laughs she already knew the meanings of. He had strengths and faults, too, but for the first time ever, they didn't prove to be a reason not to be with him. They were just there, better shaping who he was as a person.

A person she'd somehow, against her better judgment, fallen in love with.

* * *

"Are you sure this is okay?" Savannah whispered, stealing a glance behind her as she and Noah separated from the group and attempted to lose themselves in the dense rows of vines.

"I thought it was my job to always worry." He gripped her hand fiercely and tugged her along behind him, looking for...she honestly didn't know. Someplace where she could feel his lips on hers, she hoped.

The chatter of the rest of the party still reached them from wherever they were in the vineyard, but there was enough foliage in this part of the estate to keep them hidden...for now. What she wanted was to escape back into one of their bedrooms, or even a nook in the main inn. What they needed was a—

Border wall. Noah rounded it without hesitation before halting and spinning her toward him. She fell into his chest with a laugh, looking up into his whiskey eyes lit by the sun. She didn't know if it was the setting, all the romance around them, or the fact that they'd been able to explore each other more than they ever had before, or if it was simply because their real-life daily responsibilities weren't breathing down their necks, but she'd never felt freer or closer to him. Here, they could escape. Quite literally right now.

"What are we doing?" Savannah whispered, resting her hands on Noah's chest as she brushed her thumbs over the hard muscle she knew intimately.

"I needed something." His voice was husky and low, just a soft breath against her lips, and Savannah's parted in response.

"And you think you're going to find that hiding in the vineyard with me?"

"Well, I'm certainly not going to find it with anybody else."

Savannah bit her lip and stared up at him, relishing his words and the way he was looking at her. She didn't dare hope his feelings for her were growing as quickly as hers were for him, but so much of the way he was with her spoke of more than what they'd promised each other at the beginning of all this. Like maybe she meant something to him too. He showed it in the way he trailed his finger around the outline of her face and tucked her hair behind her ear. The way he skimmed his lips across her jaw, pressing a soft, delicate kiss to the hollow of her throat before scraping it with his teeth. It was in how he held her, close and tightly, as if she was someone to be cherished. As if she was someone important.

"Do you think you're going to find it in my jeans pockets?" she asked, breathless and barely able to get out the words as he slipped a hand into her back pocket.

He chuckled into her neck, the soft breaths heating her skin in a way that was wholly inappropriate for the very public place they were currently in, despite being hidden behind a wall among the overgrown vines used solely for wedding pictures and such. "This is exactly what I needed," he said, squeezing her bottom for emphasis. "And I obviously couldn't do this in the presence of others."

"Well, I think probably most of what we've done together on this trip couldn't be done in the presence of others."

"Including this," he said before lowering his mouth to hers.

The soft, slow glide of his tongue against hers elicited a moan from deep in her chest. She melted into him, pressing their bodies as close together as they could get while still being clothed. Wrapping her arms around his neck, she delved her fingers into his hair and held on as Noah drove her out of her mind with his mouth alone.

It could have been five minutes or an hour later when they finally broke apart. Noah's cheeks were flushed, his eyes dark and hungry, his breaths coming in pants. She had little doubt that she looked equally as ravaged.

"Great," she said. "Now we both look like we had sex out here, and we didn't even get the benefits of it."

Noah lifted a brow. "Would you like me to—"

She slapped a hand over his mouth. "Don't you dare finish that. We're *not* having sex in a vineyard with my brothers and our friends who knows how far away."

In fact, she couldn't remember the last time she heard their voices carried over to her and Noah. Then again, she'd been more than a little distracted by all the delicious things Noah had done to her, even with all of their clothes on.

"We need to get back. What are we going to say to them?" she asked.

He slapped her bottom lightly and then grabbed her hand, tugging her back in the direction of the tasting room where they'd begun their tour. "We can just tell them there was something wrong with the package, and we needed to discuss it with the manager."

"You're devious. Have you been speaking to Abby lately?"

"I'm plenty devious all on my own." He glanced back at her, a gleam in his eyes. "I think I proved that last night."

Savannah laughed, feeling lighthearted and buoyant and like nothing could rain on their parade.

At least until they walked out of the rows and nearly ran straight into Caleb.

"There you guys are," Caleb said, splitting a look between them.

She wasn't sure who let go first, but she and Noah untwined their hands as if jolted by electricity, though she couldn't be sure her brother hadn't seen anything before they'd done so. And despite the way her stomach dropped as Noah released her hand as if it were on fire, she knew it was for the best. Between Caleb's job pressure and his upcoming nuptials, adding this to his plate was the last thing he needed. She didn't want to contribute any more stress to his life. Still, she couldn't deny the pang of hurt that bloomed the second Noah had dropped her hand. Which was just plain stupid, because from the look Caleb was giving them, all curiosity and skepticism, it hadn't been a moment too soon.

"What've you two been doing?" Caleb asked.

Without missing a beat, Noah said, "There was a problem with the package rate."

"Oh." Caleb's gaze shifted between them, and Savannah could feel her face flame. She could only hope her brother would write it off to all the wine she'd consumed today and not that she'd nearly been caught making out with her brother's best friend. "You guys get it all figured out?"

"Oh yeah, don't worry about a thing." Noah clapped a hand on Caleb's shoulder. "We've got this. You just enjoy your time this weekend."

"Speaking of, we're probably about ready to head to

the next winery," Savannah said. "I know Abby's got us on a tight schedule today."

"Yeah, sure." Caleb nodded.

The three of them fell into step and found the rest of the group not a minute later—a little too close for comfort, if you asked her. As her brother strode straight to Issa where she stood chatting with Aaron and Spencer, not paying Savannah and Noah another bit of interest, she breathed a sigh of relief that he hadn't called them out on anything.

While she was pulled into a conversation with Becca and some of Issa's other friends about which wine was their favorite, she met Noah's eyes across the terrace, his gaze mirroring the message in hers.

That was a close one. But even so, they had no intention of stopping.

Chapter Twenty-Two

Returning to the real world after a trip away was always a harsh dose of reality. It almost made vacation not worth it, though Noah couldn't regret the days he'd spent in California, drunk on wine and Savannah's kisses. Except he'd only been home for eighteen hours, give or take, and he'd already been reminded several times of the weight of responsibility waiting for him.

When he'd arrived, Rosie had run to greet him, which wasn't out of the ordinary. It was how she always welcomed him home. Except the vise grip she had on his neck didn't cease. She'd clung to him for the rest of the night, even shooting him anxious eyes when he got up to simply go to the bathroom, and she ended up sleeping in his bed—something he'd managed to break the pattern of in the past couple months. Now it was like they were right back at square one.

Leaving to head to work this morning was heart-rending. His mom couldn't distract Rosie at all, even with excited talk of what they'd be doing at preschool today. He'd be hearing his daughter's cries as he shut the door for the rest of the day. Hell, for the rest of the *month*.

And then, as if that blow wasn't hard enough, he'd only been in the station for ten minutes before Chuck had called him into his office, just to remind him of the ticking clock that Noah was faced with. As if he'd forgotten. The end of the year was supposed to be celebratory, filled with family and friends and laughter, but all he saw was a looming ax over his neck. One way or another, he needed to figure this out, whether that was adding more childcare or giving in and finding a new job.

A run had kept him at the station past six, so he was, of course, falling right back into old habits and picking up Rosie late. Like she needed that, today of all days. He jogged up the front steps of the Sunshine Corner two at a time, like saving the extra seconds would be worth anything, and reached for the buzzer just as the front door swung open.

Megan, one of the preschooler's moms, stepped onto the porch, her dark brown hair pin straight and her blouse and slacks pressed within an inch of their lives. "Oh, Noah, I'm glad I ran into you."

His brows lifted. He'd never really had many inter-actions with the woman, other than brief comings and goings at drop-off, and he could count on one hand how many words the two of them had exchanged since the beginning of the school year. But he didn't need those words or interactions to know her son couldn't keep his hands to himself. Even if Savannah hadn't told him that little nugget of information, Rosie talked about the boy enough for him to be well versed in the situation.

"Can I help you with something?" he asked.

Megan crossed her arms and tapped her high-heel-clad foot. "Yes, actually. I was hoping to discuss our children's preschool teacher with you."

Noah's hackles rose immediately, whether from Megan's tone or simply because she was speaking about Savannah, he didn't know. He matched her stance, arms crossed over his chest, and raised a single eyebrow.

"Yes, well…" Megan cleared her throat and darted her eyes to the side before meeting his gaze once more. "I've just spoken to Abby about it. But this situation has to stop."

"What situation is that?" he asked flatly.

"Ms. Lowe *clearly* doesn't know what she's doing. She's in *way* over her head running this preschool and being the four-year-old teacher. It's clear her time is too divided and she can't devote enough of it to the children and their development."

"And what makes you say that?"

"Well, if you must know, they keep calling me down here and complaining about Austin acting out. But he never had a problem with that before moving up to preschool and being taught by that woman."

That was a bald-faced lie—Savannah had told him enough stories about Austin's time while attending the day care to know otherwise—but he couldn't see past his anger to call her on it. Noah clenched his jaw tight enough he worried he'd crack a molar. "*That woman,*" he said with emphasis, "has helped my daughter more than anyone else, including myself. So if you're looking for someone to join your unmerited cause, I'm afraid you're barking up the wrong tree."

Megan dropped her arms to her side, along with her friendly facade, and narrowed her eyes. "Fine. If you don't want to help me get her reassigned or fired, I'll find someone else who will. I'm certain the other parents are equally as fed up as I am." She didn't wait for him to respond before stomping down the front porch steps in a huff.

The nerve of that woman...If she really thought she was going to get other parents—parents of the children her kid no doubt harassed or bullied or both—to go against Savannah, she was utterly delusional. Noah exhaled a sigh before pressing the buzzer. Only a few seconds later, the door swung open, and there stood the very person Megan had been complaining about. Normally, Savannah wasn't there when he picked Rosie up, since she usually was off by five, so this was a pleasant surprise. Especially since she hadn't been in his bed last night. He only had a moment to take in how gorgeous she looked today in a brilliant red dress, her hair back in a high ponytail, before his attention was snagged by his daughter.

Rosie stood by Savannah's side, clinging to her hand, her eyes red-rimmed. When she realized it was him, she shouted, "Daddy!" before running straight to him and wrapping her arms around his leg.

"Hi, squirt." He rested his hand on her head, running it down her baby-soft hair. "How was your day?" He raised his eyes to Savannah, asking the question as much to her as to his daughter.

Savannah smiled sadly and that was answer enough for him. He'd screwed up again. He never should have gone on that trip, no matter how much he needed it or enjoyed it. He should have stayed here, with Rosie. He wasn't like Savannah's brothers—bachelors who could go off at the drop of a hat, flee on a whim to wherever they pleased. He was somebody's dad, and that someone looked to him for everything. And he'd let her down.

Savannah's voice was bright when she spoke. "I think she had fun today. We had her favorite for lunch. And she even made a few things to take home. She's getting very good at cutting, so she made a couple collages with her favorite things on them."

"Well, I can't wait to see them," he said, trying to peel Rosie's arms from his thigh. "Squirt, can you run and grab your backpack? And then we'll go home and have some dinner."

She loosened her grip only enough to stare up at him, her eyes wide with worry.

"I will not move a single inch, I promise," Noah assured her, and held out his pinky.

Rosie studied it for long moments before finally loosening her grip on his thigh and hooking her pinky through his. "That's a promise, Daddy. You can't break it."

"I won't. I know how pinky promises work."

Slowly, she loosened her grip even more until she let go entirely. She inched backward in the direction of the staircase leading up to the second-floor preschool where her cubby was, never taking her eyes off him.

He forced out a laugh, though his chest felt like an elephant had set up camp on top of it. "I won't leave. Go ahead. I'll be right here."

Finally seemingly reassured, she darted toward the rotunda, glancing back over her shoulder twice, as if to make sure he held good on his promise so far.

When she was out of sight, Noah exhaled a heavy sigh and scrubbed a hand down his face. "Let me guess—bad day?"

Savannah smiled softly and shook her head. "She really was okay. The only rocky time came after all the other kids started leaving. That's why I stuck around. She seems to do better when I'm close. It's a good thing I did, too, considering Megan showed up and dragged Abby away." Savannah rolled her eyes.

"Yeah, I had the lucky fortune of running into her outside."

"I'm sure that was fun for you," Savannah said with heavy sarcasm.

Noah breathed out a laugh and shook his head. "After the day I've had, the last thing I needed was some uptight, entitled mom attempting to sway me to get my girlfriend fired."

Noah froze, and Savannah froze right along with him, her brows arched high over wide eyes. "Your...girlfriend? Fired?" She said the words as if they were a wholly unknown language.

He didn't know if her shock came more from the fact that Megan wanted her booted from her job, or the fact that Noah so very carelessly referred to her as his girlfriend. Where the hell had that even come from? He'd never thought it, let alone said it aloud. And he knew as well as she did that what they were doing was casual. Just two people having a good time. Nothing more serious than that.

Except it had felt a whole lot more serious over the weekend...and even before that, if he were being honest.

Even thinking the word *casual* when it came to the two of them felt wrong. Not because he didn't want it to be true—because he desperately did—but because he was afraid that ship had already sailed. The weekend they'd spent together, even though they'd been sneaking around the entire time, had deepened something between them. Something that could never revert back to how it was.

Noah cleared his throat and diverted his gaze. "She, uh, she said she was going to try to get other parents on her side."

Savannah pressed her mouth into a thin line and narrowed her eyes. "That bi—"

"Daddy! You stayed right there!" Rosie said, dragging her backpack and jacket behind her.

He squatted down to catch her as she ran toward him with her arms wide open, holding her tight as he stood. He pressed a kiss to her temple. "I promised, didn't I?"

She grinned widely and nodded before glancing back at Savannah. "Miss Savannah, Daddy's home now! He let me stay in his bed last night 'cause I couldn't sleep 'cause of the monsters, and 'cause I was afraid I'd be all alone."

Savannah regarded Rosie with such tenderness, it filled up one of the cracks in Noah's heart that had been damaged since Jess left. "I'm sure your daddy's always going to be there," Savannah said. "Should I give him my special monster spray recipe to make sure that none of them can get into your room?"

Rosie's eyes lit up. "You can do that?"

Savannah nodded. "I sure can. I'll send him a text with it later so you can have it all ready for tonight." She met Noah's eyes, and he read the disappointment in them. She clearly understood what tonight would hold—a whole lot of father–daughter time and zero Noah and Savannah time.

"Thanks," Noah said, the word a rough scrape in his throat. The single syllable was completely inadequate for the gratitude he felt toward this woman. Not just for the kindness, compassion, and patience she'd shown his daughter, but also for her unwavering support of him.

He didn't know if Savannah Lowe was his girlfriend, but he was starting to think he might want her to be.

Chapter Twenty-Three

Somewhere along the line, Savannah had gotten used to spending her evenings with Noah, in one way or another. First, during their wedding scouting and appointments, and then more recently, when their time together had nothing at all to do with weddings. But since they'd arrived back in Heart's Hope Bay on Sunday, Noah had had his hands full with Rosie.

Since school had started, the little girl had made great strides in progressing from her early skittishness to someone who was vibrant and talkative and friendly with the other children. But this week, Savannah had watched Rosie retreat back into the shell she'd been in on that first day of school, and it broke her heart. So she was giving Noah and his daughter the space that they needed to bond again so that Rosie could feel secure that her dad was there to stay.

It was probably for the best anyway. With Caleb and Issa's wedding only a couple weeks away, she needed to make sure everything was in order. She didn't want anything falling through the cracks this close to the big day.

With a glass of red in one hand, she read through her scribbled to-do list—she'd finally given up on the fancy planner Abby had gifted her and instead had found a more orderly chaos sort of way of tracking what she needed to do—namely a scribbled list on whatever scrap of paper she found lying around. Maybe one day she'd graduate to an actual notebook to keep them in.

She'd already verified the photographer, the caterer, and the florist, double-checking her email to make sure that she had confirmations from them all, as well as making notes of any details she'd need to know on the day of the wedding. But the one confirmation and informational email she couldn't manage to find was from the Sage Sanctuary. She searched in her inbox to no avail and even pulled up spam, though nothing was in that folder, either.

With each minute that passed as she searched, Savannah's heart rate sped up while her stomach sank. An overwhelming feeling of dread settled over her, though she didn't know why. She'd written the check. She'd mailed it too. She distinctly remembered doing so because it was the day Austin had bit Jacob.

Exhaling a shaky breath, Savannah picked up her phone and dialed the Sage Sanctuary, closing her eyes and saying a silent prayer that her worst fears weren't coming true.

"Thank you for calling the Sage Sanctuary, this is Judy. How may I help you?"

"Hi, Judy, this is Savannah Lowe."

"Oh, hi, Savannah. How are you?"

"I'm doing okay." She forced out a laugh. "Though I'll be doing a lot better once you clear something up for me."

"I will certainly try my best. What can I help you with?"

"Well, I'm just making sure that everything is in line for my brother's wedding, but I can't seem to find the confirmation email from the Sanctuary. Could you forward that to me again?" she asked, hoping that maybe she could just speak it into existence and everything would be exactly how it should be.

Judy made a gruff noise on the other end of the line. "Oh dear. Well, I'm afraid there is no confirmation, Savannah. We never received the deposit, and I'm sorry to say, but another event has been booked for that day."

"Oh," Savannah managed, though it felt like her heart was trying to escape through her throat. "I see."

"I'm so sorry," Judy said, her voice soft and reassuring, although Savannah felt anything but reassured. "I thought you were interested but when I never received that check... Well, I had to go ahead and book someone else."

"That's okay. I understand," Savannah blurted out. "Thank you."

Without waiting for the other woman's goodbye, Savannah hung up and then sank back into her chair. She held her head in her hands as tears pricked her eyes. What was she supposed to do now? Caleb and Issa had sent the invitations weeks ago. Without a venue, there was no wedding. Sure, they had the florist, and they had the caterer, and they had the photographer—all the things Savannah had actually managed to secure—but without a venue, where did all of that go? Where would *everybody* go?

The wedding was in fifteen days. There was absolutely no way they'd be able to find something else in that short amount of time. Hell, they'd lucked out on the Sage Sanctuary in the first place, since it had been a late cancellation. But not many people in the tiny town of Heart's Hope Bay canceled their wedding with two weeks to spare. Even if they could find a new location, how would they communicate it to everybody who had already RSVP'd?

She stood up and paced the room, running her hands through her hair, as if that would help her come up with a plan. That was what she needed. To stop and slow down and come up with a plan.

Only Savannah wasn't good at plans. She never had been. That was all Abby, but after the week her best friend had had dealing with a raging case of morning sickness *and* defending Savannah from Megan's baseless accusations, Abby had enough on her plate. And Savannah was already contributing to her stress.

Besides, it was Noah who was in this with her. Noah who'd planned the wedding with her from the beginning. Who'd stood by her side, even when they disagreed on everything, and helped to make sure this was going to be an amazing day for Caleb and Issa. He may not have arranged most of the appointments or done the research, but still, he'd know what to do. He'd have to.

* * *

After a week of reassurances to his daughter, Noah was finally starting to see the light at the end of the tunnel. He'd pinky promised her each day when he'd left for work or dropped her off at preschool that he'd be there to pick her up when all was said and done. But still, she was nervous and uncertain, and he could tell it took everything in her to let him out of her sight. She hadn't even wanted to attend her dance class, or partake in her weekly Grandma time, and that broke Noah's heart.

How had he not realized exactly how far back his little trip would set her? And as if that wasn't enough to worry about, he was currently balancing his budget, trying to figure out where he could scrimp and save in order to pay for a nanny for Rosie on top of the cost of preschool, even without having to spend as much on aftercare. He didn't *want* a new job. Not only did he love what he did, but he was also good at it. He'd found his calling long ago, and how many people could truly say that? Still, there was no denying that the current situation just wasn't working.

He entered his monthly expenses one more time on the calculator on his phone, seeing the same measly leftovers he'd seen the last three times he'd done this. He swore under his breath and tossed his phone aside, resting his elbows on his knees and hanging his head. He didn't have enough money for anything extra. Period. And he didn't know what that meant for his future.

Before he could contemplate it more and spiral down a dark path he most certainly didn't have any interest in going down, there was a soft knock at his door. With a furrowed brow, he stood and strode toward it. Savannah's brothers wouldn't be that tentative in their greeting, and after this week, Savannah already knew that their after-bedtime dates were temporarily put on hold until further notice.

He opened the door, his brows shooting up when he saw Savannah on the other side, looking gorgeous if a bit disheveled. "Hey. Everything okay?"

"No," she said without hesitation, shaking her head for emphasis. "Can I come in?"

"Yeah, sure." Noah stepped aside and gestured her in before shutting the door behind her. He gripped her hip, greeting her with a soft kiss and wondering when, exactly, that had started to feel natural. "What's going on? Did Megan actually succeed in getting other parents on her side?"

Savannah's laugh shattered the silence around them, the sound too high-pitched and a little manic. "No, I wish."

At that, Noah's eyebrows flew toward his hairline. "It can't be that bad. Just tell me what this is all about."

She covered her face with her hands and shook her head before dropping them to her side. "I screwed up."

"With what?"

"The wedding."

"I thought we already went over this in Mendocino. You've been pulling both our weights with this whole thing."

"No, Noah, I mean I *really* screwed up." She stared at him for a beat before exhaling a deep breath, her shoulders slumping along with it. "The Sage Sanctuary never got the deposit."

Noah's entire body went tense at those words as his brain registered what this meant—no venue equaled no wedding…something Caleb and Issa were counting on them for. And something he'd counted on Savannah to handle. "The Sage Sanctuary never got the deposit, or you never sent it?"

"I sent it. I know I did. I just…Something must have happened. It was a bad day at preschool. Austin had bit another kid, and Tori was scrambling, and I put it in the outbox. Tori said she took it down, but…I don't know. I don't know where it went. I don't know if it got lost, or if it got misplaced, or if it evaporated, but it doesn't matter because they never received it."

And...that was it? They didn't get it, and instead of figuring this out, she showed up at his door like he'd have a solution? Through clenched teeth, he asked, "And you didn't think to check the wedding bank account to see if the deposit had come out of it at some point sooner than two weeks before the wedding?"

Savannah's forehead wrinkled as if the thought had never occurred to her. "No, I didn't."

For long moments, Noah stood very still, feeling the pressure inside slowly rising. Between his job and his dismal finances and Rosie and her increased need for reassurance, Noah didn't have anything more to give, least of all grace. Of course Savannah hadn't checked the account. Why would she? With her family's deep pockets, she'd never had to worry about money a day in her life. Her parents had always made it clear that they were ready and willing to bail their baby out. Or build a garage apartment for her, for example.

On any other day, maybe this wouldn't have hit as hard as it did, but considering what he'd been doing right before she'd shown up—worrying about money and trying to come up with a solution for him and his daughter—it was the straw that broke the camel's back.

He breathed out a humorless laugh. "Of course not."

"What's that supposed to mean?" she asked, actually sounding hurt.

Resentment and anger rose in his throat, which was good, because otherwise he'd have to feel the hint of shame and self-blame brewing in there too. She'd said she could handle everything, but what had he been thinking, trusting all of it to her? "Of course you wouldn't know to check the account balance—you probably don't even know how because you haven't ever needed to."

"I know how to balance a checkbook, Noah." She chuckled, only it wasn't funny. "It'd be great if it could stop being dump on Savannah day. I came here because I thought you might have an idea on how we can fix this."

"My idea is to have stayed focused long enough to actually make sure we had the venue secured."

Her spontaneity and free-spiritedness had been fun when she'd been showing up and jump-starting him to tackle a project that had been hanging over his head for too long. Suddenly deciding to have an impromptu picnic. Getting him to try screen-printing because she'd forgotten her mother's birthday and wanted to come up with something that looked homemade at the last flipping minute.

But he'd known there was a downside. The fun things she got distracted by came at a cost, and that cost was following through on everything else. She jerked her head back as if he'd slapped her, her eyes brimming with a hurt he'd never seen directed at himself. "Weren't you just telling me how great I've been at planning this whole thing?"

It was like he couldn't control the things coming out of his mouth. All of his frustration and exhaustion from the past week suddenly boiled over. "Yeah, well, that was before I knew how astronomically you could screw it up. Of course it had to be the most important thing, didn't it? You couldn't have forgotten to send the check to the calligrapher, could you?"

She glared at him, anger and frustration replacing the worry and unease that'd been written on her face when she'd first arrived. "You've got a lot of nerve resting this blame solely on my head. At least I tried."

"Try is all you ever do, Savannah," he said, tossing his hands up, his voice rising with each word. "For as long as I've known you, that's all you've done. Maybe you'll try knitting or bullet journaling or barre class, and maybe next week, you'll try cooking. When do you ever *do*?"

"I *am* doing. I'm the one lining things up for the wedding, making sure everything is in order, and I'm doing it on top of all my other responsibilities. In case you've forgotten, *I'm* the one there helping your daughter get through her days."

He snapped his mouth shut, his jaw ticking as he glared at her. After a moment, he said, "That's a low blow."

"And yours wasn't?"

"At least mine's true." Had it just been earlier in the week when he'd brushed off that mom at preschool with her concerns about Savannah? Then, he hadn't even given it a second thought, but now he couldn't help but wonder if maybe he'd been too quick to discount the concerns. "Maybe Megan was right. Maybe you truly can't handle all that responsibility."

"Excuse me?"

Noah lifted a single shoulder. "They say gut instincts are usually correct. And my gut told me that you're a spoiled princess who can't get a handle on her own life, much less get a handle on a group of four-year-olds."

There was only a split second where Savannah's face crumpled in shock and hurt before she crossed her arms over her chest and stood a little taller, the armor she'd shed with him in the past couple months clinking back into place, one impenetrable piece at a time. "Megan's a crappy mom who doesn't discipline her child, so *I* have to. And speaking of parents and their failings, maybe we should talk about you, Noah," she said, pure venom in her voice.

"What do you know about my parenting?"

Savannah breathed out a laugh and shook her head. "Even if I'm not around you two all the time, it's still not hard to see. You're closed off with everyone. You never let anyone in, much less admit your feelings about anything. How do you think that feels to a four-year-old little girl whose mom has already moved away? Have you ever once let her see how you're actually feeling? Or do you just hide it all behind a brick wall for her the way you do for everybody else?"

Her words hit their mark, a knife sinking deep into

his chest and puncturing his heart. He inhaled deeply through his nose and closed his eyes, hoping for some calm so they could discuss this rationally, but he was fresh out. Even if he hadn't been, it wouldn't have mattered. They'd already stepped past the point of no return. He might as well take them all the way over.

"At least I'm here for her to come home to, because I've *committed* to that. But that's something you don't know anything about, is it? You can't even commit to a hobby. You might still be able to play make-believe, but here in the real world, we don't have parents or older brothers to bail us out when we screw up. And it's about time you learned that." He reached past her and opened the front door. "So this screwup? I'm afraid you're going to have to figure it out on your own."

Chapter Twenty-Four

The last thing Savannah wanted to do after crying her eyes out the entire night was entertain fourteen preschoolers, but that was exactly what she did. She picked herself up, dusted herself off, doused herself in copious amounts of under-eye concealer, and then marched straight into the Sunshine Corner just as she'd done every day before. Because she needed to. Because it was her job, and because she was committed to it.

And a little bit, just to spite what Noah had said about her last night.

His words had cut her deep, as if he'd reached into her chest and ripped out her heart before tossing it to the side. He'd plucked out every single one of her insecurities, blasted a spotlight on them, and then dragged her in front of each and every one, making sure she saw, completely, how much of a failure she truly was.

She'd managed to miss running into Noah at drop-off this morning, but she was sure that reprieve wouldn't last forever. Thankfully it was Friday, which meant she had an entire weekend to avoid thinking about him. Or at least, that was what she told herself, when in reality, she spent every non-distracted minute replaying his cruel words from the night before.

"You okay today?" Tori asked while the children practiced writing their ABCs.

"Yeah, never better."

Tori met her expression with something that said she didn't believe a word out of her mouth. "I know I'm not Abby or Gia, and we don't have this long history, but sometimes those are the best people to confide in. Unbiased advice and all that."

Savannah swallowed the lump in her throat and was horrified to realize her eyes were actually welling up. She'd normally welcome unbiased words of wisdom, but the pit in her stomach stopped her from accepting them as a small voice in the back of her mind whispered, *What if Tori thinks Noah's right?* Because he *was* right, wasn't he? She didn't commit to things, and she hadn't ever had to stand on her own two feet. Maybe she really was nothing more than a spoiled princess who never had to face her mistakes.

"I appreciate that, but I'm okay. Promise." Savannah knew if she didn't make her escape immediately, she'd be crying a river right there at her desk with four-teen four-year-olds and Tori as witness. So she stood, smoothed a hand down her skirt, and walked toward their preschool room door. "I'm going to clean up the common area. Can you handle this for a few minutes?"

"Yeah, I've got it." Tori gave her a knowing look, one that said she didn't buy Savannah's lies and knew exactly why she was escaping, but also that she wouldn't call her on it.

Savannah offered her a small smile before she turned away and strode out into the hallway, just as a tear rolled down her cheek. She swiped it away with the back of her hand, not willing to give in to this desire to let it all out. Because even though she was alone now, there was no telling how long that would last in a preschool.

So with each toy she picked up and each center she tidied, she packed up a little piece of her emotions along with it, until she was secure that everything messy was shoved way down deep. When she got to Fairytale Lane, she squatted in front of the kids' toy mailbox and pulled a red scrap of paper poking out from it. In doing so, the whole thing popped open. Inside, it was filled with paper scraps, drawings...and three letter-size envelopes. Her stomach plummeted. She pulled it all out, sank back on her heels, and reviewed the very real mail she'd found in their very pretend mailbox.

Sure enough, there, stamped and addressed to the Sage Sanctuary, was the contract and deposit for her brother and Issa's wedding. She closed her eyes and exhaled a shaky laugh, rubbing a hand over her pinched forehead. She couldn't even bring herself to be mad at the kids for grabbing this and adding some authenticity to their pretend games.

Nope. This was all Savannah's doing. Noah's words might have been harsh, and even a little cruel, but there was no denying the thread of truth to them. She did look to others when she was in need of help. But she'd gotten herself in this mess, and she needed to figure out how she was going to dig herself out.

* * *

Later that night, Savannah was back at Abby's after her best friend had cornered her on her way out after work and demanded, in her very Abby way, that Savannah return for wine and cheesecake later. Which was fine with her. In her state, she could use a little sugar overdose, and God knew the wine could only help her bruised heart.

They'd already demolished two—okay, three—pieces of cheesecake and were currently curled up on the couch in the family room, where Savannah was trying her hardest to work her way through Abby's much-neglected wine collection.

"Where's Carter tonight?" Savannah asked.

"I kicked him out of the house and told him to go play with Marco."

Savannah laughed. "Those two don't see enough of each other at work every day?"

Abby shrugged and regarded Savannah over her tonic water and lime, her eyes sparkling. "I don't know. Do you get sick of me?"

"Depends on the day."

With a laugh, Abby shoved her foot into Savannah's thigh. "You don't really mean that."

"Don't I?"

Abby huffed. "I'm going to let that slide because I know this isn't really about me."

"No, what's it about, then?"

"Well, I'm not sure. Which is why I wanted you to come over. What I *do* know is that when you get hurt, you deflect, and you've done an awful lot of deflecting today. So, what's up? Is it Noah? Did something happen?"

At just the mention of his name, Savannah's heart gave a painful tug, her chest squeezing as a lump welled in her throat. She'd cried herself to sleep last night, had even shed some tears during work, and she absolutely refused to do any more of it.

So she put on a brave face and lied through her teeth. "Nothing could really happen when there wasn't anything there to begin with."

Abby regarded her with a pinched brow and leaned forward, resting her hand on Savannah's knee. "There *was* something there. So tell me what happened— what *really* happened, and not what you're pretending happened."

She lifted a single shoulder and avoided Abby's gaze.

"I dropped the ball. Like I always do. I guess that proved to Noah exactly the kind of person I am."

"And what kind of person is that?"

"A scatterbrained, spoiled princess who never follows through on anything," Savannah said lightly, as if the words didn't punch through her heart. As if her deepest fears about being unable to stand on her own two feet hadn't been confirmed in one fell swoop.

Abby breathed out a disbelieving laugh and stared at Savannah with heavy incredulity. "You're joking, right?"

Savannah rolled her eyes. "There's no need to pretend, Abby. I know exactly what I am, and exactly what I'm not."

"Great, then you'll know that you're none of those things."

"I wouldn't be so sure about that. How else do you explain me screwing up sending the deposit and contract for my brother's wedding and realizing with only two weeks to go that they have no location for said wedding?"

Abby gasped and covered her mouth with her hand. "Oh my God...seriously?"

"Yep. So now you see why Noah decided to call it quits. With me and the wedding. It doesn't matter anyway. It was just a fling. Some casual fun to pass the time."

Abby stared at her for long moments, scrutinizing Savannah enough to make her shift uncomfortably in her seat. Finally, Abby shook her head. "Nope. I'm not buying it."

"Not buying what? I really did screw up the deposit, and there really is no venue."

Waving a hand through the air, Abby said, "Not that. I'm talking about you and Noah, and you disregarding it so easily. You can pretend all you want that what you two had was just a fling, but I know the truth."

"Yeah? What's that?"

"You love him." Abby said it as if she were stating a fact, like the sky was blue and the grass was green and Savannah loved Noah.

She didn't know what it was about hearing the words from somebody else when she'd been rolling over the very same ones in her mind, but suddenly, the dam had broken, and she couldn't ignore the facts any longer.

Her eyes welled as her throat went tight. "Why'd I have to fall in love with a big dumb jerk?" Savannah said through her tears.

Abby breathed out a laugh, set her drink down on the table, and then enveloped Savannah in a hug. Savannah let herself be comforted by her best friend. Allowed herself to shed even more tears and purge herself of every bit of emotion weighing her down now, while she had Abby's shoulder to cry on.

"Oh dear. Another one?" Hilde's bracelets jingled as she strolled into the family room, her long skirt fluttering around her feet.

"What do you mean another one?" Abby asked as

she and Savannah broke apart, though she kept a hand rubbing small circles on Savannah's back.

Hilde sniffed and sat on the other side of Abby. "Seems to me it wasn't too long ago that Savannah was the one consoling *you*, my dear."

"That was different," Savannah said, her voice thick with tears.

"How so?"

She shrugged and accepted the tissue Abby handed her. "It was obvious those two belong together, and Carter loves her."

Hilde hummed and raised a single eyebrow. Savannah had never met anyone else in her whole life who could say so much without ever actually saying a word.

The thought of Noah loving her was laughable, especially given the words he'd flung at her only the night before. Cutting, biting words that sank their fangs into Savannah's heart and held on tight. She feared she'd be hearing the list of her failures spoken in his voice forever.

Savannah shook her head and dried her tears. "It doesn't matter anyway. And besides, Noah is the least of my problems right now. There's still a wedding happening here in two weeks. And figuring that out needs to be my top priority. I'm just not sure if I can do it."

Abby laughed, a disbelieving sound, and stared at her, slack-jawed. "You're kidding, right?"

"Why would I joke about this?"

Hilde and Abby exchanged a look and a soft chuckle,

but Savannah was still lost, as if the two of them were sharing some inside joke she wasn't privy to.

"Seriously, I don't get it," Savannah said, irritation seeping into her voice. Time was ticking, and she didn't have the luxury of beating around the bush.

"Well, honey, I think it's pretty obvious," Hilde said.

"Clearly not." Savannah gestured to her confused expression.

"Savannah," Abby said in her calming teacher voice. "You've been running the preschool for three full months, entirely on your own. Do you realize that?"

"Well, I—" Savannah cut off, her brow furrowing. "I guess, but it's..."

"Different?" Abby finished for her.

"Well, yeah. I mean I'm great with kids, but that doesn't exactly help me in this situation."

"No? You don't just spend all your time teaching the kids. You have planned their curriculum for the year, and then each week, and then oversaw and re-viewed those plans with the three-year-old teachers. You've scheduled field trips and events, as well as lined up special guests for each class. You've coordinated parent-teacher conferences on top of that, all while also planning a wedding. That, yeah, had one little snag, but otherwise is coming along amazingly."

With each responsibility Abby had ticked off, Savannah sat a little straighter, as her best friend reminded her that she wasn't the spoiled, helpless princess Noah thought her to be. And Abby was right, wasn't she?

Savannah *had* done all that on her own. She'd handled every preschool challenge head-on without thinking much about it. She may not have had a fancy paper planner like Abby, and she may come at things a little more chaotically than either Abby or Gia, but she did get stuff done.

"You're right," Savannah said, sounding shocked even to herself.

"Of course I am." Abby grinned at her.

"Takes after her grandmother," Hilde said, grinning slyly.

"But I still need to figure out what I'm going to do about the wedding. The Sage Sanctuary was seriously perfect." She thought of that location and their outdoor oasis. Of the trees strung with thousands of twinkling white lights, and suddenly had a moment of inspiration. Savannah gasped, her eyes flying wide as she stared at Abby and Hilde. "I know exactly what I need to do."

Abby regarded her with a gleam in her eye. "Yeah? What's that?"

"You remember I told you that Noah's mom had suggested my parents' backyard for the wedding, and we all shot her down?"

"Yeah…"

"Well, it really is a perfect location, especially if I decorate it just so. I think there's enough time to coordinate everything…" She told them what she was starting to envision.

"That sounds amazing!" Abby said, smiling wide. "Do you want any help?"

Normally, Savannah would have jumped at that. Abby excelled in event planning, but she found herself shaking her head. "Thank you for offering. But I think I need to do this on my own."

Chapter Twenty-Five

It didn't matter how many ways Noah crunched the numbers—the final tally never changed. He still had only a couple of weeks until the end of the year to make his decision, but he really didn't see any other choice. He needed to find another job. And in a town as small as Heart's Hope Bay, he needed to begin the search immediately. The trouble was, he wasn't qualified for, nor was he particularly interested in, any of the current open jobs available.

Though, he supposed, that didn't really matter, did it? Bills needed to get paid one way or another, and the collectors didn't care if Noah enjoyed his job, just that he was employed. Period.

He blew out an exhausted sigh and scrubbed a hand over his face, sinking back into the couch, the void of options pressing down onto his chest like a pile of bricks. The last thing he wanted to do on a Saturday off with his daughter was sort through this mess, but he didn't have much of a choice. Time wasn't going to stop for him, even if he asked nicely.

"Do you want to help me, Daddy?" Rosie knelt in front of the coffee table, a spread of Noah's mom's old magazines fanned out across the surface. Ever since Savannah had introduced Rosie to collages, Rosie had become obsessed. She wanted to create them every chance she got, and today was no different. "Maybe that will make you smile."

Her words were tied to an arrow that pierced his heart and sank deep. He'd tried hard to keep up the facade in front of his daughter, but apparently, he hadn't been so successful.

"What do you mean?"

"You've been sad," she said. "Maybe Miss Savannah can help you too!"

He breathed out a laugh and shook his head. No...the last person who'd be able to help him would be Savannah. According to her, he was an emotionally constipated brick wall.

For the most part, he'd been able to dismiss the hurtful things she'd said as her lashing out—and with good reason, considering the way he'd acted. But deep down, he couldn't help but wonder if what she'd said had contained at least some small kernel of truth.

Was he emotionally closed off? He'd always prided himself on handling things on his own. Not needing to lean on anyone. In the months since Jess had left, he'd been shouldering a heavy burden. He'd thought he was handling it well, not letting the strain show. Really, though, had he just been teaching his kid that the only way to deal with your feelings was to bottle them up and never let them show?

He hoped not. Clearly, he'd been bottling his own feelings up for too long, because at the slightest provocation from Savannah, they'd exploded. The harsh words he'd hurled at her still haunted him.

So did his callous reaction to her mistake with securing the wedding venue. Just thinking about it made him cringe. If Caleb knew Noah had basically slammed the door in her face and told her to deal with the mix-up herself, he'd have his head.

Noah had texted her a couple of times, asking how it was going, but she'd brushed him off, insisting she had it under control. Guilt ate at him. He'd kept up his end of the bargain, taking care of the handful of things he'd promised he would see to before their fight.

As for the rest of it... It made him feel like a heel, but how many times could he insist on helping without just making it worse? The ball was in her court now.

Leaning forward, he rested his elbows on his knees, focusing on Rosie. "Is that what she did for you?" He asked the question, though he already knew the answer. It was in the way his daughter had flourished since she'd been at the preschool under Savannah's care. And it was in the way Rosie had bounced back after Noah's trip to California. True, it had taken a week, and they'd had some trials and tribulations along the way, but she was nearly back to the same vibrancy she'd had before the trip. She'd even spent the past five nights sleeping in her own bed, freeing up Noah's. Not that it mattered, considering he'd kicked out the one person with whom he wanted to share it.

With a wide grin that stretched her face, Rosie nodded vigorously. "I love Miss Savannah," she said without hesitation or embarrassment.

Noah swallowed through his parched throat, his stomach churning over a realization that had arrived sometime in the past week. Yeah, he thought he might love her too.

If only he hadn't screwed everything up. He could've taken a page out of his daughter's book and just been open and honest with Savannah about his feelings. Though there was no telling if that would've helped. Not after what he'd said to her.

"I'm glad you like her so much. I'm happy she's your teacher."

"Me too. I wish I could see her on the weekends too!"

Noah opened his mouth to respond, though with what, he had no idea, before the front door opened and his mom called out, "Hello?"

"Grandma!" Rosie yelled, jumping up and running straight toward the front door, her spread of collage tools long forgotten.

Noah snagged Rosie's scissors on the way to the kitchen, tucking them in his back pocket as he headed in the direction of all the noise. His mom was no doubt dropping off another grouping of meals for them for the upcoming week, something for which he was eternally grateful.

He strode into the kitchen and lightened his mom's load by grabbing the remaining bags from her hands. "Hey, Ma."

"Hi! Noah, would you—" She froze midsentence as she took in his rumpled state, still clad in pajama pants and an old T-shirt. Her brows shot up her forehead as she stared at him. "Everything okay?"

He set the bags on the counter and started unpacking without meeting her gaze. "Fine, why?"

She was quiet for a few moments before she finally said, "Rosie, you know what I'd love?"

"What, Grandma?" Rosie asked, bouncing on her toes.

"For you to make me one of those collages you've been talking about, filled with all my favorite things. Would you do that for me?"

"Yes!" Rosie didn't wait a second before dashing off in the direction of all her materials.

"No more cutting!" Noah called after her, reaching into his back pocket and pulling out the pair of scissors he'd snatched off the coffee table. He'd learned that lesson the hard way, and it was a mistake he didn't intend on repeating.

He busied himself with unloading the bags of groceries and prepared dishes his mom had brought over, delaying the conversation he knew was coming. "Ma, you don't have to do this, you know."

"I don't think so, Noah. We're not talking about that right now."

"No? What, then?"

"How about the fact that you are in your pajamas at two o'clock on a Saturday afternoon."

He shrugged a single shoulder as he plucked more contents from the grocery bags and set them on the counter. "It's my day off. I can't lounge?"

"I've never seen you in pajamas past eight o'clock on a weekend. So, no, you can't. What's going on?"

Noah clenched his jaw, refusing to say anything else when what he really wanted was to unload everything and get it off his chest. The financial struggles. The ultimatum with the fire station. The wedding issues.

Savannah.

But he already counted on his mom for enough. He didn't need to burden her with this too.

"Honey," she said, stilling his hand with hers. She squeezed twice, the way she'd always done since he was little, and said, "You can tell me anything. You know that."

He did know that. He may not have had a large family, but he'd always had his mom. Noah braced his hands on the counter and hung his head, exhaling a shaky breath. "I'm drowning over here, Ma," he finally admitted.

It was odd that though he'd felt as if he'd been drowning for quite some time, Savannah had somehow made it better. Taken away a bit of his struggles or lessened them somehow. Like she was his life raft in an endless ocean. And he was the idiot who'd driven her away.

His mom sidled around the counter and slid in next to him, wrapping an arm around his waist. "Well, tell me about it. What's going on? Is it work or Rosie?"

He breathed out a humorless laugh and pinched the bridge of his nose. "Yes."

After long moments of silence, she huffed and gave him a light shove, her gentle coaxing clearly getting the boot. "Enough with the vault already. Just tell me. I can't help you if you don't open up. You should know that by now."

Noah wanted to tell her, but the trouble was, how did he force himself to open up after a lifetime of holding it all in? He didn't even know where to begin, but he figured the easiest way would be to just get it over with—like ripping off a Band-Aid. So that was exactly what he did.

"I'm looking for a new job."

His mom gasped. "You are? But I thought you loved it at the fire station."

"I do. But you know the concessions they made with my schedule after Jess moved away?"

"Yeah…"

"Chuck told me last month that they can't keep covering for me. It's not fair to everyone else at the station. And that I either need to find an overnight nanny for Rosie so that I can get back on the standard schedule, or I need to find a new job."

"Okay…I'm still not understanding why you're looking for a new job."

He stared at her with pinched brows. "Didn't you hear the part about needing to find someone to watch Rosie in order to keep my job?"

"I did. Did *you* not hear the thousands of times I've told you how much I adore taking my granddaughter and would take her more in a heartbeat if only you'd let me?"

Noah blew out a deep sigh and ran a hand through his hair. "Ma. We're talking about multiple overnights a week. That's more than what you should have to do. You've already been down that road once before. You're her grandparent, not her parent."

"And as her grandparent, my privilege is taking her when I want to, not because I have to."

"I don't know, Ma. It seems like a big ask of you."

"Well, that's the thing. You're not asking, I'm offering. But if you don't want me to watch her—"

He groaned. "You know that's not it, and that isn't what I said."

"Well, you mentioned a nanny, so what else am I supposed to take from that? You'd rather ship her off with a stranger than with her own grandmother."

"I would definitely rather not. I just thought it would be easier. It doesn't matter, anyway, though, because I can't afford a nanny, even if I wanted one."

She hummed, a dissatisfied sound that spoke of a flurry of withheld words.

"I know that hum," he said. "So out with it already."

"Well, I've been thinking a lot about this lately...Don't you think it's about time that you took Jess up on her offer to pay you alimony?"

He made a gruff sound in his throat, the very thought of taking financial assistance from his ex-wife seizing something deep inside him. "Ma, I—"

"That's enough," his mom cut in harshly. "Your pride just about cost you a career that you love and that you are good at because you couldn't ask for help. Isn't it about time you got over that? You don't have to forge your way through this life all on your own. There are people here who love and support you and only want to help however they can. And the sooner you accept that and let people in, the sooner you'll truly be happy."

He opened his mouth to tell her she was being ridiculous. He knew how to ask for help and let people in.

She raised a brow, and he clammed up quick. He knew that look, and it meant he better consider his words carefully before speaking.

As the seconds ticked past, a sinking feeling grew in his gut. Was she really that far off? Deep down, he hated having to rely on his mom to pitch in with taking care of Rosie. He hated the special treatment he'd gotten at the station, and he hated even the idea of going to Jess to ask for anything.

The truth of what his mother had said sent his stomach plummeting. He had been a stubborn fool, trying to handle everything on his own. And look where it had landed him. Exhausted, alone, unsure how he was going to make ends meet. Was he really so determined to never be vulnerable that he was willing to risk his job, not to mention the well-being of his kid?

Was that why he had pushed Savannah away?

Sure, she might have made a mistake with the venue, but for the rest of the time they'd spent planning the wedding together, she'd been a rock. He'd leaned on her, letting her take on way more than her fair share of the work. He'd leaned on her emotionally too. In the time since he and Jess had split, he'd never been so open with anybody. He'd never wanted to be. But Savannah had been so easy to talk to. She'd felt so perfect in his arms.

And at the first sign that she might be human after all, he'd pushed her away.

He snapped his gaze up to meet his mother's. "You're right."

"Of course I am." The confidence in her voice made him feel like he was a kid again.

Only he wasn't. He was a grown man, and it was time he started acting like one. That meant taking responsibility, asking for help—and admitting he'd been wrong.

He glanced at his phone. Step one would be taking both his mom and Jess up on their offers to help.

But steps two through fifteen would be trying to figure out how to make things right with Savannah.

All he could do was hope it wasn't too late.

Chapter Twenty-Six

Savannah stood on the back porch in her parents' yard, looking out at all her hard work and unable to believe she'd done it. She had actually pulled together a backyard wedding ceremony and reception in less than two weeks. And, despite her concerns over her ability to do so, she'd managed to take care of it all on her own.

She'd spent the past two weeks busting her butt to ensure things were getting done—and not bothering Noah with any of it. When he'd backtracked and offered to help, she'd remained firm in her response. She was taking care of everything and she'd see him at the rehearsal.

Well, it was the night of the rehearsal, and she still wasn't ready to see him. Though, truth be told, she didn't know when—of even if—she would ever be. But he was there, somewhere, because every once in a while, the low timbre of his voice would carry over to her, and she'd have to lock down her muscles just to hide the response she still seemed to have from it.

She'd decided to hold the rehearsal dinner in the backyard as a sort of dry run to the main event tomorrow so that she could make sure all the kinks were ironed out before the big day. Though she'd done the majority of the planning and preparation on her own, the one part she had called in the cavalry on was wrapping all the lights around each of the trees that surrounded the property. Even her newfound determination didn't stand a chance against twenty thousand lights.

Her brothers and parents, along with Issa's other bridesmaids and Abby, all milled about, laughing and talking. If it weren't for all the scrambling they'd had to do with getting the new wedding address to everyone, it was possible no one would have suspected the last-minute change.

"I can't believe it, Savannah. It's absolutely gorgeous." Issa stood next to her in a long ivory gown, looking every inch the beautiful, soon-to-be bride that she was. "This is better than I could have imagined."

Savannah wrapped an arm around Issa's shoulders and squeezed. "I'm so glad you like it. I was really worried that you'd be disappointed."

"How could we be?" Caleb interjected. "You saved us a fortune by moving it here."

Issa laughed and slapped a hand against Caleb's stomach. "It's more than just money."

"But the money *is* nice. It means we'll be able to go on our honeymoon all that much sooner..." He pulled Issa in for a kiss...one that quickly veered into squicky territory for Savannah to witness.

She cleared her throat, and when that didn't work, she not so gently kicked Caleb in the shin.

"Ouch," he said on a laugh as he finally pulled away from his bride.

Savannah gestured behind them toward their parents' house. "There are plenty of rooms available if you want to continue someplace your sister doesn't have to be witness to."

"Point taken." He tucked Issa into his side. "But seriously, thank you for this. How'd you manage to get all these lights up?" He gestured at the transformed space of their parents' vast backyard. Thousands of white lights were strung up on every tree and every branch. Mason jar candles hung suspended from draped tulle zigzagging between each tree, the overall look resembling a magical forest.

On top of it looking amazing, it was functional, too, thanks to her brother Jackson. He'd worked out a deal with his friend Ben, the owner of Heart's Hope Bay's favorite bar, Last Call, to loan them their outdoor space heaters for the weekend, making sure the backyard never got too chilly.

Becca, Jackson's platonic plus-one for both the

rehearsal and the wedding, smiled as she looped her arm through the crook of Savannah's elbow. "Savannah has a lot of friends who are always here for her."

Savannah's chest squeezed. Did she ever. And unlike some people, she wasn't afraid to lean on them when she needed help.

Not that her brothers would ever give her credit for that.

"Actually, it was all child labor." Aaron held up a hand in Caleb's face, showing the Band-Aids he had wrapped around his fingertips.

Caleb laughed and swatted Aaron's hand away. "What about you two? Were you dumb enough not to wear gloves too?" he asked.

Both Spencer and Jackson held up their bandage-free hands.

"The smart genes skipped over him, apparently," Spencer said, tipping his head in Aaron's direction.

Caleb glanced over Savannah's shoulder and lifted his chin. "How about you, man? Did Savannah work your fingers to the bone?"

She didn't need to turn around to know who was standing there. She could feel it. At one time, a sentence like that may have made Savannah blush while in Noah's presence, thinking of all the deliciously naughty things those fingers had done to her. But now she couldn't even think about Noah without hearing him throw all of her worst fears in her face.

Noah cleared his throat. "Actually—"

Actually, she wasn't interested in letting the man get a word in edgewise. If it were up to her, he wouldn't even be here. But best man and all that. "Actually, Abby just gave me the thumbs-up, so everyone's here. We can get started with the ceremony rehearsal, and then dinner should be ready at six."

"Thank *God*, I'm starving," Jackson said, leading Becca back toward the house.

Aaron clapped a hand on his shoulder, walking alongside them. "When *aren't* you starving?"

"While he's eating?" Spencer said, sliding into step with them. "And even then I'm not so sure."

Her brothers continued their banter all the way up to the back porch where Abby stood chatting with Savannah's parents and the other bridesmaids.

Issa pulled Savannah in for a tight hug. "I seriously cannot thank you enough for this."

Savannah returned the embrace, closing her eyes and allowing herself to revel in this feeling of accomplishment. "Don't worry about it. It was no big deal."

Caleb laughed and hooked an arm around Savannah's neck as soon as she was free from Issa. Tugging her to his side, he pressed a kiss to her forehead. "Now you're just flat-out lying. Noah told me about all the work you've done with the wedding, not to mention doing it all while keeping him in line too." He shook his head. "That can't have been an easy feat."

No, Savannah most certainly had not kept Noah in line. And when had he told Caleb any of that?

Obviously before her epic screwup, which she'd already come clean on to the two of them, thankfully, so she didn't have that hanging over her head. But it didn't matter when Noah had said it, because it was clear he no longer felt the same way.

The rehearsal went smoother than she'd thought it would. She'd been prepared for absolute disaster, but in actuality, there was only one near catastrophe with an uncleared fallen branch. But thankfully it had been Noah who'd tripped on that and not Issa. After the ceremony practice, they'd feasted on the most incredible barbeque—luckily, catered by the same company who'd be handling the wedding tomorrow—and drank enough wine to give even their trip to Mendocino County a run for its money.

Later, once things were winding down and the raucous laughter had tapered off to a lull, she and Abby stood off to the side, hidden by a garden trellis. Finally, Savannah allowed herself a moment to breathe.

"You seriously did an amazing job," Abby said, squeezing Savannah's hand. "I can't believe you've played me all these years, and really, you had these skills in your back pocket the whole time."

Savannah laughed and shook her head. "I assure you, I most certainly did not."

"Well, you do. And I hope they're here to stay, because…" Abby clasped her hands together in front of her face and pressed her lips together, her eyes shining brightly at Savannah.

"Because what?"

She grinned widely and dropped her hands...and if Savannah wasn't mistaken, actually bounced a little. "I haven't talked to your mom about it yet, but I was sort of hoping you would help me do the exact same thing with mine."

"Seriously?" Savannah asked, unable to soften the incredulity in her voice. Her best friend, event planner extraordinaire and hard-core perfectionist, wanted to copy the cockamamie scheme *Savannah* had dreamed up? And at the last minute at that?

Abby laughed. "Yes, seriously! Have you looked around?" She gestured to the backyard, where, even in its disarray thanks to the cleanup that still needed to happen—ugh, something else she needed to take care of tonight—it was still stunning. "It's breathtaking. Any couple would be lucky to be married here."

"Well, if that's where you want it, I'm sure my parents would be happy to host another wedding, especially yours."

Abby squealed and enveloped Savannah in a tight embrace. "Oh my God, I'm so excited!"

"Take it easy," Savannah said on a laugh. "Don't get too worked up just yet. I still need to make sure my parents are okay with keeping the lights strung, because Lord knows it'd take an act of God to get my brothers to help with any of that again. As it is, I'm going to be hearing about this for at least the next ten years.

Actually, I'll be lucky if they let it drop when I'm on my deathbed."

"I bet I could sweet-talk your parents," Abby said before glancing over Savannah's shoulder, her face softening slightly. "I should run. Your mom wanted help with, um, something..." She spun around without another word and took off toward the house.

Savannah stared after her with furrowed brows. What the hell was that all about? But her answer came a second later when someone cleared their throat behind her. She didn't even have to turn around to know who was standing there. Now that she was truly paying attention, she felt it in her body. In that hummed awareness that she always got when Noah was around.

She wished there was some way she could go back to before. Before she knew what it was like to be held in his arms. Before she knew what it was like for his lips to be on hers, to hear her name whispered in his gravelly voice, to feel him come undone with her.

"Savannah, I wanted to say—"

Without turning around, she held up her hand to stop him and shook her head. If this had been two weeks ago, she might've listened, but the truth was, no, she wasn't interested in what he wanted to say. Because, in the end, it didn't matter. He'd said it all, hadn't he? As far as she was concerned, there was nothing he could do that would erase the hurt he had heaped upon her, cracking open a lifetime of insecurities she'd never managed to work through.

But she was beginning to.

It may have taken her a while to get here, but these past couple weeks had taught her that she was a force to be reckoned with. She was smart and successful and imaginative. So what if she didn't have a hobby that stuck, and so what if she wasn't as organized as her best friend, and so what if she still lived right next to her family? She *liked* all those things about herself. Liked not being rigid and trying new things and being close to support when she needed it most. Heck, without her improvisational skills—and her family's help—she never could have pulled this wedding off.

While she didn't expect to be with someone who also liked or needed all those things, she certainly expected to be with someone who respected her and her choices.

And there was no doubt in her mind that that wasn't Noah. He'd shown her over and over again that he never had respected her. Worse, he never would.

So she was going to do what he'd been telling her to for so long. She was finally comfortable standing on her own two feet, just as he'd told her she needed to. The trouble was, in all the times he'd said as much, he probably never thought she'd use her newfound confidence to walk away.

Chapter Twenty-Seven

The day Noah had thought would never arrive was finally here.

They were doing pictures before the ceremony at a park outside of town, and everyone else seemed to be having a ball. Too bad Noah couldn't seem to get out of his funk.

He should've been enjoying the time with his closest friends, beaming with pride as Rosie awed everyone in her frilly dress, her hair in some fancy updo his mom had spent an hour on this morning. He should've been sneaking in kisses and lingering touches and whispered words with Savannah.

Instead, they'd maintained their distance, interacting with one another with nothing more than cool detachment.

Rosie was still hanging fairly close to him, but she'd

warmed up to Grayson, the ring bearer, and Grayson's sister, Mia, the other flower girl—Issa's maid of honor's kids—who she'd met last night, and he couldn't have been more relieved that she seemed to be enjoying herself.

The three kids were currently playing hide-and-seek while the rest of the wedding party took turns posing. Noah stood with the Lowe brothers, allowing himself to be directed by the photographer and trying to remember to look at the actual camera rather than where his gaze had been drawn to over and over again.

Namely, Savannah.

She stood off to the side, laughing with Issa and the other bridesmaids, looking for all the world like some sort of goddess come down to earth just to torment him. Her hair was pulled up, showcasing the long line of her neck. The dress she wore was navy blue and had both far too little and far too much fabric. Her shoulders were bare, which did nothing to encourage him to avert his gaze.

"Hey, best man," Greg, the photographer, called. "Eyes over here, please."

Jackson snorted. "And you call me the troublemaker."

"Nice try, but I hardly think him asking for my attention means I'll suddenly take that moniker off your hands."

"Once, maybe, but I'm pretty sure he's had to do it, like, four times," Caleb said, glancing at Noah with a smirk. "I *wonder* what could possibly have your attention over there?"

Noah had to work very hard to keep his expression carefully blank as he stared back at his best friend.

"Got the hots for a bridesmaid, Adams?" Aaron said.

But before he could answer, Jackson chimed in, "I sure as hell do. Dren is *hot*. She's not who you're looking at, right?"

"Fellas?" Greg said. "A little less chatting and a little more smiling, please."

Noah gratefully clung to the life preserver he'd just been tossed and sent up a silent thank-you that Greg was the one he and Savannah had decided to book for the wedding.

"Okay, ladies," he called. "We're going to do some group shots, so why don't you come on over."

The bridesmaids ceased their conversation, grabbed the kids—Noah wasn't surprised in the least when Rosie ran straight up to Savannah and gripped her hand—and headed their way.

"All right, we're going to do this a little different." Greg glanced at the ladies, then at Noah and the other guys. "Savannah, since you're related to every grooms-man besides Noah, I'm going to put you with him. That okay? Might make some of the closer shots a little less weird."

She didn't even spare him a glance. "Sure, no problem."

As Greg directed the other bridesmaids and

groomsmen to get into place, Savannah squatted down and had a quiet conversation with Rosie. He couldn't hear what they were saying from where he stood, but with how Savannah gestured toward him and regarded Rosie with a soft smile and nods, he could guess that she was reassuring his daughter that they'd be just a few feet away.

Finally, she stood, rolled her shoulders back, smoothed a hand down her dress, and strode toward him. He now knew her so well, he could read everything he needed to in that walk. She'd stand next to him, pose however they needed to, and even smile for the camera, but there wasn't an ounce of her that would enjoy it.

"Thank you," he said when she stepped up in front of him.

She must not have been expecting him to say anything, because she glanced back at him in surprise, her brows raised. "For what?"

"Making sure Rosie's been okay."

"Yes, well, all I can really do is try, right?"

He cringed, wishing he could go back in time and never say those idiotic words to her in the first place. They were callous and cruel and completely untrue. He'd had a stressful day—hell, a stressful few months— and he'd taken it out on her. She hadn't deserved any of it.

"Savannah, I'm—"

"Okay, everyone look this way," Greg called. "Noah,

I need you to get a little closer to Savannah. Step right into her and wrap your arm around her waist, please."

And thus began fifteen minutes—give or take—of pure torture.

At least the last time they'd been close like this with prying eyes watching, they'd been able to sneak off for some adult enjoyment. But this...holding her close, breathing her in, feeling every curve and dip of her body pressed up against his, all without knowing if it'd be the last time, was agony.

"All right, everyone, that was great!" Greg grabbed his camera bag. "I think we should probably head back to the Lowes'. I don't want to cut it too close to the ceremony time."

Rosie ran straight toward them, a grin stretching her mouth. "Daddy, Savannah, it's wedding time!"

Her words snapped him out of the trance he'd been in, and he realized he still had his hand resting on Savannah's back even as everyone else had started heading toward the limo bus they'd needed to rent to fit everybody. Though he didn't want to, he finally dropped his hand from her skin and smiled at his daughter.

"Almost, squirt."

"But it's time to go, right?" She didn't wait for an answer before grabbing his hand and then Savannah's and tugging them toward the parking lot.

Savannah laughed, the sound drawing his eyes. "Are you excited, Rosie?"

His daughter grinned up at Savannah. "Yes!"

Still smiling, she turned toward him and met his gaze, then seemed to remember he wasn't exactly her favorite person and wiped it clean off her face.

Once in the bus, Rosie sat with the other kids, playing and laughing, and Noah and Savannah joined the rest of the bridesmaids and groomsmen, where they'd already dug into the bottles of bourbon and wine they'd opened.

"There they are!" Caleb called, holding up his glass in a toast. "The couple that made this whole thing possible."

"You're an idiot," Savannah said, though she was smiling. She accepted the glass of wine Issa handed her.

"If I agree, are you going to call me an idiot too?" Issa asked.

"Are you one of my brothers? Then no."

Issa laughed and held her glass toward Savannah and Noah. "In that case, we couldn't have done this without you both."

"Adams, what are you doing?" Jackson yelled. "Grab a drink already! We've got some toasting to do."

Figuring he could use a little bit of numbness, he accepted the proffered glass from Spencer with a nod. "I'll take the bourbon but not the praise. That all goes to Savannah."

"To Savannah!" the group cheered.

He met her gaze above the rim of his glass, and for one fleeting moment, all the noise and chaos and laughter around him faded out until all he could focus on was the undeniable connection that still simmered between them.

And then he was forcibly yanked out of the trance by the squeal of brakes, a sharp jerk to the side, and the earsplitting sound of metal on metal.

In the seconds that followed, time seemed to stand still. He wasn't even aware he was moving until suddenly he knelt in front of Rosie, cupping her face and scanning every inch of her for injuries as she stared at him, her eyes wide with panic.

"It's okay, squirt. You're okay. Does this hurt?" He asked the question over and over again as he poked and prodded every inch of her body.

Groans and curses sounded behind him, and he glanced back to see everyone righting themselves in the wake of the crash.

"Daddy!"

At her ear-piercing scream, he snapped his head toward her. "I'm here. Everything's okay. We're okay. But I need to check on the others, okay?"

She started crying, and as much as he wanted to comfort her, to hold her in his arms and tell her over and over again that everything was going to be fine, he needed to make sure no one else was hurt. He checked over the other kids, both of whom were fine physically but shaken nonetheless, then turned to find Savannah.

It took him a moment to locate her, and in those brief seconds when he couldn't find her, his heart practically leaped straight out of his throat, worry seizing him. Once he found her, he ran a scan of her body, noticing her ripped dress, her hair a little askew, but otherwise no visible injuries. He finally breathed a sigh of relief and continued forward, Rosie gripping his hand for dear life.

He scanned the rest of the group, his pulse kicking up at all the red, until he realized it was nothing more than a spilled bottle of wine. "Is everyone okay?"

There were several calls of, "I think so," and "mostly," and a few groans intermixed with it all. Noah did a quick scan of everyone, including the driver—there were cuts and scrapes, none deep enough to need stitches, thankfully. Aaron's arm was hurt and would need to be in a sling, but that was it. All things considered, they'd lucked out. He glanced out the window, noticing for the first time that they weren't the only ones in this accident and that the only reason they'd gotten out mostly unscathed was because their driver had veered them off the main road and onto the shoulder, where they'd run into the divider rather than one of the other multiple cars in the pileup.

There were so many other cars. At least ten, from what he could see, and no ambulance in sight yet. He needed to get out there, and he needed to do so immediately.

"Daddy!" Rosie screamed again, terrified, her face tear-streaked.

He picked her up and held her close, cupping her head as she burrowed into his neck. The last thing he wanted to do was leave her right now, but there was no way he could do his job properly with her clinging to him. And there was also no denying how very much he needed to do his job right now. The familiar battle of duty warring with loyalty overwhelmed him. He loved the Lowe brothers like they were his own, but he still didn't trust them with Rosie. Not when she was in this state. If his mom were here, she might be able to help, but when Rosie got like this, it took a force to distract her.

A force like Savannah.

His eyes locked on her and everything inside him settled, his mind easing with the absolute certainty that he implicitly trusted her to give his daughter everything she needed. "Savannah," he called through a tight throat—or maybe he hadn't spoken at all.

But then she whipped her head in his direction, her gaze connecting with his, and she didn't hesitate. She strode straight toward them without a backward glance. "What's wrong? Is she okay?"

Later, when he was safe at home with his daughter tucked into bed, he'd allow himself to relish the worry in her tone, but right now, there wasn't time.

"I need to go out there and help with the other accidents. Can you . . . Would you watch Rosie?"

"Of course," she said without hesitation. She reached

out and ran a hand over Rosie's head. "Hey, sweetie, will you come sit with me for a bit? Your daddy needs to go be a hero."

* * *

Savannah's heart seized as she watched Noah dash out of the limo bus and straight into the chaos that had erupted around them. Rosie clung to her hand, tears still streaming down her face and her bottom lip quivering. And she wasn't the only one crying. Grayson and Mia, the ring bearer and flower girl, were also in tears, and their mom was attempting to console them, while at the same time attempting to check the rest of the wedding party for what they needed.

Savannah knelt down in front of Rosie, gripping the little girl's arms. "I know you're scared, sweetie, but everything is going to be fine. We're all fine."

"But Daddy!" she wailed, more tears spilling out over her bottom lashes.

Savannah smiled and rubbed her shoulders. "Your daddy is helping people right now. Do you know what he does when he goes to work every day?"

Rosie nodded, her bottom lip pushed out in a pout. "He helps people with owies."

"That's right. He helps people who are hurt, and right now, there are a lot of people out there who need him. But you know what?"

"What?" she asked, her tears finally tapering off.

"There are people in here who need help too."

"There are?"

"Yeah. Your new friends are scared just like you were. And there are lots of cuts and scrapes. They're not serious enough for your daddy, but they still need some help. What do you like to put on when you get an owie?"

"Unicorn Band-Aids!"

Savannah grinned. "I bet they're so pretty. I don't think we have any of those, but I bet we can find some plain ones around here." Thank God Savannah had packed an emergency wedding kit, complete with enough bandages for the entire wedding party, should the need arise. If only she'd known just how much it'd be needed. "Do you want to pretend that we're EMTs like your daddy and help the people in here?"

Rosie's eyes brightened and a shadow of a smile crept across her mouth. She nodded vigorously. "Okay."

Savannah pulled the kid in for a hug. "It's so brave of you to help other people while you're still a little scared."

"I'm gonna help just like my daddy."

"You sure are. Should we go find your friends and see if they want to help us?"

Rosie nodded and then, without waiting for Savannah, ran down the bus aisle, straight toward the still crying Grayson and Mia. It warmed Savannah's heart to watch Rosie greet them with soft words and reassuring touches.

Dren, Issa's maid of honor, glanced up toward Savannah, relief and gratitude shining on her face. She mouthed the words *thank you*, and Savannah waved her off. This was second nature to her. Commanding a space—especially one with kids—and entertaining them, possibly distracting them if necessary, was what she excelled at.

It was what she was born to do.

She loved her job. Loved molding little minds and helping to shape them into the people they'd one day become. And she was *good* at it.

The thought was so jolting, so *certain*, like a final piece clicking into place inside her, that she almost missed the kids running straight toward her.

"We're here, Savannah!" Rosie said, her arms around her new friends.

"Thank you for bringing your friends, Rosie," Savannah said, smiling at the kids. "Have you come to play EMTs with us?"

All three children nodded vigorously, a chorus of *yeah*s going up from them.

Savannah's smile widened. "I'm so glad. What do you think the first thing we need to do is?"

Rosie raised her hand, and Savannah gestured for her to go ahead. "Find Band-Aids!"

"Very good. Normally, there's a first aid kit on the bus, but Rosie's daddy took that with him."

"Oh no!" Grayson said, slapping his hands to his cheeks.

Savannah chuckled at him. "It's okay. I've got a special pack I was saving just in case anyone got hurt. We can use those." She held out her hands toward the kids, and Rosie and Mia immediately held on, Grayson grabbing his sister's hand as she led the charge to help the rest of the wedding party.

For the next several minutes, Savannah corralled the children, while at the same time providing the noncritical but still essential first aid supplies to the rest of the wedding party. They were all a mess. Ripped dresses and tangled updos, cuts and bruises, spilled wine, and even Aaron's arm in a makeshift sling. But at least they were there. They were safe and healthy. No one had gotten seriously injured.

In the split seconds that had followed the crash, Savannah's thoughts hadn't been on the glass of wine that had streaked down the front of her skirt, or the bone-jarring jolt as she'd slammed into the side of the bus. In that moment, she hadn't even thought about her brothers yet. Instead, her mind screamed one word: *Noah*.

She'd attempted to freeze him out for the past couple weeks, had shot him down anytime he'd tried to talk to her. More from hurt than anything else. But death-defying instances certainly had a way of clearing things up and making her desires crystal clear. There was no denying anymore that she wanted Noah. Loved him, though she'd already known that. And it didn't matter what he'd said to her.

She wasn't able to turn her feelings off like a light switch. They were there, blooming in her chest, an ever-present hum that only intensified in his presence.

And as she watched him from the bus window, Rosie perched in her lap and the other kids nestled beside her, Savannah realized he was it for her. It had taken this to have happened for her to have an epiphany about her profession, to realize that she was doing exactly what she was meant to. What she loved. It seemed it had done the same for her personal life, putting into sharp focus exactly what—*who*—was important.

The only trouble with that was, she wasn't able to call Noah hers. Not yet anyway.

Chapter Twenty-Eight

In all the years Noah had been an EMT, he could honestly say he'd never had to provide medical care to those injured in a thirteen-car pileup and then immediately stand up in a wedding. He was exhausted, a bone-deep tired that always came after the letdown from the rush of adrenaline felt at a major scene. It was a miracle that the ceremony had started only a few minutes late, but that hadn't been the only miracle they'd experienced today. The fact that they'd all avoided any sort of major, life-threatening injuries in a crash of that magnitude was nothing less than astounding.

Once they were absolutely certain everyone was okay, there was no question the wedding would go on. Caleb and Issa had been hesitant at first, but the bridal party convinced them that surviving the accident virtually unscathed was a sign that they should celebrate after everything that happened.

Just thinking of what could have been made Noah's throat grow tight. He looked over, past where Caleb and Issa were reciting their vows, their voices both thick with an emotion Noah was all too familiar with right now, and allowed his gaze to rest on Rosie and the woman whose hand she was currently clutching. If it hadn't been for Savannah and her warm and calming spirit with his daughter, there was no way he would have been able to perform in any sort of capacity. He would've spent his time unfocused, thinking only of Rosie and how she was doing.

But that hadn't happened today.

He hadn't had to worry about his daughter at all. From the moment he'd stepped off that bus, first aid kit in tow, and dashed into the melee of crash victims, he'd been able to put concerns about his daughter aside and focus on the job at hand.

Rosie's hair was mussed, the fabric of her dress smudged, but otherwise she was smiling. No bumps or bruises or cuts. And for that, he couldn't have been more grateful. Savannah, on the other hand, hadn't fared quite so well. Her hair, too, was a little wild. It was no longer in its updo, now lying loosely down her back. She had a cut on her hand and an angry-looking bruise blooming on her shoulder, but that was the extent of it, thankfully. They hadn't gotten out unscathed, but he was beyond grateful that they'd gotten out at all.

He had no idea how long he'd been staring at
Savannah when her eyes finally met his and a knot
tugged deep in his chest. He wished she could read
everything that he wanted to say in his expression.

I'm so glad you're not hurt.

I'm sorry for the things I said.

I love you.

Can you ever forgive me?

But when cheers erupted around them at the
pronouncement of Caleb and Issa as husband and
wife and she glanced away, he knew that was a pipe
dream.

Later, after dinner and numerous retellings of the
events from earlier in the day, Noah sat at one of the
tables, beer bottle in hand, surveying the loose crowd
assembled on the dance floor. His mom was out there,
swaying slowly to the music, as were Jackson and
Becca, though the goofy tango he was leading her in
could barely be classified as dancing. What kept drawing Noah's gaze, though, was the heart-squeezing sight
of Savannah dancing with Rosie under the twinkling
lights she'd painstakingly put up.

"My sister is a lot of things, but a mind reader she is
not," Caleb said, startling Noah as he pulled up a chair
and sat next to him.

Noah straightened, cleared his throat, and regarded
his best friend. "I don't— What?"

Caleb breathed out a laugh and shook his head,
glancing to where Noah had just been looking. "I know

you've always thought I was an idiot, but come on, man. I'd have to be blind not to notice what's been going on between you two."

Noah was tongue-tied, his mind whirring a mile a minute at what was the best response to this. In the end, he decided on a very eloquent, "Um..."

"Don't look so shocked. I was pretty sure about it at the bachelor/bachelorette party—you're welcome for staying with Issa, by the way—but now there's not a doubt in my mind."

"And...that doesn't bother you?"

"Why would it? Is it only casual for you?"

Noah shifted his gaze back to Savannah, his heart squeezing painfully in his chest just at the sight of her. "Not even a little."

"Then why the hell would I be upset? My best friend and my baby sister?" Caleb grinned. "Hell yeah, man. I can't think of a better man for Savannah."

"Yeah, well, you might not say that if you knew why she's not speaking to me right now."

Caleb laughed and shook his head, his gaze seeking out his bride across the lawn. "I can probably relate— God knows I've done my fair share of idiotic things. But you know what I learned through it all?"

"What's that?"

"Not a single one of them was something that a heartfelt apology and a major grovel couldn't fix."

Noah breathed out a laugh and glanced down. "I don't think an apology is going to cut it this time. And

I'm not sure I have the resources for the kind of grovel she deserves."

"No? Looks to me like you've got the world's most romantic stage right here. I'm sure you can figure something out." Caleb clapped a hand on Noah's shoulder as he stood and strode straight toward his wife, sweeping her up in his arms before kissing her soundly.

What Noah wouldn't give to be able to do that with Savannah right now, and every day hereafter. He wanted to be the one to give her all the things she'd said she wanted that day so long ago at the Sage Sanctuary. It felt like a lifetime had passed since then. He certainly felt like he'd grown as much.

As he recalled her words and stared out at the beautifully decorated space in front of him, a plan started forming in his mind. It wouldn't be easy, and he'd need to call in some favors. A lot of favors, actually. But he no longer felt shame in doing that. His friends and family would support him in any way that he needed. Sometimes, supporting him even when he didn't deserve it. He only needed to ask.

And he'd finally gotten to a point where he felt brave enough to do so. First, he'd see if his mom could take a very exhausted Rosie home with her for the evening. Then he'd check in with Savannah's parents about a few details before recruiting the bridesmaids and Abby to help bring his plan to life.

He only hoped his newfound bravery would stick

with him long enough to hold him up as he approached the rest of Savannah's brothers, told them how he felt about her, and then begged them for their help in getting her back.

* * *

Savannah had already agreed to help Abby with her wedding, but she could honestly say that if she never had to do this again, it would be too soon. She was exhausted, a bone-deep heaviness that had sat on her shoulders the entire evening that only partly was due to making sure everything ran smoothly for the wedding. Which, to be fair, was totally unrealistic, considering each and every member of the wedding party had shown up bruised or battered, their dresses torn and tuxes stained. But Savannah sort of loved all the imperfections of the day. It had made the ceremony and the vows all that much more romantic in their realness.

Life wasn't perfect. It was messy and ugly sometimes. But it was bolstering to know that true love didn't waver, even when faced with a tremendous storm.

"There you are," Abby said.

Savannah sat hidden in a corner of the backyard, her legs tucked under her and her shoes discarded on the ground. "Here I am. Not sure I'll ever move again, to be honest."

"I hope that's not true."

"Why, you and Gia have some sort of alcohol-free

pregnant people revenge party you want to drag me to after? I'm afraid I'm going to have to pass."

Abby laughed and shook her head. "Nothing quite as eventful as that. But there is something I think you're going to want to see."

Savannah glanced up at Abby's extended hand, finally grabbing it with a sigh. "If there's not wine at the end of this trail, I don't want it."

Just then, Savannah's stomach grumbled, a reminder that she'd been so busy today, she'd barely had time to eat, even during the actual dinner service. She'd had to deal with a mix-up of not enough vegetarian meals, and by the time she'd made it back to her chair, her plate had already been cleared away.

"Scratch that," she said. "If there's not food at the end of this, I don't want it."

"Well, then, I think you're going to be pleasantly surprised." Abby tugged Savannah off to the side, away from the festivities still happening around them, and pointed to the arched trellis strung with white lights and flowers, a path of sprinkled rose petals beyond it.

Savannah glanced at Abby with confusion. "What's that? I didn't decorate over there."

"No, you sure didn't. As for what it is, well, you better go find out. And while you do that, I am going to enjoy dancing under the stars with my handsome fiancé." Abby started walking away and then turned back around. "And, hey, you better call me tomorrow and give me the whole scoop. I want every last detail."

Without explaining any more, Abby strode toward Carter, who scooped her up in his arms and began immediately swaying to the soft music playing through the backyard.

Savannah slipped her shoes back on, the ground too chilly to walk on, and grabbed her shawl, wrapping it around her shoulders as she headed in the direction Abby had pointed. She never was one to turn away from a good mystery. She followed the path of scattered petals through the archway and around the portion of the yard she hadn't decorated. These petals looked an awful lot like the ones used in the bouquets and centerpieces.

The path was scarcely lit, just a few mason jar candles to let her know she was on the right track. And then, as she rounded a large evergreen, she found her favorite nook completely transformed, much like the ceremony site had been. The trees weren't strung with white lights, but a few fairy strands were wrapped around a blanket laid out and covered in rose petals. A bottle of wine, two glasses, and an array of plates sat upon it.

"What—" she whispered to herself, just as someone stepped out of the shadows. She startled, her heart racing for a moment from the scare, and then skipping a beat entirely when she realized who had put this all together.

Noah stood there, his white shirt unbuttoned, tie hanging loose around his neck, his hands tucked in his pockets as he regarded her with hope and apprehension and...something else that made a lump form in the back of her throat.

"Noah, what..."

He strode toward her, his gaze never straying from hers until suddenly, he was directly in her space. She breathed him in, despite a voice that whispered it would be too painful, but it didn't matter. She couldn't help herself. Neither could she help how her body came alive like it always did around him. Her heart drummed, and her toes curled, her entire being aware of his presence.

"I figure the apology needs to reflect the level of the screwup. And considering how badly I screwed this up, I hope this suffices."

"What?" She'd said the word too much, but she was still royally confused. She glanced behind him at the picnic he'd set up.

He smiled at her, a soft lift at the corner of his mouth. "Will you come sit with me?" He held out his hand toward hers.

She glanced down at it, not hesitating to place hers inside. His smile widened, relief seeming to wash over him, and he walked backward, pulling her along with him toward the blanket. He sat down, patting the space next to him, and she took the invitation, lowering herself to the surprisingly plush ground.

"How many blankets have you got under here?" she asked.

He chuckled under his breath and shook his head.

"Your mom was a little overzealous when I asked for one."

Savannah's eyebrows flew up. "You asked my mom...for help...with this? For *me*?" she asked, her words stuttering over themselves.

He nodded in confirmation. "I did. I asked your dad too. And your brothers—that was a fun conversation, by the way—as well as Abby and Becca, and my mom, and Issa, and the rest of the bridesmaids."

"How did I not realize this was happening?"

Noah chuckled under his breath. "Because you were very busy doing what you do best—entertaining my daughter, along with the other kids, and making sure everyone was having a good time."

It was easier to focus on how she'd missed this than to really drill down on the fact that, somehow, her entire family now knew about her and Noah. She'd wondered about those smirks her mom had kept shooting her, but had been too tired to truly pay attention.

"What is all this?" she asked.

Noah straightened, his gaze growing serious as he regarded her. "You told me one time that it was the little things that were truly romantic. When the person who loves you notices what you need and gives it to you without you having to ask."

She knew immediately the conversation he was referring to—the one they'd had at the Sage Sanctuary when she'd admitted she'd love it if she came home after a long day to a bath strewn with rose petals and dinner ordered in. But that wasn't what she was focusing on, because his words repeated over and over in her mind as her heart leapt in her throat. He *loved* her.

Before she could say anything in response, he pulled off the silver dome from one of the plates, presenting an untouched meal. The very meal she hadn't had a chance to eat earlier, in fact. And next to it on its own plate was a sliver of the strawberries and cream cake she'd loved so much but also hadn't been able to taste tonight.

With two fingers pressed lightly under her chin, he lifted her face toward him, his eyes beseeching. "I know this isn't as much as you deserve, Savannah. And maybe if I'd had more time, I could have put together something even more romantic that would be worthy of you." He slid his hand back and held her face, brushing his thumb across her cheek. "But the truth is that I didn't want to wait even another minute to tell you that I love you, and I'm so sorry for what I said to you at my house when you came to me with a problem. It wasn't you—it was everything else I'd been dealing with. I took that frustration out on you, but you didn't deserve it. The real kicker is, what I said wasn't even the truth. I haven't thought of you as that spoiled princess in a very long time, but it was easy to fall back on old habits when I was hurting."

She couldn't look away from his eyes, lit only by the soft, twinkling lights surrounding them. But even in the low light, she could see the regret flickering there.

The worry that he truly feared he may have screwed up things between them beyond repair.

He lowered his hand to her neck, his thumb resting over her pulse point. "I just hope that what I said didn't ruin what we have because I will be kicking myself for the rest of my life if I don't get to spend it with you."

Savannah's vision went blurry, and tears welled in her eyes before spilling down her cheeks. Noah made a gruff sound in his throat and swiped a thumb across her skin, catching each of her falling tears. She wanted to get closer to him, to tell him that she'd been missing him beyond belief, and that had only ratcheted up after the eventful afternoon and a glimpse at a world in which he could've been seriously injured.

She reached up and gripped his forearm, her other hand resting on his thigh. "I said things I'm not proud of too."

Noah shook his head. "You were right, though. I *am* a brick wall. I never realized how much of one I was until you. But it's something I'm working on." He swallowed, his gaze tracking all over her face, lingering on her lips before lifting to meet hers once more. "I was just sort of hoping you'd be there while I did."

She glanced around at the space he'd set up in a matter of hours. A space tailor-made with her desires in mind. He'd listened to what she'd said, hadn't written them off as frivolous or dumb or a passing interest like so many other things in her life. He'd found a way to work them into *their* storybook as part of their happily-ever-after. And she couldn't have loved him more for it.

"I'll make you a deal," Savannah said, holding out her pinky toward him.

He glanced down at it and raised an eyebrow. "What's that?"

"I'll help knock down that brick wall if you help me explore whatever new hobby or interest the wind blows me toward."

He sat there for long moments, just watching her. "I'm afraid I'm not going to be able to accept those terms as is."

Her stomach plummeted right along with her heart. She darted her eyes between his, wondering if she'd somehow gotten this all wrong. That he hadn't meant that he wanted to be with her. But no...he'd said he loved her. He'd said he wanted to be with her. So then what—

"I'm going to need to make sure that the expiration date on this is forever, because I love you, and I don't intend to stop at any point in this lifetime."

She breathed out a laugh and hooked her pinky through his. "I love you too," she said before throwing her arms around him and fusing their mouths together. He crushed her to him, pulling her directly into his lap, all while never breaking the kiss. It'd only been two weeks since she'd been wrapped up in his arms, his mouth pressed tightly to hers, but it felt like a dozen lifetimes had passed. She never, ever wanted to go that long without him again.

She might have lived her life, exploring different avenues and jumping from interest to interest, never finding the perfect fit to settle on. But it wasn't like that with Noah. She knew, deep in her heart, she was ready to dive headfirst into committing to him. Not just today or tomorrow or next week, but forever.

Chapter Twenty-Nine

Four months later…

It wasn't that long ago when Noah was dreading the time after he got off work, stressed and overwhelmed at all he was failing at. He'd been constantly late to pick up Rosie and always felt like there was never enough time to do anything but the daily grind. But now, in only a few short months, his life had been flipped on its head. Instead of dread and anxiety after a long day of work, now the only thing he was anxious for was to get home.

He pulled into the two-car garage next to Savannah's car and barely managed to remember to shut off the engine before he was out of the car, stepping into the house in four long strides. His schedule had switched back to twenty-four on, forty-eight off at the beginning of the year, but he'd worked out a plan with his mom. And now that Savannah had officially moved in, she was able to be there with Rosie whenever he couldn't be. Asking for help had come with a bit of a learning curve, and he still stumbled from time to time, but he was getting there. Partially because Savannah had no trouble reminding him when he was being ridiculous.

It was early still, but not so early that his two favorite girls wouldn't be awake, so he didn't bother to try to quiet his entry. "Hello?" he called out, listening for signs of life in the house.

The space smelled of freshly baked goodies and the kitchen was strewn with various baking pans and mixing bowls—an online baking class had been this week's new adventure. Rather than give it up completely, Savannah had leaned into that curious part of herself, even pulling him and Rosie along for the ride. And he was more than willing to join her.

"Daddy!" Rosie called, the *thump, thump, thump* of her feet as she ran toward him bringing a smile to his face.

She rounded the corner, still clad in her pajamas with her bed head on full display. He tossed his keys on the counter just in time to free his hands to catch her. Lifting her up, he pressed a kiss to her temple while she did her level best to choke him with the strength of her hug.

This hug wasn't in terror, though, or worry that caused her to fret about when he'd be back. This was just pure, unadulterated joy that he was home. It was miraculous, really, the strides she'd made at becoming more comfortable with him being gone. That had been a group effort, though, and he'd realized a lot of it actually fell to him. When he'd become more comfortable asking others for help—welcoming it, even—she'd relaxed. It wasn't hard to believe that her reluctance had been feeding off of his.

He'd been leaning more and more on the people who loved him—and not just his mom. He'd begun to realize that family was so much more than who he was related to by blood. It was the people who had his back, who held him up when he couldn't do it himself, and who stood by him no matter what. People like everyone he worked with down at the station. Like the Lowes—both Savannah's brothers and her parents. And then, of course, Savannah herself.

She'd been one of the biggest culprits in not only Rosie's newfound ease, but also his own. Now she stood in the hallway, leaning against the wall as she watched him and Rosie with a contented smile. Savannah was clad in one of his old T-shirts and those short shorts that nearly drove him out of his mind. A fact she damn well knew—and exploited, he was sure of it.

"Hi, squirt," he said, pulling back and running a hand down Rosie's hair. "How was your day yesterday?"

"So fun! I made you something special in school. But I hid it, so you have to find it." She pointed a finger within an inch of his face, fixing him with a stern expression. "Don't try to cheat, either, Daddy. I'm not gonna tell you where it is."

He laughed and nodded. "Got it. No cheating. What'd you do last night?"

"We watched *Frozen!*"

Noah's brows flew up as he shot Savannah a questioning glance. "Again?"

Savannah shrugged in response as if they hadn't watched it approximately three hundred times in the past few months. "That's the one she wanted."

"Vanny let me pick the movie *and* the pizza!" Rosie grinned, her smile no less bright even with the missing front tooth.

"She did? That was awfully nice of her." He lifted his gaze toward the woman who'd stolen his heart—and his daughter's as well. He'd always known they'd gotten along well—that had been clear enough from the start of the school year—but their bond had only intensified since Savannah had officially moved in.

"Uh-huh." Rosie nodded. "And then we baked muffins this morning and talked to Mommy, and Vanny said she'd help me pack for my night at Grandma's!"

It hadn't been that long ago that sending his daughter off to an evening with his mom had made him uncomfortable. Made him feel like he was somehow inept, unable to live up to the responsibility that he'd signed up for. But he now realized that simply wasn't true. Both his daughter and his mom looked forward to their special evenings together. And who was he to stand in the way of that?

"It sounds like you've had a fun day already. Are you excited for your night?"

"Yes! Grandma said we could go get ice cream!"

"Sounds yummy," Noah said. "We don't have to leave for a while, but do you want to go and pick out what you'd like to bring with you?"

Rosie nodded and pushed to be let down. Once he obliged, she didn't spare him a backward glance as she ran off in the direction of her bedroom, her hair flying out behind her.

As soon as she was out of sight, he turned his attention to Savannah. He'd been home for five whole minutes and he hadn't kissed her yet—something he intended to rectify immediately.

"A whole night to ourselves, huh?" he said as he stalked toward her.

She bit her lip and grinned as she tracked his movements. "Yep. What ever will we do with our time?"

When she was within reach, he grabbed a handful of her backside, pulled her up against him, and lowered his head to press his mouth to hers. What he'd intended to be a brief greeting quickly dissolved into something else entirely—which was wont to happen when they were together. Pressing her body even closer to his, she slid her fingers up through his hair as their tongues swept against each other, and a low groan rumbled in his chest.

After far too little time, he forced himself to break the kiss and pull back. They both knew from experience not to tempt fate with a curious five-year-old just down the hallway who could interrupt them at any moment. Could and *would*—it was almost like Rosie had a radar for it.

"I'm pretty sure I can come up with something," he said, his voice a low rumble.

"I have no doubt you can." She lowered her hands and rested them against his chest. "I have to help Abby with some wedding-slash-baby stuff this afternoon, but then I'm all yours to do whatever you want with."

"Just the words I love to hear," he murmured against her lips, getting lost in her taste all over again.

Long moments later, Savannah broke away, breathing out a laugh. "I'm not sure why you insist on making this so hard for yourself." She pressed a hand to the front of his jeans, cocking her eyebrow knowingly. "We've got hours before we can even *think* about grown-up fun."

He groaned, dropping his head to her shoulder. "I'm a masochist, apparently."

"I guess so."

After taking several deep breaths to calm his body, he lifted his head and met her gaze. "How was the call with Jess this morning?"

"Good. I think things are getting serious with that guy she's been seeing."

"Oh yeah? Good for her." He knew just how lonely

it could be to forge through life as an island, and he was happy his ex-wife could find some companionship since she was without a support system in Texas.

"How was work?" Savannah asked. "Did you manage to make it through a shift without anyone giving you grief?"

Noah groaned and scrubbed a hand over his face. "Of course not. They *live* to torture me."

She laughed. "Yeah, it must be *so* hard to relive your fifteen minutes of fame, Mr. Fancy Pants."

Noah's fifteen minutes of fame had all started thanks to that pileup on the interstate, where a candid video of him leaping into action to help crash victims had gone viral. A local news station had picked up the story, and then it spread nationwide. The headlines were all some variation of *Home Town Hero*—except for the one everyone down at the station still ribbed him about: *Hero or Hunk? You Decide.*

The funny thing was, to Noah, it hadn't felt like heroics, but rather just another day on the job. The only difference was he usually didn't perform first aid while wearing a tux.

"Laugh it up," he said. "They still haven't let up on calling me *GQ*. And it's an off day if I don't find an old issue somewhere—under my seat, in my locker…Hell, they even slide them under the door when I'm in the bathroom."

"Well, I'm sure they'll run out of copies at some point."

He shook his head. "I wouldn't count on it. People around town are all too willing to help with their cause. They're begging everyone they come in contact with for any old copies. I caught Cash doing it on a run last night."

"You poor thing," she said, her bottom lip pushed out in an exaggerated pout.

"Your sarcasm isn't appreciated."

"No? I quite enjoy it."

"Well, I'm glad one of us does." Though who was he kidding? He loved it too—loved everything about her, and he was no longer afraid to admit it. "How was your day?"

"Good." She beamed as she pulled away.

One of his greatest pleasures, beyond the obvious, of course, had been watching her grow into herself these past few months. Nowhere was her increased confidence in who she was more evident than in her work at the Sunshine Corner.

To absolutely no one's surprise, Megan's attempt to have her fired had been met with little more than blank stares, and in one case, he'd heard through the grapevine, outright laughter. Even if any other parents had been on that witch's side, Abby had Savannah's back, a fact Savannah no longer doubted in the least.

"None of the kids gave you any trouble?"

"No more than usual," she assured him. "Austin even gave me a hug after we read the Feelings Monster book—again."

Noah hid his wince behind a smile. Savannah had put a ton of effort into helping that kid work through his emotions in a healthier manner. The Feelings Monster book was one of the ones she turned to when he was dealing with some serious anger, so it must have been a tough day. But the fact that they'd come out of it with him ready to give her a hug was a huge success, and he was proud as hell.

"Have I mentioned recently that you're amazing?" he asked.

"Not recently enough."

He tugged her in. With his mouth hovering over hers, he breathed, "Let me correct that."

They were in danger of getting lost in another toe-curling kiss, but their moment of peace and quiet was over.

"Vanny!" Rosie yelled from her bedroom. "Will you come help me?"

Savannah smiled at Noah, then called, "Be right there!"

"Looks like you're being summoned, *Vanny*." He grinned when her only response was an eye roll. "Are you mad at Caleb for teaching Rosie to call you that? You hate that nickname."

She lifted a shoulder in a shrug and grabbed his hand, pulling him toward Rosie's room. "I hate it coming from my thirty-four-year-old brother. From Rosie, it's sweet. Makes me feel like I'm...I don't know. Important to her, I guess."

He tugged Savannah to a stop and gathered her up in his arms, brushing her hair from her face. "You are important to her. To both of us. I don't know what either of us would do without you."

Her eyes softened and she pushed up on tiptoes, pressing a sweet kiss to his lips. "Luckily, you won't have to find out." She raised an eyebrow, holding up her pinky and hooking it through his. "I think we still have a bit of forever left."

Look for Becca and
Jackson's romance in the
next charming Sunshine
Corner story

Available Winter 2023

About the Author

Phoebe Mills lives near the Great Lakes and loves her family, coffee, and binge-watching, in that order. During the day, she wrangles kids and by night she dreams up strong women, dreamy men, and ways to wreak havoc on their lives—before making sure everyone lives happily ever after, of course! It's a tough job, but there's nothing else she'd rather do.

You can learn more at:
   http://authorphoebemills.com/
   Twitter @phoebe_writes
   Facebook.com/authorphoebemills
   Instagram.com/authorphoebemills/

*Can't get enough of that small-town charm?
Forever has you covered with these heartwarming
contemporary romances!*

THE INN ON MIRROR LAKE
by Debbie Mason

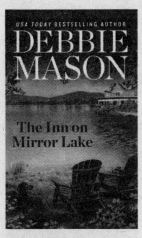

Elliana MacLeod has come home to whip the Mirror Lake Inn into tip-top shape so her mother won't sell the beloved family business. And now that Highland Falls is vying to be named the Most Romantic Small Town in America, she can't refuse any offer of help—even if it's from the gorgeous law enforcement officer next door. But Nathan Black has made it abundantly clear they're friends, and nothing more. Little do they know the town matchmakers are out to prove them wrong.

FALLING FOR YOU
by Barb Curtis

Faith Rotolo is shocked to inherit a historic mansion in quaint Sapphire Springs. But her new home needs some major fixing up. Too bad the handsome local contractor, Rob Milan, is spoiling her daydreams with the harsh realities of the project...and his grouchy personality. But as they work together, their spirited clashes wind up sparking a powerful attraction. As work nears completion, will she and Rob realize that they deserve a fresh start too?

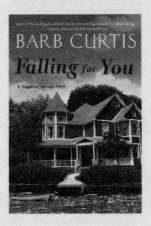

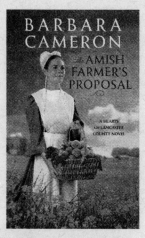

THE AMISH FARMER'S PROPOSAL
by Barbara Cameron

When Amish dairy farmer Abe Stoltzfus tumbles from his roof, he's lucky his longtime friend Lavinia Fisher is there to help. He secretly hoped to propose to her, but now, with his injuries, his dairy farm in danger, and his harvest at stake, Abe worries he'll only be a burden. But as he heals with Lavinia's gentle support and unflagging optimism, the two grow even closer. Will she be able to convince him that real love doesn't need perfect timing?

AUNT IVY'S COTTAGE
by Kristin Harper

When Zoey returns to Dune Island, she's shocked to find her elderly Aunt Ivy being pushed into a nursing home by a cousin. As the family clashes, Zoey meets Nick, the local lighthouse keeper with ocean-blue eyes and a warm laugh. With Nick as her ally, Zoey is determined to keep Aunt Ivy free. But when they discover a secret that threatens to upend Ivy's life, will they still be able to ensure her final years are filled with happiness...and maybe find love with each other along the way?

THE HOUSE ON SUNSHINE CORNER
by Phoebe Mills

Abby Engel has a great life. She's the owner of Sunshine Corner, the daycare she runs with her girl-friends; she has the most adoring grandmother (aka the Baby Whisperer); and she lives in a hidden gem of a town. All that's missing is love. Then her ex returns home to win back the one woman he's never been able to forget. But after breaking her heart years ago, can Carter convince Abby that he's her happy-ever-after?

TO ALL THE DOGS I'VE LOVED BEFORE
by Lizzie Shane

The last person librarian Elinor Rodriguez wants to see at her door is her first love, town sheriff Levi Jackson, but her mischievous rescue dog has other ideas. Without fail, Dory slips from the house whenever Elinor's back is turned—and it's up to Levi to bring her back. The qui-etly intense lawman broke Elinor's heart years ago, and she's deter-mined to move on, no matter how much she misses him. But will this four-legged friend prove that a sec-ond chance is in store? Includes a bonus story by Hope Ramsay!

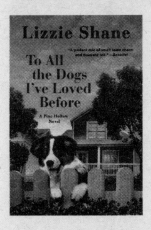

COMING HOME TO SEASHELL HARBOR
by Miranda Liasson

After a *very* public breakup, Hadley Wells is returning home to get back on her feet. But Seashell Harbor has trouble of its own. An injury forced her ex-boyfriend Tony Cammareri into early retirement, and the former NFL pro is making waves with a splashy new restaurant. They're on opposing sides of a decision over the town's future, but as their rivalry intensifies, they must decide what's worth fighting for—and what it truly means to be happy. Includes a bonus story by Jeannie Chin!

SUMMER BY THE SEA
by Jenny Hale

Faith can never forget the summer she found her first love—or how her younger sister, Casey, stole the man of her dreams. They've been estranged ever since. But at the request of their grandmother, Faith agrees to spend the summer with Casey at the beach where their feud began. While Faith is ready to forget—if not forgive—old hurts, she's *not* ready for her unexpected chemistry with their neighbor, Jake Buchanan. But for a truly unforgettable summer, she'll need to open her heart.

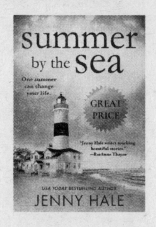